THE RIO CASINO INTRIGUE

A Major North Intrigue Novel

Van Wyck Mason

The Rio Casino Intrigue

CLEVELAND AND NEW YORK
THE WORLD PUBLISHING COMPANY

Published by THE WORLD PUBLISHING COMPANY
2231 WEST 110TH STREET · CLEVELAND · OHIO

By arrangement with Reynal and Hitchcock

TOWER BOOKS EDITION
First Printing June 1944

To

THEODORE B. PITMAN, JR.,

LONG A STEADFAST FRIEND

The characters in this story are entirely imaginary and any similarity to actual persons, living or dead, is purely coincidental.

The names of newspapers presented have been selected at random and bear no relation to actual so-named newspapers.

Contents

CONTENTS

THE RIO CASINO INTRIGUE

O Cruzeiro do Sul

STEADILY the sunlit skyscrapers and soot-smeared factory chimneys of São Paulo commenced to sink, to blend into a smoke-veiled horizon. The lush verdure of a wide countryside began to rush past, punctuated by thatched, white-walled huts and groups of brown, wooden-faced natives who stood staring in wonder on this great, glittering train. As if determined to anchor the track on the horizon, the distant metropolis seemed to tug twin strands of steel from beneath the express.

Now the twilight was deepening and the already insufferable humidity increased. The locomotive's frequent whistlings reverberated louder. A trainboy, neat in a white uniform lavishly adorned with many small gold buttons, approached from the direction of the buffet. Traveling half the length of the club car, he expertly balanced his tray as he bore down upon a lean individual apparently absorbed in the many little points of light beginning hesitantly to twinkle through the dusk.

"As the estimable senhor has ordered, a chilled rumswizzle."

"Obrigado." Major Hugh North of G-2, United States Army, accepted the well-frosted glass, fumbled for change in neatly

pressed gray gabardine trousers. Deftly, the trainboy caught a five-milreis piece and, holding his tray before him, bowed deeply.

"*Milhares de obrigados gravados no coração, oh, mais distinto, estimado senhor.*"

A smile curving his wide, good-natured mouth, Major North relaxed in a wicker armchair situated near the center of the club car. Odd, though he had been in Brazil now for over a week, he had not yet accustomed himself to that incongruous mixture of formality and simplicity characterizing its people.

Picture an American porter murmuring, "A thousand heartfelt thanks, most distinguished, estimable sir" for a trifling tip.

"The luggage is in my compartment?" North inquired.

As he bowed, the trainboy's teeth flashed against the café-au-lait background of his face. "It has been placed, Senhor, in *Camarote* Two, second car forward."

North nodded. He had seen small point in sweltering in a cramped compartment, so, by promptly seeking the club car, he had observed that basic precaution—a choice of seats. He found it most agreeable to sit thus under the slowly clacking fans and so utilize a certain lucidity of thought which leisure and the possession of creature comfort usually afforded him. The wide windows, rich paneling, deep-seated chairs and subdued lights became allies, but on this late February evening it was still stickily hot.

Before commencing the swizzle, Hugh North passed a handkerchief over deeply tanned features dominated by high cheek-bones and a thin, straight nose. Mechanically, he smoothed black hair growing a bit gray above ears that lay flat to his skull. Thus the Intelligence officer conducted an appraisal of his fellow passengers as swift as it was inclusive. Since they appeared satisfactorily self-engrossed, he plucked from his pocket a telegram received at seven o'clock—barely an hour ago.

He had had, therefore, just time to toss his things into his bag and, since all planes were reported grounded, to rush for the *Cruzeiro do Sul*—the Southern Cross—that crack night express between São Paulo and Rio de Janeiro. Certainly, until now, he had had scant opportunity to deliberate upon the implications presented by so utterly unexpected an order.

Once he had enjoyed a long pull of his swizzle, and the click-clicking of wheels over rail joints had begun to play a soothing obbligato, the man from G-2 unfolded the telegram.

It was most concise:

> HOWARD NORDHOFF
> HOTEL ESPLANADA
> SÃO PAULO, S. P.
> 24F—139—KLG—61—X290
> M.

The Intelligence officer again referred to his swizzle, then stared with unseeing eyes out of the window opposite. Not much to Maitland's message, yet it clearly suggested a disaster of some sort. Why should he, all in an hour's time, be so abruptly relieved of an assignment important enough to have brought him flying down from Washington? Why was he being recalled to Rio de Janeiro? What *could* be more vitally important than the Companhia Americus matter?

Completely at a loss, he tore the telegram to minute fragments and dropped them into a shiny brass cuspidor beside his foot.

"Twenty-four F, one thirty-nine, KLG, sixty-one, X two, nine, zero," he reflected. In simple English this meant: "Relieved of present assignment. State Department directs you report immediately to Rio. Extreme urgency. Maitland."

What in the world might have caused Captain Stuart Maitland thus to get the wind up? The Junior Military Attaché to Brazil habitually was as imperturbable as a croupier.

Settling deeper into his armchair, Hugh North brooded; and the more he brooded the less he liked the immediate prospects. It wasn't often that the State Department interfered with the Army in the pursuit of its lawful occasions. Not since Budapest,* back in '33, had the State Department thus pled for help from the Military Intelligence Division.

When a south-bound train suddenly passed on the adjacent track and shattered the quiet of the club car, everybody jumped. As the uproar faded, Hugh North became aware of a tiny, golden-brown monkey leaping down the blue carpeted aisle in obvious terror.

The little animal made a flying leap for his leg, climbed hurriedly up it and then hid under the skirt of North's gray gabardine coat. Though the Intelligence officer glanced about in search of the marmoset's owner, no one exhibited the least interest.

It was odd, he reflected, how often the perceptions of people on trains and aboard ship became dulled. Gently, he shifted the little monkey onto his lap and tickled its tufted ears until it chittered in an ecstasy of enjoyment and wrapped fragile arms about his thumb. Still no one appeared to take even a mild interest in the fugitive.

North was lighting a cigarette when the passing cars clattered out of sight with a brief winking of scarlet tail lights. Amid the sudden resultant silence he heard, quite distinctly, a voice observing,

---

* See *Budapest Parade Murders*.

"It is as I say, Pedro! I insist I know whereof I talk. These worms are never at rest. Take, for example, the Companhia Americus—"

The speaker was a plump, thick-bodied business man who, with two fellow Brazilians, occupied a small table near the observation platform.

"Are you aware, Roberto, that the management will employ no workmen who are not members?"

Obliquely, North considered the trio, found them well set up and alert of manner. Obviously affluent, the three were sipping tiny cups of very thick coffee—*cafezinhos*—with obvious enjoyment.

Major North sat a trifle straighter. What a touch of irony that these three should discuss the Americus Arms Corporation of São Paulo—now that he had been relieved of that fascinating, if perilous, investigation.

Hell's bells! To be pulled off a job just when certain delicately calculated moves, when laboriously gained contacts were beginning to produce results, was exasperating. He experienced a savage impatience with such interference. Besides, Manuela, back in São Paulo, had such a delicious singing voice, such an art in pleasing a man. Dear white-skinned, red-haired Manuela! For a long time their light-hearted excursion to Campinas would glow like a rich jewel in the treasure chest of his memory.

Still absently fondling the marmoset, Hugh North crossed long legs and sighed, for now the conversation of the three men in rumpled linens was too low-pitched to be well heard over the club car's rhythmic clatter. Only snatches of it reached him.

"*Desculpe-me!* I repeat, you are wrong. Luis da Evaristo would never permit such a thing. The family da Evaristo is too old, too respected, too honorable. Never would he allow activities approaching treason—"

One of the Brazilians, who greatly resembled Lewis Stone, slowly shook an iron-gray head.

"But, my dear Rodrigo, it does not follow that, merely because he is of a respected house, da Evaristo is not Patriotista. Alas, that certain of Brazil's best families credit every word Dom José Pujol either says or writes. I know—" he tapped his friend's knee—"that Dom Luis has given Pujol thousands of contos of reis."

Unluckily, at that moment the *Cruzeiro do Sul* began to roar past a local waiting humbly on a siding. The resultant uproar put pause to North's eavesdropping so he took a thoughtful sip from his swizzle, was vaguely aware that the marmoset had begun gently to play with his tie clip.

Damn! In less than a week he'd unearthed some very curious facts concerning the Americus Corporation—facts hard to reconcile with the policy of a supposedly pro-government corporation.

For a man who had supported President Getulio Vargas so openly and repeatedly, it seemed a trifle paradoxical that Luis da Evaristo, president and principal stockholder in the Americus Works, should employ so many Italians and ex-members of a now illegal Nazi Bund.

The directors proclaimed, of course, that a profound difference existed between Nazi and Patriotista ideals. Yet the more Hugh North investigated, the less he had been able to perceive any variation worth a pinch of ashes.

Once the local had been overtaken and voices were again audible, the heavily built Brazilian could be heard.

"—And the reason? It is that the United States Government, in the interests of hemisphere defense, has made available to the Companhia Americus certain secrets of ordnance. *Deus!* Do either of you really believe that the North Americans will for long tolerate a Patriotista—an Axis sympathizer—in control of the Companhia Americus?"

"Either the North Americans are not informed of the true state of affairs—or they do nothing about it," snapped the smallest of the three.

North squirmed. That remark struck uncomfortably close to home. Damn it all! Allowed but a few hours' more time he would have run down certain communications between Pujol and Dom Luis da Evaristo proving, at the very least, the munitions maker's implication. To prove that Dom Luis, apostle of patriotism, democracy and loyalty, was hand in glove with Pujol's Fascists would hand Brazilian officialdom a nasty jolt.

What the this-and-that *could* have prompted Washington to recall him at the last instant? Only today, he had played on the unquestioned republicanism of da Evaristo's principal vice-president to such an extent that that worthy was prepared to filch Dom Luis' correspondence with Pujol for discreet photostating.

If said correspondence contained a half of what North expected, the newspapers of Rio and São Paulo tomorrow would have printed certain disclosures very unwelcome to certain foreign gentlemen known to hold the Patriotista cause close to their chilly hearts.

Under straight black brows Hugh North's gray-blue eyes narrowed and, irritably, he tugged at a close-clipped mustache.

Because American experts already were tooling the Americus plant for machine guns and anti-aircraft guns of the latest type, the investigation would not be abandoned. Very likely M.I.-8 would designate Gaines MacMillan or Harry Clarke, both extra-competent men, to complete the assignment.

A sudden hope warmed him. Possibly this abrupt summons to Rio had still to do with the affair Americus?

Since little was to be gained by mulling a necessarily insoluble question, he decided to make the most of this comparatively peaceful evening and ordered another swizzle. For the diminutive guest now happily exploring his coat pockets he ordered a biscuit. He found it very odd that no one appeared in search of the straying pet.

Smoothly, the express thundered northwards through fast-deepening dusk past great coffee fazendas, past a succession of hamlets glowing with golden pin-points of light. A shadow fell across a copy of a daily newspaper North had salvaged from a chair recently vacated to his left. Though his knowledge of Portuguese was sparse, he could, through a fluent knowledge of French and Spanish, grasp the gist of the news.

What he read was not pleasant. More than ever the Patriotista movement appeared to be gaining ground. Its leaders were openly flaunting green shirts and brown breeches cut in the most approved storm-trooper patterns. Not one, but several, articles aimed especially vitriolic attacks against England and the United States.

When, profoundly irritated and alarmed, the Intelligence officer glanced up, he saw that a blonde young woman was seating herself directly opposite. With brilliantly tinted finger-nails she was occupied in opening a package of Astorias cigarettes.

Presently this young woman, with almost insolent deliberation, surveyed—nay, appraised—him over the flame of a wax vesta. Yet the very openness of her inspection somehow rendered her interest quite impersonal. As the marmoset snatched a bit of cracker, her rather full but discreetly colored lips formed a smile.

"He is yours?" North inquired, silently blessing the small creature in his lap.

"Oh, no, but I had a marmoset once." Eyes, smoky blue like a young kitten's, dropped. "Poor Mimi died."

"Poor Mimi," North murmured. "Pneumonia?"

"No. Misplaced affection," explained the blonde young woman, poising her cigarette. "Mimi fell desperately in love with a macaque and, during a tender moment, he squeezed her to death. A romantic way to die. But it was very sad all the same."

"Quite tragic," agreed North brightly. "May I offer a drink in her memory?"

The girl deliberated an instant, smiled, then said, "I think you may. With this trip I am bored—tired, also."

"What will you drink?"

"A Barbados and seltzer, please."

Gradually an impression burgeoned in North's mind that this blonde young woman's features were not wholly unfamiliar. Yet recollection, like a drop of mercury, kept escaping through his groping mental fingers.

While giving his order, the Intelligence officer found opportunity to scan his vis-à-vis more thoroughly than she might have suspected. All in all she reminded him of an expensive new car, stream-lined, efficient—and metallic.

The name 'Paula Harte' was written in flowing brass wire letters across a handbag of pale blue leather. Her white silk blouse of smartly simple design harmonized with a gray-blue suit which did subtle justice to a really superb, if rather mature, figure. A lapel watch that the Harte girl wore looked expensive, as did also neat pumps of gray suede.

Those smoky blue eyes set attractively far apart were always on the move under brows so pale that, to be noticed at all, they had required retouching with a brown pencil. Quickly, North deduced that the girl opposite was accustomed to handling matters of importance.

When their glances met unexpectedly, bright lips rippled from flawlessly white teeth.

"Do you know, Señor," she began in an unusually rich voice, "I have just been wondering where I could have seen you before?"

A single wavy lock of silver blonde hair escaping her turban complimented the darkness of very long lashes—also retouched.

"I am Major North, Major Hugh North." There seemed to be no sense in clinging to his *nom de guerre* of Howard Nordhoff.

"And I—" She held up her bag. "But then, you have already noticed."

Miss Harte accepted a Barbados highball and took a sip with evident enjoyment.

"You have been in Brazil long, Major?" When he told her, she asked, "And what do you think of us?"

"Us?"

"Oh, yes. I am quite as Brazilian as they." She inclined her pale head towards the three men lingering over their *cafezinhos*. "And they—" Her eyes flickered to a pair of Japanese firmly preëmpting the observation platform.

After an instant's scrutiny, North concluded that these two on the observation platform were not part of that influx of Japanese immigrants which, for fifteen years, had been pouring into Brazil in ever-increasing numbers. They did not carry themselves with that stiffness which seems to characterize a Japanese in Western surroundings. Their mode of dress, moreover, indicated the likelihood of their being native born. North put them down as first generation Japanese-Brazilians.

Near them and absorbed in a copy of the *Deutsche Rio Zeitung* was a powerfully built individual who was obviously as Teutonic as Göring. Sitting bolt upright in his badly cut sack suit, the fellow suggested a caricature Boche, complete to short, bristle-like blond hair, cold blue eyes and a thick neck climbing straight up to the base of a conical skull.

"Is one to assume that yonder amiable-appearing hombre is also Brazilian?" North demanded. He had seen dozens of German schools and churches and gymnasiums in and near São Paulo.

Before the Harte girl could answer, the *Cruzeiro do Sul's* locomotive emitted an abrupt, ear-piercing shriek. Immediately the whole train commenced to shudder under a sudden application of air brakes.

Unceremonious Exit

MAJOR HUGH NORTH instinctively went limp, several years of high-goal polo having proved that those who stiffened against an unexpected fall most frequently came to in a neat white room—if at all.

The *Cruzeiro do Sul* continued to buck like a mustang with a sandburr under its saddlecloth, and a series of shrieks from female occupants of the club car rose, all but drowning out the crash of a trayful of drinks which the trainboy had been serving to a prosperous gentleman and his dark-eyed *chère amie*.

The German, catapulted from his wicker chair, landed half in the car, half out upon the observation platform.

"*Himmelherrgottkreuzmillionen!*" he roared.

The girl with the bag marked 'Paula Harte' was pitched onto hands and knees, displaying an intriguing length of beige stocking secured by a garter with a jade-and-diamond clasp. Under other circumstances, the exposé would certainly have aroused the Intelligence officer's approving interest.

When the train finally ground to a shuddering halt, North hurried to help up the Harte girl. In doing so he was distinctly interested to note that sudden uneasiness with which her eyes flickered to the car windows. Outside, however, there was nothing to be seen but darkness and myriads of whirling fireflies.

Next, North retrieved the marmoset, squeaking in tiny terror from its refuge on a sconce bracket.

Amid a chorus of queries from the passengers a bewhiskered and well-fed conductor appeared, scarlet with emotion.

"*Mil perdões,*" he panted. "A pig is to blame. A little pig, a filthy small pig has dared to get itself run over by the *Cruzeiro do Sul!*" Quite needlessly, he added, "The pig is dead. The train will proceed immediately. *"Desculpe, muito obrigado!"*

"Then there is no station here?" queried the blonde girl just a trifle too casually.

"No, senhora."

"Was there not even a signal?" demanded the German.

"No, senhor," the conductor murmured. "Pigs do not understand their use."

"What stupidity, what wretched management! In our Reich such stupidities are not tolerated—they do not occur. Nor will they——" He broke off, retrieved his newspaper, and plunked himself angrily into his chair.

When air brakes hissed and the express gave a premonitory quiver, North was sure he heard a small sigh escape Paula Harte. He was still soothing the twice-rescued marmoset when a female avalanche came bursting in from the sleeping car just ahead.

"Alesandro!" wailed the apparition, rolling ardent black eyes. "Alesandro! Where art thou, my beloved?"

Instinctively the passengers recoiled before the advance of a vast, black-silk-clad figure complete with triple chin and perceptible mustache. Jet earrings flashed like sable storm warnings.

"Which of you has Alesandro? Where is my precious? Ah, ha!" Gasping, the woman lunged towards North, snatched the monkey from his grasp and submerged her pet in a flurry of moist kisses.

"*La Madonna,*" murmured Paula Harte, setting straight the seams of her stockings. "How beautiful is mother love."

"Oh, senhor." The apparition turned on North like a benevolent juggernaut. "*Muito obrigado!*" Suddenly she clasped him to her bosom with an arm as thick as a hawser, and bestowed a lusty smack on his cheek.

"So it is you, senhor, who have preserved my adored Alesandro? Command what you will. I can never thank you. To me Alesandro is like a child."

Meditating the obvious comment on a family resemblance, North backed hurriedly away.

"It was nothing," he assured her. Then in a hasty, inspired lie added, "It was really this young lady who saved him from being crushed."

"Indeed?" gurgled the vision in black, and a necklace of colossal diamonds flashed blindingly as she swung about. She tried to kiss the Harte girl, too, but the latter was on the alert.

"The Señor is only being modest," Paula Harte cried. "It was indeed he who rescued your pet."

A fearfully coy gleam entered the woman's beady black eye as she swung back to face North. "Now are not you the modest one? You will stop at my *camarote,* my stateroom, please— Number Ten, next car? Here, one cannot properly offer thanks." Her mustache quivered with emotion. "You will come? I—I have refreshments."

Embarrassed as he had not been in years, North was aware of the amused glances of Paula Harte, the three Japanese and the three Brazilians. The German, however, still glowered, cursing Brazil and all in it beneath his breath.

"Why—er—I will try to, Senhora. But I am retiring early. I—"

"You will not regret your call, Senhor, I promise it." With an arch giggle the woman waddled out of sight.

"Cad!" smiled the blonde young woman.

"Self-preservation is the first law of nature," North reminded. "A fresh drink, what say?"

"One, and then, Señor, I must retire—and leave you to your conquest."

"I'll never observe Kindness to Animals Week again," North complained. "What's yours? A Barbados and soda?"

"Um, let me see." Slender brows merged, she narrowed her eyes and for quite a while studied the card. Meanwhile the German treated her to that sort of stare which left her without a stitch of clothing.

"That print is very fine," North pointed out, "and the train's motion doesn't help. Suppose I read it for you?"

"Oh, I can see all right. I was merely attempting to make up my mind. I'll have the third from the top—a Copa de Bahía."

"Sounds impressive. What's in a Copa de Bahía?"

"I haven't the remotest idea," confessed the blonde young woman, "but I have a persistent curiosity about things—about drinks, that is."

Once the glasses had been brought, Hugh North felt better, yet could not rid himself of an impression that Paula Harte's original jaunty manner had not quite returned.

After a perfectly commonplace conversation, the blonde young woman bade him a cheerful "Good night—and thank you."

As he watched her sway out of sight, Hugh North silently reviled G-2, the Companhia Americus, Stuart Maitland, José Pujol and everyone else for holding a prior claim to his attention. He shrugged and, perforce, began to deliberate his course in Rio.

Obviously, he must first see Captain Maitland. Most likely the Junior Military Attaché would be at the station to meet him, but maybe not; it would be safer so.

Um. Why should the Harte girl have been so bothered by the unexpected halt? Smart both as to body and brains, she was an unusual type. She must be of German extraction, if Harte really was her name. Charming, all right, but wasn't she a bit hard under it all? Well, maybe. Below the Equator blondes usually had a rough time of it.

Since there was no use in pondering this business, he might as well go to bed. Thank God he'd been inspired in São Paulo to secure a *camarote* all to himself. Tonight he wanted no snoring, no struggle for fresh air to keep him wakeful.

In the corridor he encountered the conductor.

"One hopes that O Senhor will repose well," the official observed. "You are mos' fortunate, Senhor. Tonight the Express is fill' up."

"Thank you. Good night."

"And a very good night to o senhor," the conductor murmured. As he turned away, North could have sworn that that bewhiskered individual tipped him a wink as of intimate understanding.

In tarnished silver the Roman numeral, II, marked a door of solid mahogany. After checking the number of the car and compartment against his ticket stub, the Intelligence officer took a last look at a moon-drenched landscape and turned the knob of his stateroom door. Instantly a voice charged with menace warned,

"Stand quite still!"

North obeyed. There was too much metal in the speaker's undertone and, for once, that cut-down .32 automatic he customarily carried in a shoulder holster was inaccessible.

Though his compartment stood in semi-darkness, he could, nevertheless, discern his suitcase on a rack above the washstand.

Poised in a half crouch in the center of his compartment stood Paula Harte looking anything but sweet and glamorous. In her left hand she clutched the blue pocketbook bearing her name; her right hand was plunged into its interior, gripping some object. North needed no diagram to tell what that was.

"Oh, it's *you*, Major?" Slowly, the Harte girl's hand came away from the gaping bag and, mechanically, she flexed long, capable-appearing fingers. "What do you want?"

"Hello," he greeted almost affably. "Er—small train, isn't it?"

"Not too small to be packed with surprises," replied Paula Harte. She began to appear not altogether displeased. "Nice of you to stop by."

"This is a pleasure, Miss Harte," he murmured warily, "a really unexpected pleasure. By the bye, you don't happen to have a roommate?"

The Harte girl shot him a coolly inquisitive look, then half smiled. "No. I was fortunate enough to secure this compartment to myself."

North grinned, emitted a small whistle of surprise. Wariness in bucketfuls chilled a not unpleasurable sense of uncertainty. Um. His eye flickered up to his battered suitcase. It appeared not to have been tampered with, but the aspect of the situation seemed a bit thick.

Could Miss Harte really have failed to notice his valise up there? Possibly. People so seldom took in details above eye level.

Subdued curiosity marked Paula Harte's manner as a smile parted ripe, evenly rouged lips. Smoothly she seated herself upon a berth running the width of the European-type compartment.

"Well, Major, please do come in for a moment. I am interested to learn how you found where I was."

A brown and wiry figure, North remained before the compartment door after he had pushed it shut with his heel. Not until she had closed her bag and placed it on the blanket cover beside her did he relax.

"Am I mistaken, Miss Harte, or weren't you expecting—someone?" A speculative and faintly ironical gleam lit his gray-blue eyes. "Your welcome was most *attentive.*" He inflected the last word to its French meaning.

"Not precisely, Major." She shoved aside a fragile blue nightgown liberally inset with lace at various strategic points, and indicated the foot of the berth. "Won't you sit down?"

"I shall be delighted," he murmured, then added, "but perhaps I should be inviting you to sit on *my* bed?"

Paula Harte instantly colored and her smile vanished.

"I do not understand your meaning, I am sure. Perhaps, Major, you had better—"

"Go? Oh, no. I wouldn't dream of leaving now."

"What?" Her hand started towards the bag.

"Don't," he advised sharply. "I can move pretty quick when there's reason."

As, coldly, she stared at him, he perceived that this was a singularly determined and self-possessed young woman.

She shoved aside a long lock of blonde hair which was

dangling before one eye. "Unless you leave at once, I shall call the conductor!" She reached towards a push button.

"I wouldn't ring. If the conductor comes, my dear, charming as you are, he would be forced to throw you out of here."

"Throw me— Have you gone mad?"

"No."

Anxiously she considered him an instant, then asked, "What is it you want?"

"Only my compartment. I'm hot and uncommonly tired." He nodded to the rack. "Incidentally, that little item up yonder is my bag."

"What!" It was clear that Paula Harte had not noticed the suitcase. "Then your porter has made a stupid mistake."

"Possibly. But suppose you inspect this?" North offered his stub. Once she had read it, Paula Harte dug frantically into her bag and produced an exact duplicate.

She began to laugh a little too heartily for sheer amusement. "But this is ridiculous! They are identical!"

Warily, North compared the slips of pasteboard. "Identical, yes, except that mine was bought in the station while you seem to have gotten yours on the train."

The girl in pale gray-blue bit her lip, considered her companion with fresh interest. "Mine, then, is invalid?"

"Under the law, I suppose so. However—"

She brightened. "Then it is all very simple. I will get another compartment."

It was only then that North sensed the real entrepreneur of this ambulant bedroom farce. That confounded conductor!

Quietly, Paula Harte commenced to collect her belongings.

"Before you pack," he suggested, "suppose we consult with the conductor?"

"You talk. I—I prefer to remain in here. There are—well, reasons why. Please go."

Five minutes later North returned, irritation written large across his features. Behind he had left a sadly puzzled would-be promoter of romance lamenting the astonishing unpredictableness of the North Americans.

"Well, Miss Harte. Seems we're up against it," he reported. "There's not even a vacant berth aboard, let alone a whole compartment. Fate and the E.F.C.B. railroad seem to have decreed that you and I are to be—well, traveling companions. I must say, though, the Central Railroad carries 'courtesy of the road' to extremes."

Paula Harte laughed softly, followed his gaze up to the luggage rack. "For an American, Major, you display an astonishing appreciation of the whimsical."

"I suppose I must be a great, gallant gentleman and sit up in the club car."

"You must not!" Paula Harte contradicted, looking up at him. "You are very tired, I see it plainly—and so am I. But neither of us need do without rest. No, Major, we shall manage. We are not prissy children, are we?"

Who the so-and-so, North kept wondering, was this young woman? No ordinary passenger, else why those dramatics at his unexpected entrance?

The girl, too, conducting a reappraisal, found this gaunt and humorously alert gentleman with the high cheek-bones, bronzed complexion and the slightly ironic smile distinctly attractive.

With a supple movement Paula Harte swung her legs up onto the edge of the berth. "Well, Major, since this is to be *our* compartment, shall we make ourselves comfortable? Do you mind if I put my feet up?"

"If you don't object to my shedding this beastly hot coat."

Where the hell had he seen this girl's face before? That she was not either English or American was certain; and, unless she had lived long years in Brazil, she was not German; too much taste in clothes. Could she be a Swede perhaps? Possibly.

As a gentle hint, he made no effort to conceal his shoulder holster when he removed his coat. Surprisingly, she failed to comment at all on the automatic, so he reluctantly dedicated himself to a night of vigilance.

After he had rung for two *abacaxi refrescos,* they relaxed, vis-à-vis, comfortably propped against opposite ends of the berth. Pleasantly reminiscent of Manuela was an aura of Flor do Noite perfume arising from her bag lying half opened beside the berth. Um. Flor do Noite surely was catnip to him.

"You are quite sure, Major," she was observing with a mocking curve to her lips, "that it was not *Camarote* Ten that you were seeking?"

"Compartment Ten?"

"Men are incredibly forgetful," Paula Harte complained, wrinkling her nose at him. "Surely you cannot already have forgotten your conquest?"

"Conquest?"

Taunting lights sparkled in the smoky-blue eyes. "Alesandro's mamma, remember?"

North flinched. "Oh, my God! Don't ever bring that up."

"But you were looking ever so thoughtful."

"Was I? Well, I was only trying to decide on your nationality."

"I am Brazilian, Major. A Carioca of the Cariocans."

"You're a liar, even if a lovely one," North told himself. Though the faintest imaginable accent in her speech suggested a Latin background, he guessed it stemmed from some other part of South America. Despite the fact that Spanish and Portuguese were kindred tongues, there was nevertheless a shading which differentiated the two when English was spoken.

Again, though Paula Harte usually had addressed him as senhor, in moments of tension she called him señor, the Spanish equivalent.

As the express tore on through a night made glorious by a three-quarter moon, he suggested, "You have been in São Paulo on business?"

The dark blue eyes swung to consider him and a hitherto unnoticed dimple appeared in her chin. "Your intuition is terrifying, Major. Yes, I have been engaged in a delicate mission for—a great banking house of Rio de Janeiro."

To North that rang about as true as a pewter bell, but he let it pass.

"And you?"

"Why, I've been on a hunting trip," he replied, truthfully enough. "There is a surprising variety of game to be found in the vicinity of São Paulo."

"So I have heard," came her enigmatic assent.

Time flowed by in tempo with the surging pace of the *Cruzeiro do Sul,* and presently the now heavy-eyed trainboy entered bearing drinks and as silently withdrew.

Against the soft blue-gray velour of the upholstery and the richly gleaming panels of mahogany, Paula's blonde head glowed pleasingly by the subdued light. For greater comfort she cast loose the cuffs of her white silk blouse. All at once she nodded to herself and her mouth relaxed.

"I remember now."

"Remember what, my dear?"

"Where I have seen you."

"You are sure?"

"Yes. You were leaving the Companhia Americus proving grounds," she observed, her breast trembling gently to the train's vibrations. "I am very sure of it."

"I am flattered but also puzzled," North confessed.

"Puzzled? Why?"

"Because I am sure I have seen you, or a picture of you, not so long ago."

Recollection came to him so suddenly that he almost cried out. Great God above! It was this girl's picture which stood on *Captain Stuart Maitland's desk!* What could this chromium-nerved young woman have to do with the United States Embassy's Junior Military Attaché?

"And where was that?" sweetly inquired Paula Harte.

"It must have been on some society page," he evaded, still mentally reeling from the implications of his recollection.

The steady droning of an electric fan above their heads sounded very loud in the brief silence.

"Me, in society?" The possibility seemed to afford Paula Harte boundless amusement. "Heaven forbid! You must guess once more, Major."

"Can't. I'm fagged out," yawned the Intelligence officer. "You are familiar with Brazilian hospitality? It's genuine, it's unique, it's complete—but my God, it's exhausting."

Cigarettes dissolved themselves into gray smoke and stubs littering a bronze ash tray, and North found himself rendered speechless by the dexterity with which his companion recognized—and evaded—certain innocuous, but leading, remarks.

At length Paula Harte politely smothered a yawn, kicked off her pumps and, blinking, slid lower onto the berth.

"I am going to sleep," she announced. "If you wish to read, Major North, a light will not annoy me."

"No. Think I'll catch forty winks, too," North replied and, switching off the light, stretched long legs upon luggage arranged for that purpose.

By the time the *Cruzeiro do Sul* was rocketing into Santos, he was fighting to stay awake. By now the sultriest corner of hell wasn't half hot enough for that blasted, interfering conductor.

The Harte girl seemed sound asleep, her delicate profile turned and her pale head pillowed on one arm. Her position created a fascinating sweeping line down from her hip to one slim ankle; there were no worn or stained patches on the stocking's sole, either.

If only Brazil were not so luscious an international plum! Vastly underpopulated, yet abundant in rubber, sugar, tobacco and coffee, what temptations did not lie in a growing beef industry, in vast herds of sheep and in amazingly rich mineral deposits?

Small wonder that all three Axis powers had agents busy everywhere, stealthily sapping the Republic's strength, stealing her secrets and trying to confuse her people. A country so sparsely settled, so polyglot must represent Fifth Columnists' idea of Heaven.

Once the last lights of Santos had swept past the compartment windows, North resettled himself and, titillated by elusive whiffs of Flor da Noite, sought consolation in reminiscences of little Manuela—expertly affectionate Manuela!

His introspection was not fated to last long. Although no evidences of a town were visible, the *Cruzeiro do Sul* sounded its whistle twice and commenced to slow its plunge through the night.

North half opened his eyes. Paula Harte sighed, turned cautiously on the berth. When, slowly, she turned her rumpled blonde head, he batted his eyes almost shut and watched his companion study him very intently. Apparently reassured on this point, she swung long and muscular legs over his body with the ease of an athlete and sat peering out into the moonlit night. Acute tension was expressed in every fiber of her body.

North was interested to note that she did not put her face close to the window either, but stayed well back, as a well-trained observer should. When, presently, a clump of kerosene flares drew squirming bright patterns on the stateroom ceiling, she flinched away into the dark.

Reflected in the highly polished mahogany paneling above his head, North beheld the outlines of several uniformed figures; also the wicked and significant profile of a number of carbine barrels. Voices called something unintelligible; then a succession of dim kerosene lamps jogged slowly past the compartment windows.

Just before the express came to a halt, when the jolting might presumably rouse her companion, Paula Harte replaced her head on the pillow, feigned sleep. The halt proved brief. Almost at once, the brakes sighed and a lantern flashed.

Because North continued to puff in apparently unbreakable slumber, Paula Harte got quickly and very silently to her feet. Under cover of the noise made by the train in gathering way, she lowered a window still farther. Then, squatting on her heels, she must have made a rapid selection of objects from her suitcase. At any rate he heard various catches click. This done, she slipped on her pumps, donned her hat and hesitated in the center of the stateroom with her purse clutched nervously before her.

North deliberated interference but, as rapidly, decided against any overt act—not that he entertained the least respect for that miniature automatic in her purse. He had plenty to worry over without becoming involved in skulduggery not his own.

He certainly had to admire Paula Harte's self-control. Quite still she stood waiting, listening as the train commenced to clank on towards Rio; then, quite as calmly as if she were stopping a bus, she reached up and pulled hard on the emergency cord. Immediately the air brakes whistled and chattered and when once more the express stood still, she climbed nimbly upon the seat and thrust a cleanly modeled leg through the open window.

Gripping the purse handle between her teeth, Paula Harte swung her weight over the sill as, on all sides, arose shouted queries evoked by this third emergency stop.

Grinning, North sat up as the blonde young woman's blue skirt, fashionably brief and tight, rode up and snagged itself on the window crank handle. The more she struggled, the higher rode the hem, until a noteworthy length of pallid skin showed above Paula Harte's stocking top. When a hubbub of voices and feet resounded in the corridor she gasped.

Awkwardly astraddle the sill, she jerked, tried desperately to free her skirt. *"Nombre de Dios! Que mala suerte!"*

"Señorita, permit me the pleasure." North jumped up and released the imprisoned cloth.

"Mil gracias!" Paula Harte flashed him a look of unutterable gratitude, planted a warm kiss full on his mouth, then dropped lightly to the ballast and ran like the very devil until she disappeared amid a moonlit tangle of coffee trees.

North had just time to grin, to sink back on the berth and savor her lipstick ere a pass-key commenced to rattle in the compartment's door.

Mr. Prescott Explains

MAJOR HUGH NORTH made it a point not to react too rapidly to the sudden irruption into his compartment of a rotund plainclothesman and two saddle-complexioned gendarmes uniformed in gray. The latter held ready a brace of short-barreled cavalry carbines.

"*Perdão, senhor,*" began the plainclothesman as he switched on the lights. "One regrets exceedingly the necessity to interrupt your rest, but we seek for someone, a blonde young woman, a beautiful blonde young woman."

"Eh, wha'-wha's that?" North rubbed his eyes, managed a none-too-intelligent stare and mumbled in Spanish, "*Qué quiere Usted?*"

"*Perdão, senhor.*" The speaker bent immediately over Miss Harte's bag; it stood half open with fragile and intimate feminine garments overflowing onto the compartment's floor. From these the fat man's gaze flashed to the wide-open window. "There was a lady in here with you?"

Immediately North noted that a destination tag was missing from the handle of Miss Harte's bag; also that the bag bore no initials whatsoever.

"I—yes, that is to say, a lady *was* in here. Where is she?"

The fat man's dark features contracted. "That is what we wish to learn."

"Ask me another, *amigo mío*. One is not clever at riddles."

Silently Hugh North began to curse the accident of his meeting with Paula Harte. Or was it not so much of an accident? He thought fast. Wouldn't it be the devil to get dragged off the express in order to answer a set of questions posed by some thoroughly worried provincial police official?

The two gendarmes put broad-brimmed straw hats together, conversed with the plainclothesman in rapid Portuguese.

"Senhor, we have been informed that a person most urgently desired for questioning boarded this Express in São Paulo," explained the official. "We see reason to believe that she has—er—occupied this compartment. Please, senhor, when did the Senhorita leave?"

"I regret that I do not know, Senhor," North lied with the facility of a veteran in Intelligence work. He heaved himself to a sitting position and straightened his tie. Was this a genuine check-up, or some wheel turning within wheels?

The man in the doorway looked very unhappy. Clearly he was beyond his depth.

"But, senhor, since you have shared the same *camarote*, you must know something of this desired lady?"

"To be sure," North admitted sleepily. "There was a stupid error about the tickets, arranged by the conductor through a mistaken weakness for romance. This young lady, whose name I do not even know, was most annoyed at having to share a compartment. We hardly spoke."

Fervently, North prayed that this tired-looking, olive-skinned man would not notice the two glasses standing so convivially together above the wash-basin—one of them yet bore lip-prints done in bright carmine. Nor was the fact that only one ash tray had been employed at all helpful, especially since there were several in the compartment.

The *Cruzeiro do Sul* had started its oft-interrupted progress once more when a second group of highly excited officials appeared in the corridor. One, a thin, hook-nosed individual with an unmistakable air of authority, waved his underlings aside, politely introduced himself as one Miguel Carvalho of the railroad police. By the time he had seated himself beside North, the latter had managed to dump the ash tray and to divorce those too cozy-appearing highball glasses.

"It is, senhor, for the good of the State that you inform us of this young woman's name. Surely you must have learned that?"

"I have already explained that we were barely on speaking terms," North returned. If he must make any disclosures concerning the remarkable senhorita Harte, they had better be reserved for the ears of higher officials.

As the express clattered over a series of switch points and its whistle screamed like a fiend ejected from heaven, North demanded with genuine interest, "What can this young woman have done that you should hunt her so urgently?"

To make up lost time, the *Cruzeiro do Sul* was fairly flying now and a cold night wind came beating in through the open window and bringing the sour-sweet smell of sugar cane fields.

"The charge," the man in white gravely returned, "is one of the gravest, of activity against the safety of the State and—" he hesitated, "of complicity, at least, in a theft."

The man in white fixed him with penetrating dark eyes. "Senhor, you are *very* sure you have had no conversation with her?"

"None beyond the most casual," North assured him.

The thin-faced man sighed, shrugged. "Then I shall leave you to your rest. My apologies and *bôa noite,* senhor."

As the plainclothesman and his superior bowed and backed out into the overflowing corridor, North smothered a small sigh of relief.

"The answer is obvious," he heard the hawk-faced man mutter. "We must look for this wretched female on the road between Lorena and Rio."

The two gendarmes gathered up Paula Harte's bag but left her negligee and that fetching crêpe de chine nightgown swaying from a hook behind the compartment's door.

Once more alone, Hugh North thoughtfully lit a cigarette. So *this* was the kind of girl Stuart Maitland kept a picture of? Well. Well! *Well!*

Towering above the noisy crowd at the E.F. Central railroad terminal loomed Captain Maitland's broad shoulders. Eagerly, his clear gray eyes scanned the crowd. A fine face that, clean looking, capable and typically American in its structure. The only possible criticism was that his mouth was a bit small and had a hint of stubbornness about it.

Beside the Junior Military Attaché North glimpsed a shorter individual whom he recognized as Edward Prescott, precise, almost prissy, veteran First Secretary to the Embassy. Once Maitland discerned North's wiry figure advancing through the highly scented swarm of passengers, he jerked a barely perceptible nod, turned on his heel and, with Prescott a step or so behind, sauntered off.

Eyes alert, Major North pushed through a good-natured and varicolored throng of sailors in striped jerseys and with small gold rings in their ears. There were also gauchos in from the North, peasants from the interior carrying cages of pets and rolls of blankets, gold-spangled officers, soldiers on leave, trollops, ordinary commuters from the suburbs and hundreds of grinning little Bahianas in colorful costumes. On all sides vendors and newsboys shrieked at the top of their lungs, *"O Globo!" "Diário Car-r-rioca!" "Re-fresco lar-r-anjada!" "Doces! Doces!"*

Posters advertising the impending Carnival do Rio blazed on all sides, together with gay advertisements announcing various balls, Carnival Club costume contests and excursions galore.

North groaned mentally. Carnival, he knew, would commence on the morrow. For two reasons he had cause to feel resentful. There could now be no chance of his joining wholeheartedly in that fascinatingly colorful musical madness which for nearly a week renders Rio de Janeiro spontaneously gay. Also, he foresaw that during the next four days government services would be curtailed or altogether inoperative; persons would be very hard to find.

It came as no surprise to Hugh North that also quitting the *Cruzeiro do Sul* was the hawk-faced railroad police inspector who had taken charge of Paula Harte's luggage. He seemed at once agitated, puzzled, and in a hurry.

Waiting with motor running before the gaily decorated station platform was Captain Maitland's gray club coupé. The Junior Military Attaché sat behind the wheel while on the rattan-covered rear seat lounged the First Secretary, smoking and surveying the passing traffic as if he had not a care in the world.

Once North had swung his bag aboard and stepped inside, the Military Attaché put the car in gear and commenced expertly to weave a hair-raising course among trucks, bicycles and cabs dashing about with an abandon exceeding even that of Paris or Havana.

"Well, Major, I'll confess we're mighty relieved to see you here," Prescott greeted and offered a nervous hand.

"Thanks. As a matter of fact, I had an interesting trip."

"Did you?" Prescott demanded sharply, then said absently, "Want to hear all about it—but later."

The First Secretary fixed a quizzical eye on the Intelligence officer's bronzed features. North braced himself. Since eavesdropping on a moving automobile was next to impossible, he guessed he would soon learn what was up.

"No doubt, Major," the First Secretary began, his hands slowly tightening on his lap, "you are wondering what in God's world could have justified our relieving you of the Companhia Americus assignment?"

North smiled wryly, confessed to having suffered a certain amount of curiosity.

Mr. Prescott's rather thick fingers commenced to drum on plump, pongee-covered knees.

"As you certainly know, the Axis nations are determined to forestall—if they can't wreck—the Brazilian-United States plans for hemisphere defense. You, better than anyone else in the service, are familiar with the Axis technique in such efforts. The Haushofer system of political infiltration, is it not?"

North nodded.

Prescott said, "Will you refresh my memory?"

"Very well," North replied earnestly. "For the amazing success of his campaigns to date, Hitler has a certain Major-General Karl Haushofer to thank more than any one man."

"Major-General?"

"Yes. This Haushofer, you see, was the inventor and perfecter of the so-called *Stützpunkte* system of political infiltration."

North had to raise his voice over a sudden furious

pandemonium of taxi horns and the insistent shrilling of police whistles. "When a country is to be softened, strategically located base points are set up, complete with arms, ammunition, radios, explosives. Such *Stützpunkte* are usually located near prime military objectives.

"This activity goes hand in hand with the other subversive activities such as the organization of bunds, the buying or suborning of newspapers, the establishment of camouflaged U-boat bases and of landing fields. Next comes the stirring up of internal dissension by the bought newspapers, the bribery of officers and politicians and the organization of 'tourists' and traitors into a Fifth Column.

"Oh, it's all very ugly and complete—and effective!"

Hugh North broke off, glowered upon a line of porters trotting by balancing a bedroom set complete to wash-basin and chamberpot on their kinky heads.

Prescott frowned. "Yes. I know. We gather that this sort of infiltration has had a good start here in Brazil."

North's voice grew edged as a surgical instrument. "Down in São Paulo I learned that once Pujol's Patriotistas get established, we can look for a northward drive by the Axis. There'll be slow encroachments, little advances, unimportant except to the wary." He held up a succession of fingers. "First Venezuela, then Colombia, then, without warning of course, comes the attack on their main objective—the United States."

A hard little smile flitted across North's lips. "I know. I risked my life to see what would—and what did—happen in Holland. But nobody in Washington would listen—not until after the ax had fallen."

304 G-2b

SMOOTHLY, Captain Maitland's long-snouted car sped across the Praça Republica, then down the bunting- and flag-draped Avenida Maréchal Floriano. Increasingly the distinctive roar of the city beat on North's consciousness. Acrid-sweet, the scent of roasting coffee grew stronger in his nostrils. In animated groups Cariocans stood before various cafés gossiping about the impending carnival and sipping their eternal *cafezinhos.*

Absently North rubbed his hands on his knees, said briskly, "Well, Mr. Prescott, suppose we come to cases? I suspect we haven't much time?"

"Right. We—you will have to move fast—very fast, indeed, if anything is to be accomplished."

The First Secretary turned a face by no means as fresh and jaunty as the rosebud in his buttonhole. He spoke agitatedly. "Yesterday afternoon a code clerk at the Embassy brought in to us a pair of wireless messages picked up and relayed to Brazil by the State Department's listening station at Anacostia."

Having long since learned that silence is a very able questioner, North made no comment.

"At no matter what cost," Prescott informed him with a

simple air of gravity that was enormously effective, "you are to locate the destination of a certain freighter now presumably nearing the coast of Brazil."

"You are positive, of course, that this vessel *is* headed for Brazil?"

"Reasonably so."

"You don't know its name?"

"No."

"Nor where it is due to make port?"

"We have no idea."

"Or when?"

"No," the secretary admitted gloomily. "Worse still, we can't even be sure of the reliability of the information. You'll have to estimate that for yourself, when you've heard the whole story. The danger is so grave, however, that the Department cannot afford to ignore any possibility."

Prescott's forehead became creased with concern. "If these wireless messages *are* authentic, then the most viciously expert and experienced corps of saboteurs, technicians, aviation experts and Fifth Columnists the Gestapo has ever sent abroad are, at this instant, nearing the coast of Brazil!"

Hugh North passed a hand slowly over his chin, tried to grasp the terrific implications of such a move. Over the roar of traffic the First Secretary's voice droned on.

"Further, enough gold is reported on board this vessel to finance a very sizeable revolution. Ready cash, by the bye, is just about all our local brand of Führer, José Pujol, lacks to take over."

North felt his mouth go dry as he inquired, "You are certain Pujol and his Patriotistas are expecting the arrival of this freighter?"

"Not at all certain. You can never be sure about the Gestapo and their methods," came the disconcertingly prompt reply. "But to us it seems quite logical that they should. The Brazilian Intelligence informs us that Pujol requires only a gesture of outside assistance; then he and his Patriotistas will become a deadly menace. It's the old, old story of a belligerent and well-organized minority."

North nodded soberly, then suggested, "Suppose we leave Pujol for the moment? May I see those wireless messages?"

As the car swung past the ever-astonishing monument to Marechal Peixoto, Prescott delved into his breast pocket, passed over two slips of pale blue paper. "That's the pair of them. The first was heard very faintly and, therefore, not effectively tuned in until after the name of the ship had been transmitted."

"Oh, I see."

"The second came in fairly strong but—" Prescott paused significantly— "incomplete."

North listened, found no time to appreciate the handsome buildings, the flower-filled window boxes everywhere, the graceful, sun-dappled trees and the very broad sidewalks of checkered black and white mosaic. As from another room, he heard the First Secretary's voice saying,

"The sender gave only an approximate position in his first message, you understand." The secretary's blood-shot eyes swung to meet North's. "Suppose you look them over yourself?"

In scanning the first message, North noted that the receiving operator had at least recorded the time.

3/19/41

10:01 a.m.

LATITUDE THREE DEGREES SOUTH LONGITUDE SEVENTEEN WEST. CALLING U.S.

NEUTRALITY PATROL BRITISH WARSHIPS.
HIGH AXIS PROPAG AGTS RADIO TECHNICS
FLYERS ABOARD AS REFUGEES. GREAT SUM
GOLD DESTINED U.S.B. INTERCEPT NO TIME
MORE NOW STAND BY.

304   G2b

The second message was terse, obviously hurried:

3/19/41
12:45 p.m.
    SUSPECT WATCHED AXIS PASSENG PLAN
SEIZE SHIP TONITE FOR GODS SAKE HALT
FREIGHTER—

North, while digesting the essence of these messages item by
item, was aware of a bitter, icy tide rising and spreading in his
being. U.S.B.? Of course that designated the United States of
Brazil. A great sum of gold? Gold. Just the bait with which to
lure into the Axis camp a set of treacherous politicians, would-
be viceroys and bush-league Gauleiters. It seemed entirely prob-
able that aboard this vessel must be equipment for a radio
station capable of penetrating to even the remotest states of
the Brazilian Republic.

Again and yet again, North reread the messages. Then, with
high cheek-bones unusually prominent, he faced Prescott.

"Have any steps been taken?"

"None except to warn vessels of our Neutrality Patrol—and
the British, of course—to be on the lookout for a freighter
suspicious in appearance."

The First Secretary turned a drawn pink and gray countenance. "What do you make of all this? Every few hours
Washington has been demanding information."

"What is the Brazilian reaction to all this?"

"Their Ministry of Foreign Affairs is worried, but a majority of the officials there are inclined to think these messages the work of some lonely radio operator trying to amuse himself."

North's deepset gray eyes narrowed momentarily. "I might be inclined to agree with them—"

"What!"

"Except for the signature on that first message," North added deliberately.

"We have investigated that point," the secretary told him, "What does 304 G-2b suggest to you?"

"304 G-2b? Um," North mused, his eyes straying out to view a detail of the National Guard tramping by. "G-2b, of course, indicates the counter-espionage subdivision of G-2."

"Do you happen to know what officer had number 304?" Prescott inquired.

"Can't say; there are so many changes nowadays."

Tires screamed as Maitland's gray sedan first dodged a huge, gaudily painted truck, then narrowly missed a mild-looking old gentleman who was attempting to cross the street while reading a newspaper.

Prescott said, "Three hundred and four was the number assigned to a Lieutenant Paul Sturtevant."

"Sturtevant? Sturtevant?" The Intelligence officer's chin tightened as he tilted back his head in concentration. "Um. Wasn't Paul Sturtevant reported killed when the Nazis blitzed Belgrade?"

"Yes," the Embassy official confirmed, his eyes fixed unseeingly on a small donkey which pattered by bearing two large cans of milk in a canvas sling-saddle. "That is what G-2 was informed and so reported last night when I phoned Washington."

"Good Lord! You *phoned*?"

Prescott looked annoyed. "Should have encoded and cabled, I suppose, but we were very short of time and—this reported death of Sturtevant raised some delicate and very critical questions."

"For instance," North muttered, "the certainty that Sturtevant *really* was killed?"

"Yes. His body was never found. There's the unpleasant possibility that the Foreign section of the Gestapo—"

"UA-1, if you are curious."

"Thank you. That UA-1 has taken over Sturtevant's number and is using it. Or did Sturtevant have to lie low and finally manage to smuggle himself aboard this ship?"

"A neat series of questions," North admitted heavily, "and not easy to answer. It's a damned shame Sturtevant—if it was he—didn't send the name of that freighter at the beginning of his second message." He needed to do a lot of deductive reasoning about that vessel.

Prescott collected himself, anxiously studied his companion. "Well, Major, I'd like your opinion. Is this genuine, or maybe a clever scheme to decoy British auxiliary cruisers into a trap?"

"At this point I have no opinion," explained the Intelligence officer. "I can't have until I learn what, if anything, there is to be picked up at this end."

Momentarily, the car halted to permit the passage of a funeral. To North's amazement the hearse, flower cars and cortège all went tearing by at not less than forty miles an hour with the hearse driver repeatedly sounding his horn and the mourners doing likewise.

"'Horns are more fun than brakes.'" Prescott quoted. "That's a primary Cariocan belief. But you soon get used to the racket—or go crazy.

"The Department hated to take you off the Americus

matter," he continued, "because, as we both now know, these 304 G-2b messages may very well be a lot of moonshine. Some of the Brazilian officials, though, are not inclined to be skeptical. They have assigned to collaborate with you a chap called Lieutenant Ramon Nabuco—one of the best men from their Department of Naval Intelligence. I believe he met you when you came in on the Clipper?"

"Yes. Seemed a steady sort."

"If these radiograms prove bonafide, the urgency of the situation is self-evident," Prescott observed as Maitland guided his car along the Avenida Rio Branco. "Let this freighter unload and—as I've already said, the Patriotistas will find the chance they've been waiting for."

"Yes, I know. Down in Santos I came across whole towns in which I heard nothing but German or Italian, and up north the same is true of the Japanese, I'm told. What kind of a surveillance can be arranged?"

"Do you know how long the Brazilian coast-line is?" acidly inquired Prescott. "It has literally hundreds of small river-mouth ports; why, there are dozens in the Amazon delta alone. It would be utterly impossible to keep any kind of watch over all those ports."

Um! North saw he wasn't going to be allowed much opportunity for groundwork; this was all of a piece with those callous preparations which had preceded the destruction of Norway, of the Netherlands and of the Balkans.

North experienced a sensation of grim anticipation. He had fought the Boches before—but those Boches had been not so subtle, not so utterly cynical as these of Himmler's breed. Yes, it would be interesting, damned interesting, to take another crack at that people which, within a quarter of a century, had twice deluged the world with blood, tears and despair.

The Military Attaché

TWO blocks east of the handsome new United States Embassy on the Rua São Clemente, Edward Prescott asked to be let out.

"I hope you'll have some real news for us soon, Major," he said anxiously. "The Department is raising more hell every hour that goes by."

As Major North was joining Captain Maitland on the coupé's front seat, he noticed again the presence of a small blue sedan which, for some time, had been cruising very unostentatiously in the gray coupé's wake.

"I say, Maitland," North demanded, "haven't we some persistent admirers?"

The Junior Military Attaché's laugh was brief and hard. "You bet. Our Embassy staff—the British, too, of course—is being tailed night and day."

"Police protection?"

"Hardly," Maitland grunted, turning his car away from the curb. "Those fellows back there are members of what we've come to call the Axis Touring and Chowder Club."

North felt a trifle taken aback at so frank an admission. "Can't you give 'em the bum's rush?"

Maitland's squarish jaw tightened. "There's not a thing we can do so long as the bright boys back there never get actively objectionable—and so far they haven't. If you say 'How come?' they claim to be only sightseeing. Funny, isn't it? They all look like Phi Beta Kappas out of a school for parachutists."

It was with wariness that Hugh North entered the Military Attaché's rooms in a huge modernistic apartment house on the Avenida Atlantica. It was a shock to realize that, much as he had hoped his memory to be at fault, it was not. Yonder on Captain Maitland's desk a studio portrait of Paula Harte smiled from an expensive green leather and gold easel frame.

"Praise Allah for air conditioning on a day like this," Maitland sighed and, after stripping off his coat, eased a wiry five feet ten inches into a chair. After lighting a cigarette he smiled almost boyishly at his black-haired guest.

"Say, it's mighty good to have you on deck, Major."

"Thanks."

"Where will you be staying?" he inquired.

"At the Copacabana Palace, I expect," North returned. "I like lots of people about when things are getting hot. None of your sleepy pensions or second-rate hotels where you'll generally find the night clerk dozing. *That* error nearly got me done in in Cuba once."

A Negro servant brought in a pair of small coffee cups and a tall pot which gave off aromatic feathers of steam.

"Where's your boss, Maitland?"

"Colonel Adams is away observing Second Corps maneuvers in Rio Grande do Sul. I'm holding the fort while he's gone."

Once the *cafezinho*s had been served and the servant gone, North inquired, "What can you add to what Prescott told me?"

Maitland frowned. "Not an earthly thing. I've been up to my

ears in the Americus investigation. You can believe I hated like hell to see G-2 relieve you of the São Paulo assignment, and I'm not sure yet it was justified. I'll bet you were really getting places."

The Intelligence officer's dark head inclined briefly but, with matters as they were, he framed a cautious answer.

"There *are* illegal arms shipments leaving the Americus plant, all right. There was a letter I—"

"Illegal exports?" the Junior Military Attaché leaned forward, his small pale gray eyes intent.

"That's the catch," North replied between sips of the almost syrupy coffee. Nuisance about Colonel Adams being absent. For all his obvious keenness Maitland had certain things still to learn. "Though the shipping cases were *marked,* and the invoices billed for export, I discovered something interesting—"

"They weren't being shipped at all?"

North kept rein on his impatience, said, "No. For instance, I found out that if a munitions shipment was destined for Paraguay but showed a period after the word 'Paraguay,' then said case was placed aboard a truck which subsequently headed straight *into the state of Rio Grande do Sul!* Any shipment marked 'Venezuela' in dark blue paint never even starts for Santos and shipment north. Such cases I find disappear in the general direction of Minas Geraes and so forth."

Maitland's gray eyes rounded themselves. "The hell you say! Anything else?"

With the strident whistling of a ferry leaving the Praça Mauá beating faintly into the apartment, North hesitated. A recollection of Paula Harte climbing through the sleeping car window was yet very fresh in his memory—for more reasons than one.

"Anything else you learned?" Maitland insisted.

It was the devil to have to hold back information. North didn't like it; but if Paula Harte was an intimate of Maitland's—

"No, there is nothing except that extra-confidential mail seems to be passing between Luis da Evaristo and the Estrella del Mar Company."

"How do you know that?"

"I got next to one of da Evaristo's secretaries."

"Da Evaristo's secretary!" Maitland ejaculated, then said, "Which one? Da Evaristo has many."

"Fellow named Pombo. Why?"

"I just wondered," returned the attaché, then went on hurriedly. "Estrella del Mar? That sounds Spanish."

"It does," came North's curt assent. "But this corporation isn't Spanish; it's German—lock, stock and barrel."

"What does this company do?" the attaché wanted to know, leaning forward, his handsome sunburnt head outthrust.

"Theoretically," North explained, watching his word, "the chairman of Estrella del Mar's board, a certain Dr. Hermann Rupp, is trying to arrange for the liquidation of Nazi credits tied up by the war. They have chiefly to do with shipping."

Maitland shrugged broad shoulders, started to put a question but checked himself and said, "First minute you get time, Major, I'd like to go over your São Paulo data. I've developed some theories in that direction." He got up. "Meantime I expect you'll want to get settled at the Copacabana and get rolling on this queer 304 G-2b matter?"

"There's no time to throw away," North agreed. "By the bye, who's the gorgeous gal?" He nodded towards the photograph on Maitland's desk.

Maitland's rather broad red face lit. He seemed at once

pleased and a trifle hesitant as he took up Paula Harte's portrait, tilted his blond head to one side and beamed on it.

"Pretty, isn't she?"

"Fascinating," was North's ambiguous verdict. "I'd say there's a good deal of character about that chin of hers."

Maitland colored like a schoolboy, blurted, "I'm sure glad you admire her, Major. You see—I—I—" he glanced up with a singularly engaging smile, "well, I expect to marry her very soon."

Marry! Had the floor opened and permitted Hugh North to drop five floors, he could not have been more taken aback. A flirtation, an attachment with the Junior Military Attaché—a liaison at most—was all he had anticipated. He must have betrayed a measure of his surprise, for Maitland demanded quickly,

"What's the matter? Why do you look like that?"

"Oh, I—oh—" For the first time in many a moon, Hugh North found himself floundering. "I was thinking how lucky you were to win so—unusual-looking a girl."

Maitland put down the picture, stood very stiff and West Point before his guest. "I don't think you were, sir," said he slowly. "I can guess, though, what you were thinking. You have heard gossip concerning Paula." Belligerency entered his tone. "If you have, Major, I'll thank you not to repeat it." Then he made an appealing little motion with his hand. "Paula *is* different from most girls, I'll admit that, sir, but—well, you see, she has had to make her own way."

"Oh, then she's working?"

"Yes. As confidential secretary to Luis da Evaristo. Paula has a very responsible position in his Rio office."

So this was why Maitland had been so anxious about his having seen da Evaristo's secretary?

"Since when has it been disgraceful for a girl to work for a living?" Maitland's expression was like that of a mule getting ready to kick.

"Don't be an idiot," North smiled. "I'm sure Miss Harte is very capable. If I ever marry, it will be a girl who has worked—" And he wondered what ever could have become of Vanessa Byrne.* "Working girls think straighter than most women."

Maitland hurried forward, his hand extended. "Please excuse me, sir. Sorry I flew off the handle. But some people—well, you know how folks are about a person they can't understand. On my word, Paula is everything that is fine and loyal and true!"

Momentarily, North deliberated a revelation, an account of his trip on the *Cruzeiro do Sul;* but he decided against it. Men who felt as Maitland so obviously felt wouldn't listen to logic. All he said was, "I'm sure of it," but he felt a fine perspiration breaking out on the backs of his hands. Were he looking for fineness, truth and loyalty, it would not be in Paula Harte.

---

* *Washington Legation Murders.*

The Butterfly and the Tycoon

HUGH NORTH'S cab raced along but remained well within Rio's sixty-two-mile-an-hour limit and entered an insignificant street. Here the curbs were crowded with shiny black fruit vendors. These either strolled sedately about with heaping, glowing baskets of abacates, goiabas and abius balanced on their heads or squatted on their hams with bandannaed heads held close together.

A wizened, brown-faced individual in a ragged straw hat and a glaringly yellow shirt risked his life by suddenly pushing a small white cart, with many tin cups hooked along its edges, squarely across the street. Over the agonized shrieking of brakes he grinned, waved a friendly salute and kept on intoning, "Laranjadas! Laranjadas!"

North leaned forward, inquired of the cabby, "What is a laranjada?"

"A native drink, Senhor. Ver' good. Coconut water wit' much sugar."

After depositing his bags at the Copacabana Palace and engaging a small suite, the Intelligence officer headed downtown and, a few minutes later, stepped briskly across the marble floor toward the elevator-starter of the A Noite building.

"*Desculpe-me,*" he struggled in Portuguese. "*Avise-me quando devo descer o Companhia Standley Steamship?*"

"On tenth floor, sir," the smiling recepção returned in perfect English. "Room 1001."

Well, here began the campaign, North mused as the car shot skywards—a campaign the outcome of which might shape the destinies of two great nations for generations to come. The thought of his responsibility was almost unnerving. If he guessed wrong, if he only wasted time . . . !

A large, double door of glass displayed the familiar green-and-yellow globe and trident insignia of the Standley Steamship Company. Smaller print indicated that the Line operated freighters between New York, New Orleans, Recife, Belém, Rio de Janeiro and Buenos Aires.

Since it was the luncheon hour, the Company's office, a large room with dozens of desks aligned in three rows behind an expensive railing of acupu wood, appeared all but deserted; but, beyond a mahogany guard-rail, the Intelligence officer noted a door which bore the elegantly lettered inscription, "Office of the President. Private."

North knocked and entered when a girl's voice called, "Come in."

He found himself in a dimly lit reception room smartly finished in copper and sheet-cork. Opposite was a metal door marked "Junius P. Standley."

While his eyes were accustoming themselves to the gloom, North noticed the Line's trade mark repeated on the floor in very shiny linoleum. Two deep leather lounges flanked the door, each equipped with ash trays, cigar boxes, thermoses and coffee tables. A deep blue rug muffled the visitor's tread.

"Like this set-up?" drawled a lazy young voice. "I think it's too, too ducky; too damned ducky for words."

Promptly, North forgot all about the furnishings, for, seated behind a stenographer's desk, was a singular, eye-filling figure; to all intents and purposes a replica of the exotic Carmen Miranda. The girl's get-up was complete down to the least detail, fruit-basket turban, enormous necklaces, bared midriff and dangling earrings.

"Want to see J.P., I expect?"

Placidly, the apparition continued to buff almond-shaped fingernails while beside her a cigarette burned away its life in spirals of white-blue smoke.

Hugh North all but chuckled. Heretofore, he had deemed Junius P. Standley, formerly of New Haven, Connecticut, as a very direct individual with a literal mind, a good taste in cigars and possessed of unusually shrewd business sense. That the president of the enormously influential Standley Steamship Company should indulge—to put it mildly—in so exotic a secretary was infinitely amusing. But no simple secretary could have afforded the expensive hair-do, the subtly perfect make-up of this girl. Before her a small brass plate marked "Miss Louise Clark" nestled amid an incongruous clutter of papers, toiletries, cigarettes and dictation pads.

The girl glanced vaguely up at the tall and wiry figure across the room and, aware of his interested glance, languidly straightened on her chair and in so doing hinted at bosoms of geometric perfection sketchily concealed by a scanty bandeau.

"Want to see somebody?"

North dropped onto one of the lounges. "I *am* seeing somebody—or something. Since when has Standley gone in for inner-office theatricals?"

The girl flushed and stood up, revealing a slim, fresh young figure, rendered enticing by the fidelity with which her costume fitted it. Her eyes of tawny gray, however, somehow suggested that they belonged to a much older person.

"How *very* amusing you are." Her effort at sarcasm dissolved as it made no visible impression on the caller.

"Oh, I see. You—I—well, Miss Clark is Mr. Standley's secretary. She is still out to lunch. Why *do* people try to do business at lunch time? It's barbaric."

"I agree," North said solemnly. "But I still don't understand."

"This is carnival week." Coolly she put down the buffer. "I wanted to try on my costume, so, if there are alterations—" She broke off almost angrily. "I'm sure I don't know why I'm explaining all this to a perfect stranger."

"Carnivals are fun," North observed helpfully. "In Venice once, I—"

"The one here in Rio is superior."

"The costume is most effective—if I may say so."

Involuntarily, North was impressed by this girl's patrician self-assurance. By a narrow margin it missed being condescension. Quite tall, she was, nevertheless, well proportioned. The studied perfection of her poise, posture and her expressions suggested stage experience. Everything about this young woman seemed to murmur, "Look. Of course you will look and admire." He felt that he should know her, yet could assign no reason for this impression.

One really shouldn't readily forget such a cascade of pale brown hair, such faintly slanted eyes, such a delicately formed nose. Yes, those brows, with their faintly quizzical lift, seemed definitely familiar.

Before Hugh North could put mental fingers upon her identity, a door to the left opened and the comfortable, shirt-sleeved rotundity of Junius P. Standley emerged; his gaze was fixed on a sheaf of typewritten correspondence. Still puffing on a panatela cigar, Standley ran a white silk handkerchief across a fringe of receding hairline, then passed it over a rather pudgy jaw line.

"Damn this heat!" he growled, thumbing through his papers. "What's gone wrong with our air conditioner? Miss Clark! Damn it, Aurora, where is Miss Clark?"

"Out to graze."

"Eh! Oh!"

"Gone to lunch, in words of one syllable."

Glancing up for the first time, the shipping man caught sight of the costume. "Great God in heaven! What in blazes goes on here?"

"Remember the old blood-pressure, J.P. I'm just giving the okay to my costume for Opening Ball," the girl informed him carelessly. "Going tomorrow night to the Tenentes do Diabo with Freddy Thomas."

"Christ in the foothills! How dare—"

"Now don't be cross. It just came, and I didn't want to have to buzz way back in from Urca if it needs refitting. Rather super, eh what?" Arising, the tall young woman executed a little pirouette which set spangles on her skirt to flashing. "How do you like it? Pretty bitchy, eh what?"

"In my office I'd like it better off," gruntled the shipping man, but he wasn't really as displeased as he pretended. North, still unnoticed, couldn't exactly blame him.

The girl called Aurora gave Standley a look of pretended shock. "Off? Why, J.P. *How* you talk! But then Aunt Evelyn claims you've always had a weakness for a snappy strip-tease."

"Your Aunt Evelyn knows a lot of things she shouldn't. Dammit, girl, after this please remember that my office is no fitting room!" Junius P. Standley scrambled hurriedly back on his pedestal of official disapproval. "Merely because my sister was careless enough to wish an aristobrat onto the family rates you no privileges."

Carelessly Aurora blew him an airy kiss and closed her nail kit. Mimicking a telephone operator's tone, she turned lightly toward a door to one side. " 'Scuse it, please." She paused, flashed the openly amused Intelligence officer a mechanical smile. "Incidentally, J.P., this tall, dark and handsome gentleman has been waiting to see you."

"Waiting? Why the hot coals of hell didn't—?" The shipping man turned, stared open-mouthed an instant, then hurried over to the lean figure in gray, booming,

"Hugh! You old son of a bitch. How? What in hell are *you* doing in Rio?"

The enthusiasm in Standley's voice was genuine and he clapped his caller heartily on the shoulder.

"Well, well! This sure *is* a treat! Say, *amigo,* I'll turn this burg inside out for you." He turned suddenly to the girl. "Suppose maybe you'd like it if I were to say 'we'? Or is Major North too damned ancient for you sun-dodgers?"

Carefully posed, the girl halted at the door to a washroom. "Oh, he'd do, I guess. Incidentally, J.P., I haven't had the pleasure."

"Sorry, thought you must have met. This is my niece, Aurora Morrow." Standley quickly changed his tone. "And this is Major North. If you'd ever read anything but Winchell and Sobol, you'd know he's the smartest Intelligence officer in the United States Army."

"Charmed, I'm sure." Aurora's voice had become languid and very soft.

Standley cut in, "For the love of Mike, will you get out of

that silly rig? How can I maintain office discipline when you pull such damnfool shenanigans?" Standley flung back his office door. "Come on in. You're as welcome as a raft at a shipwreck. To begin with, let's have a wee touch in celebration. What say?"

Without awaiting North's reply, J.P. Standley slid back a panel let into the side of a huge walnut desk. Revealed was a silver-trimmed decanter of Scotch surrounded by several similarly patterned glasses.

"Sun's over the yardarm and personally I'm fed up with all these goddamned *cafezinhos*. Too much coffee makes me bilious as a goat."

"Good idea," North agreed. "I'm short on sleep and right now I've more worries than a Mexican's dog has fleas."

Standley prepared tall drinks with an almost professional deftness, passed one across his desk and smiled. "Talk about worries! My God, I've been up to my ears in worries, what with mountains of freight in our warehouses and bottoms of any description scarcer than blond Zulus."

North, with deep appreciation, savored his drink while eyeing a collection of gleaming ship half-models decorating the office walls.

Standley was saying, "What few of my freighters the government hasn't grabbed for naval auxiliaries I have had transferred to Panamanian registry so's I can maintain a run to England. But there's *mucho bueno dinero* in that, you know. Since last fall two of those Panama boats have been sunk, so right now I've a dozen shipping firms yelping for me to take cargoes off their docks." He smiled wryly. "I'm not going to bore you with my troubles, Hugh. What are you up to here— or shouldn't I ask?"

North relaxed in his chair, summoned a faint smile. "Up to

my usual tricks," he admitted, studying a huge map of the South Atlantic painted onto the wall behind Standley. "I'm going to need your help, J.P.—but in the strictest confidence."

"Go ahead, and if it's to give those Axis bastards a kick in the pants, it will be a special pleasure."

The Intelligence officer, for the first time, found room for encouragement in the uncomplicated quality of this fellow American's responses. For years the Standley Line had prospered because this barrel-shaped individual had been alert and forehanded; Junius P. Standley, however, had grown rich chiefly through keeping his mouth shut at the right time.

"This affair isn't particularly involved," North explained, "but that doesn't detract from its importance." He hunched forward in his deep armchair and, in lowered accents, offered his flattery cut thin and delicately seasoned. "I presume that here and elsewhere you have certain sources of information through which you can discover facts of shipping interest?"

"Yep."

"And in far less time than official channels would require?"

"Possibly," Standley murmured. "Go on, man, come to the point."

"Well, then, J.P., here is what I most desperately need to find out. Somewhere in the South Atlantic there's a freighter heading for Brazil."

"There are probably several hundred," Standley corrected, clipping the end from a long perfecto. "Of what line is she?"

"That's the trouble. I haven't the least idea," was North's succinct reply. "But that's only one of the difficulties. What little I know indicates that this freighter is not likely to be flying a belligerent's flag."

By pairs Standley joined stubby, hirsute fingers before him and from behind shiny, octagonal-lensed glasses surveyed his guest with shrewd attention. Said he, "Well, Hugh, that's some indication, at least."

"In reasoning this thing out," North continued, "it would seem that this freighter must have cleared from some port either in South Africa, Spain or Portugal."

"What about Dakar in West Africa?"

"That *is* a possibility."

"Why so?"

"Because she's supposed to have left the other side crammed with refugees."

Standley frowned. "Can she have been sunk?"

"She won't be sunk, J.P.," North sighed, absently tinkling the ice in his glass, "but I wish to God she could be!"

Standley lit his cigar, looked fixedly at his guest through its smoke. "Do you realize you're talking riddles?"

"I suppose it sounds like it. You see, this freighter I'm interested in is en route to Brazil with enough political and military propaganda dynamite aboard to blow this Republic and the Vargas régime sky-high."

"The hell you say!"

"The hell I say."

Agitatedly Standley chewed the butt of his cigar. "Can you tell me if this business has any connection with Pujol and his pack of fascists?"

"It might very well, J.P., but I'm saving that to worry about later. The most critical need is to identify and locate this freighter *muy pronto.*"

The executive removed the cigar from his mouth, laid it precisely across a heavy bronze ash tray bearing the Standley Line's device. "I see your point."

"You can see how important it is to discover that freighter's identity but, failing that, it would be a great help to know for which port she's headed. Here's the rest of the story."

Briefly, but omitting nothing of significance, North repeated what Prescott had told him during their ride along the Avenida Rio Branco.

Standley considered his cigar with absurd intensity. "To identify such a vessel in peacetime wouldn't be extra difficult. But when there's a war on—well, that's a very different story," he pronounced. "Still, it might be done, even in these days. But it will take time." Reaching into a desk drawer, the shipping magnate produced a Lloyd's register through which he thumbed hurriedly. "Tell you what, Hugh. I'll drop everything to help you. It will cost me plenty but what the hell? America's done a heap for me and I'm grateful, and getting more so every day. What data I can collect we can analyse and sift tonight. Eh? What is it?"

North had held up a sensitive, yet powerfully constructed hand.

"J.P., I'm wondering if you could arrange a small party on short notice and yet make it seem entirely-casual?"

"Sure. How soon?"

"Tonight?"

"I can do it," Standley announced after a brief deliberation. "With the carnival coming up, everything goes. Why?"

"I most urgently want to meet certain persons, but it must be under friendly and disarming circumstances, *entiende*?" the Intelligence officer replied. "Some of them are prominent."

Standley caught up a pen from a desk holder and prepared to write.

"It's a cinch, son, it's in the bag. I only have to let drop that Aurora will be on deck to bring the local lads of all ages a-running. Whom do you want?"

"Luis da Evaristo. Can do?"

J. P. Standley took a gulp of his drink. "*Seguro*. That's easy. He's flying up from Santos today."

North's interest sharpened. "Flying up? How do you know that?"

Standley pointed to a heap of invoices. "A shipment of his is overdue, and I expect he's coming to raise hell about it. These local manufacturers are short-tempered as the devil these days. Won't be a bad idea to placate him. Next?"

"Dr. Rupp. Know him?"

The shipping magnate's keen blue eyes widened momentarily, but all he said was, "Yes, the Nazi bastard. While we're on that subject, how about Count Gino Altrocchi?"

"Who's he?"

"Used to be Lloyd Triestino's agent here. Right now he claims to be an authority on maritime law and feminine pulchritude. He's fallen for Aurora in a big way. Who else?"

"A certain Ito Setsukada."

"The coffee exporter?" Standley looked a trifle astonished. "Where'd you hear about him?"

"In São Paulo," was North's terse reply. "Then there's the Junior Military Attaché of our embassy," the Intelligence officer spoke thoughtfully, "and any gal he wants to include. And I also would like you to include Lieutenant Ramon Nabuco of the Brazilian Navy."

Questionably, Standley's pale blue eyes sought North's rather Indian-like countenance. "Say, this is getting interesting."

"Too many?" North queried, conscience-stricken.

"Hang the expense! Ask as many as you like. None of us businessmen want any part of the Axis in Brazil." Standley finished his drink. "Yep, it should be real fun, this blow-out tonight. Aurora really knows how to arrange a smart, star-spangled binge. She should. That's about the only useful accomplishment they taught her during four very expensive years at Miss Chapcroft's School."

North expressed thanks, caught up his palm-fiber hat and offered his hand.

"You're a real comfort, J.P. When, where and how will this shindig take place?"

Standley wrung his hand, said, "Say about nine-thirty, black ties, at the German Yacht Club? No, don't flinch—it's German in name only."

"The Woman, Harte"

LOST in furious speculation, Hugh North descended to the street, stood blinking in a brilliant sunshine which revealed in full detail the façades of the many imposing structures lining the Avenida Rio Branco. He decided he had better return at once to his hotel. There Lieutenant Nabuco shortly should appear in answer to an urgent telephone message.

"*Jor-r-nal do Commercio!*" shrieked an incredibly ragged newsboy. Hopefully, a straw-hatted vendor of *jogo do bicho* tickets furtively fluttered his illegal offerings before the Intelligence officer as he stood watching a party of workmen arranging flags and bunting across the front of a smart couturier's shop.

The day was growing very warm and the smell of roasting coffee all but overpowered the reek of a thousand nearby exhausts. Taxi horns shrieked and blatted, brakes screeched, and in the distance sounded the clattering bells of street cars derisively christened *bondes* by saddened Cariocans who had, long, long ago, subscribed to a fantastic bond issue sold to procure them.

North had left the wide, tree-shaded sidewalk and was heading for a cab rank in the center of the Avenida when something stung him in the side. As, instinctively, he clapped a hand to the injury, he heard a vicious, hollow *thock!*, glimpsed a slender, cruel-looking knife sinking deep into the highly varnished side of a delivery truck. Still quivering, the weapon was borne away in the traffic streaming by at that headlong speed so characteristic of Rio.

Though aware of a burning sensation, North freed his .32 from its holster and wheeled. Nobody appeared to have even noticed that near-murder had just taken place. All about the coldly furious Intelligence officer were only the good-natured faces of Cariocans ranging in color from jet through brown to pure white.

Warned by a hot stream beginning to trickle down over his ribs, North at once hailed a cab, gave his address and got in. Placing the .32 on the seat beside him, he removed his coat hurriedly, pulled up an already sodden shirt and examined a gash in line with his heart. It proved to be nothing serious, just a painful cut which was not even deep.

"We'll give that lad A for effort, though," he thought when he fastened his belt tight over a handkerchief arranged as a pad. The bleeding was thus effectively checked. Once he had resumed his coat, few would have guessed that he had been hurt. It wouldn't by any means do to draw undue attention when entering the Copacabana Palace Hotel.

Whether this attempt had to do with recent activities in São Paulo or had been prompted by the 304 G-2b matter, there could be no telling; but somebody, very evidently, had spilled the beans about his mission in Rio, and the opposition, whoever they might be, were losing no time.

This had been a damned sight too close to be amusing. Had

that knife flown four inches to the left, he would now be sprawling limp and lifeless on the hot asphalt of the Avenida.

What annoyed him most of all was that he had failed to obtain even a glimpse of his assailant. For all he knew, his would-be murderer could come up, smiling, for a second try. This, decidedly, was not a pleasing prospect.

In the security of his suite at the luxuriously smart Copacabana Palace, North once more examined his wound and found the gash no more serious than he had at first decided. The application of a disinfectant and a simple compress secured by an adhesive tape occupied little time and the donning of a fresh shirt and a suit of crisp white linens effectively concealed all outward evidence by the time Lieutenant Ramon Nabuco rang up from the lobby.

Very slim and straight in a pale blue palm beach suit, Lieutenant Nabuco presently appeared, shook hands warmly.

"My dear Major," the Brazilian smiled, his dark eyes flitting rapidly about the sitting room. "It is such a pleasure to welcome you back in Rio. All this past week I have been consumed with impatience to learn more of that method for restoring charred manuscripts. Do you recall we were speaking of it?"

Beneath the naval officer's manner, impatience struggled hard for release.

"Of course I remember. But what is it you really wish to ask?"

"About this—these radiograms," Nabuco burst out, his thin and sensitively handsome face aquiver. "The Ministry of Foreign Affairs is, it seems, not concerned but I—we at the Naval Intelligence Bureau are—well, shall I say most worried over them."

His teeth looked very white in the pale olive hues of his features. "What is your opinion, Major?"

"Concerning what?"

"The validity of those messages."

The Intelligence officer's gaze wandered out of the window, out over the aching blueness of Guanabara Bay; out there a class of six-meter yachts was heeling in a close-hauled reach.

"I credit the radiograms, Lieutenant," said he simply. "I believe they were sent in as deadly earnest as a certain knife." He touched his side.

"What do you mean, Major?" the Brazilian demanded instantly.

The taller of the two laughed shortly. "On my way up here some *caballero,* with bad intentions and a worse aim, tried to murder me on the Avenida Rio Branco."

.."*Deus!*" Nabuco exclaimed and went a little pale. His lively dark eyes commenced to snap. "Tell me, please, how did this occur?"

North summarized the incident, then continued, "Are you aware that Dom Luis da Evaristo, the president of the Companhia Americus—"

"Flew in from São Paulo this morning? Yes. It was half after eleven at the Condor Company airport."

"You keep yourself well informed."

"We try to," the Brazilian Naval Intelligence officer murmured modestly. "*They* do. All too well." He tossed his panama onto a chair and leaned forward. His whole body was quivering gently, like a hawser under heavy tension. "Major, am I a fool to speculate on this so unexpected trip of Senhor da Evaristo? Does it not, perhaps, have to do with those radiograms?"

"That, my dear Lieutenant, is entirely possible," North admitted and felt it politic to make an inquiry of his own. "But before we go any further, I wonder if you'll tell me what you make of something which happened to me last night aboard the *Cruzeiro do Sul?*"

"I shall be flattered, Major, to be of any service. And what was this business?"

Omitting not the least detail, North related the affair but made no mention of Paula Harte's name.

Lieutenant Nabuco cocked an alert dark head to one side as he selected from his case a very long and thin cigar. "You refer to Senhorita Paula Harte. Am I correct?"

"Quite right." North's respect for his colleague mounted by leaps and bounds.

The Brazilian's narrow brows momentarily merged themselves. "So? Paula Harte. *Deus!* It must certainly have been she whom those in São Paulo wished—detained."

Instantly North asked, "Detained on what charge?"

Nabuco shrugged. "This young lady was an intimate of a certain employee of the Americus Company in São Paulo—one Hugo Becker. He traveled on a Swedish passport but we knew he was German, nonetheless. Yesterday he was found dead, his papers plundered. She is only wanted for questioning, however. Of the murder itself she is not suspected."

"I see. What do you know about Miss Harte?"

"This young woman is very clever, and because she is also beautiful, she is all the more dangerous. Listen to this." North's guest sighed, produced a notebook and, after taking a puff or two on his cigar, said, "I have here the dossier of the lady in question. Shall I read it?"

Eagerly North nodded and prepared a mental notebook.

"'Full name, Paula Graham Harte.'"

"Graham?"

"Yes. Her mother was an American," Nabuco explained through a cloud of fragrant cigar smoke. "'Age 27. Born the daughter of Colonel Manfred Stoltz-Harte in St. Jago de Chile. Colonel Harte, a German subject of Saxon origin, was detailed to the Chilean Government in 1910 as head of a military mission.' Is this too detailed, Major?"

"No. It's most instructive," murmured the Intelligence officer. "Please continue."

" 'Colonel Harte returned to Germany during the first World War, was killed in Ukrainia, October 1918.' " Nabuco glanced up, then went on reading. " 'The mother, Edna Graham Harte, originated in St. Louis in the State of Missouri, U.S.A.' A strange alliance, no?"

"Please go on," urged the Intelligence officer, wondering how much of this vivid family background was known to Stuart Maitland.

" 'On the death of the father the mother became the mistress of a rich Peruvian and the child, Paula Harte, attended a convent school near Buenos Aires. In 1934 the mother died in Colòn in the Republic of Panama. She left no property.' "

Evenly, clearly, Nabuco's voice continued, " 'From the age of fifteen, the woman, Harte, has earned her living. Her knowledge of languages, including French, German and Spanish in addition to English, is extensive.

" 'She has been employed successively by the Standard Oil of New Jersey in Montevideo, the Ford Motor Company in Buenos Aires. In 1936'—this should interest you, Major—'she worked in the Rio office of the Hamburg-Sudamerikanische Line.' "

Nabuco's voice rose. " 'Then in 1938 in the Condor Air Line office in Recife.' Significant, eh?"

"Very. Sounds as if the father's blood was telling over the mother's. Where next did the woman, Harte, work?"

Nabuco resumed his reading. " 'In October, 1939, she entered the employ of Luis da Evaristo as ordinary secretary, but in 1940 she became confidential secretary—at a greatly increased salary.' *Voilà tout!*"

"Quite a fascinating career," North observed and shifted to ease the painful throbbing of his side. "Has she a police record?"

"Listen to this. 'The woman, Harte, has never been proved involved with any crime, civil or political.'"

"Please go on."

"'The woman, Harte, now occupies a small apartment at Number 1081 Estrada do Redemptor.'" Nabuco's clear voice continued. "Among her recent associates this report lists a 'Dr. Hermann Rupp, Pierre Reneau,' the French coffee millionaire, you know, 'Conte Gino d'Altrocchi, former representative for the Lloyd Triestino Line.'"

"And now practising maritime law?"

"Eh?" A short laugh broke from Nabuco's lips and he considered North with frank astonishment. "But you are amazing! In so short a time you have already learned that."

"This is a rush job," North reminded. "Does the dossier mention other friends?"

"'The woman, Harte, has been, from time to time, escorted by one Baron Ito Setsukada, owner of seven large coffee fazendas in the State of Amazonas. Within the last three months she has been most frequently observed in company with—'" A gesture of both embarrassment and apology separated Nabuco's expressive hands. "Major, I hesitate, I regret to mention—"

"Captain Maitland?"

The naval officer appeared vastly relieved. "*Sim.* I am glad you know. You understand that a matter involving the military attaché of a friendly nation is indeed most delicate. My

Bureau must know what goes on but has not the least wish to offend.

"'Captain Maitland and the woman, Harte, are continually together; bathing, playing tennis, riding horseback and'—this we do not encourage—'motorboat riding out among the government-controlled islands of the bay.' This, Major, completes the report."

North looked his gratitude. "My thanks, Lieutenant. And by the way, I intend taking a hand in the Maitland matter. You said Senhorita Harte lives on the Estrada do Redemptor, number 1081?"

"Yes, that lies in the Ipanema suburb. Shall I write it down?"

"Thanks, no." With wind of chance blowing as ominously as it had since his arrival in Rio, North had no desire to carry about on his person anything of a leading nature.

The cut along his ribs continued to throb painfully. To forget it North arose and commenced to pace back and forth before a window overlooking the long, ultramarine sweep of Guanabara Bay and its pale yellow-white streaks of beach.

"What's that?" He cocked his head in the direction of a drumming which sounded in the far distance. The reverberations varied constantly in pitch and tempo.

"Macumba drums in the Praça Onze—the Negro quarter," Nabuco explained promptly. "The inhabitants are getting ready for the carnival. All over the city we have carnival clubs such as the *Fenianos,* the *Democraticos.* Today they impatiently prepare for tomorrow. Many spend their last reis on costumes. Yes, Major, tomorrow you will see strange and amusing sights."

In spite of his correct bearing, enthusiasm entered Ramon Nabuco's manner and his eyes commenced to sparkle. "Tomorrow Rio will be at its maddest, its pleasantest and perhaps its best! Imagine it! For four whole days there is a perfect democracy. The bootblack is equal with the worst *granfino* snob at the Regatta Club. During carnival anyone may enter anyone else's home and sit right down to dinner. It is most exciting and dramatic. Sometimes things of the oddest may happen."

"So I imagine," came the Intelligence officer's grim comment. "Especially this year."

"Eh?" The elation departed from Nabuco's sensitive features, then his mouth tightened. "I understand. You fear many Patriotistas will seize the opportunity to enter Rio?"

"Yes. What is there to stop them?"

"Nothing. An assassination or two would be very simple to arrange."

"Wish to God carnival came at any other time," North said.

Nervously the Brazilian naval officer began to flex his fingers. "Tell me, Major, you feel confident that our enemies have taken this carnival into their calculations?"

North halted, spoke with a gravity unusual for him. "That is the principal reason I feel those radiograms are genuine."

"If that is true, the situation is extremely serious," stated the Brazilian, staring into space. He turned. "Is there anything my Bureau can do? Is there any information we can furnish?"

"Yes. I'd like to know more about the Patriotista leader. So far, I have seen only newspaper accounts, most of them biased in one direction or another."

Swiftly, the naval officer lifted a brief case to his knees and produced a dossier, a clear photo-portrait and a series of action snapshots.

Briefly, the man from G-2 studied the vulpine, heavily mustached features and intolerant expression of Dr. José Pujol. From a summation of characteristic poses, North deduced that

Dr. Pujol fancied himself as a second General Vincente Gomez, that ace and inspiration of South American dictators who, for twenty years and more, had confined the liberties of Venezuela in a steel garotte.

José Maria Luis Pujol y Rau—to give his full name—North discovered was fifty-three years of age, a native of Salamanca, Spain, and had received an A.B. degree from the local university. He had earned an M.A. from the Sorbonne and also a Ph.D. degree from the University of Dresden. He had been twice imprisoned: once by the government of Primo de Rivera; then, paradoxically, for communistic activities in Seattle, Washington.

There was appended a list of Dr. Pujol's principal supporters. To North the only familiar name among them was that of Luis da Evaristo.

"Remarkable, isn't it?" North queried. "So few of these men are really Brazilian. Dr. Pujol is a Spaniard while two of his lieutenants are Chilean. A big majority of his backers seem to be either Argentine, Italian or German."

Lieutenant Nabuco's fragile-appearing shoulders rose in a sigh. "Like your own most estimable country, Major, Brazil now pays a high price for her too-generous hospitality."

It grew so still in North's pleasant little gray and pink sitting room that that distant drumming crept indoors over the nearer noises of the traffic.

Lieutenant Nabuco abandoned his restless prowl about the room, said abruptly, "On the chance that it will prove useful, I have warned all government-operated radio stations between Belém—or Pará—and Rio Grande do Sul to record any suspicious message or call. They are to note the precise instant of receipt."

"That's splendid." North felt a renaissance of hope. "I presume you are having Luis da Evaristo watched?"

"But certainly."

"Tonight, Lieutenant, will you bring a pair of dependable operatives to the German Yacht Club? By eight o'clock at the latest."

"That will be attended to." Nabuco's eyes shone. "Somehow, Major, I have a feeling that this dinner party of Senhor Standley's will prove memorable. Here is my private telephone number. If you desire protection, do not hesitate to call the Bureau at any time. It pays to be careful."

North hesitated but immediately foresaw that he must move swiftly, unencumbered by a shadow. Care certainly paid large dividends but what was one to do when the identity of myriad foes was not even to be suspected? What precautions could one adopt in the face of those abnormal conditions which, for the next four days, would make a madhouse of this great and unusually polyglot city?

Once Lieutenant Nabuco's figure, slight, erect and very neat in its pale blue palm beach cloth, had vanished, Hugh North realized that his hurt side was throbbing infernally, really more than one might expect of so trifling a gash. Suppose the knife blade had not been sterile—perhaps quite the contrary? Silently cursing this complication he phoned the Embassy, inquired of Mr. Prescott the name of a thoroughly discreet physician.

In order to clear his mind, he sought his bedroom and, completely weary, prepared to snatch half an hour's rest. In the middle of the room he halted, however, sniffed. Yes? No? Yes. A faint breath of perfume *did* tinge the air—a fashionable, but most unmanly perfume. He recognized instantly Flor da Noite.

The scent recalled São Paulo, a moon-silvered terrace, glowing maracujá blossoms and a sea breeze stirring whispers from a grove of jaboticabas. He felt immeasurably relieved. The scent undoubtedly originated from a bottle of perfume he had purchased as a gift for dear little Manuela. Um. He'd better post it tonight as *amende honorable* for his abrupt departure. When would he again behold her Dresden china doll of a figure and really noteworthy eyes?

His peace of mind was rudely shattered when, on opening his suitcase, he found that the perfume came not from a leaking vial but from a cake of soap which, inexplicably, had appeared among his socks and shirts. Yielding automatically to the dictates of experience, he phoned below for two similar bars of Savon Flor da Noite.

Tête-à-Tête

A BRISK young Brazilian doctor, who proudly mentioned having completed his training at Johns Hopkins, appeared and began an examination. He pulled a long face as he cauterized North's wound.

"This hurt should have been treated much sooner, Senhor," he commented. "If any infection *is* present, it has had opportunity to take hold. Should the wound grow any worse, you will get in touch with me at once?"

North promised, thanked the doctor and sent him on his way. Then for a moment he remained in the center of the little living room deliberating his next move.

One thing was certain. Captain Stuart Maitland must be interviewed—and at once. Aware that his side was still smarting like fury, he called the Embassy, suggested that the Junior Military Attaché stop by immediately.

Now about that soap? His mind functioning well once more, he deliberated and soon found a plausible explanation.

Paula Harte in her hurried departure had, in snatching some garment from her bag, let the soap fall into his bag. Or had she deliberately *put it there?* Such a dodge, but of a really compromising sort, had been practiced on him in Rumania* and not so long ago, either.

After swathing the soap in a fine linen handkerchief, the Intelligence officer compared the cake with two others delivered in haste by the Ceará Pharmacy's errand boy.

He started when his door buzzer sounded, then put away the enigmatic piece of soap while leaving one of his purchases in plain sight. Grown warier than ever, North took the precaution to remove the .32 from his shoulder holster and drop it into his coat pocket. Decidedly, it was much too soon for Captain Maitland to have completed his trip from the Rua São Clemente. Keeping his body well out of line with the door, he called, "Who is it?"

"Paula Harte," a low voice informed him. "Please, may I come in?"

With his left hand he turned the knob, remained alert. She entered, graceful and trim as a millionaire's yacht, in a well-starched white dress. A necklace of excellent amber accentuated the perfection of her fair complexion. To his astonishment, Hugh North experienced a sense of warm satisfaction when she gave him a radiant smile.

"I'm so glad to find you in, Major. I was hoping against hope."

"And I—I was just—" North smiled while easing the .32's safety catch back into position—"thinking about you."

"You were thinking of me? Really?"

"Yes. Really."

"Then indeed I am flattered," she murmured, a shade of color brightening the pink-white sheen of her cheeks.

Her expression softened as she entered and then quite coolly surveyed this pleasant apartment with its superb view, its com-

---

* *Bucharest Ballerina Murders.*

fortable furniture, its demure French-gray walls, pink and gray upholstery and curtains.

"Do you always do as well for yourself, Major?"

"Even as a shave-tail—second lieutenant, that is—I'm afraid I appreciated the good things of life," confessed the dark-haired host. "But I seldom got them."

She interrupted her appreciation of the view in looking over her shoulder. "Would it annoy you if I remove my hat? It is warm and I have hurried."

"Not in the least, Miss Harte, but I must warn you, I am expecting company."

Annoyance flitted over features somewhat reminiscent of Alice Faye's. "Oh, bother! But that is all right. Really, I am only stopping for a moment. I—I wished to thank you so very much about last night."

North offered a box of cigarettes, kept his guard up despite a pleasant crinkling at the corners of his eyes and mouth.

"*De nada, Señorita*," he exclaimed. "It has been a long while since I've seen such an—er—breath-taking exposé. That Belgian embroidery on your—"

"On my scanties?" she supplied laughingly.

"When I went to school such were not called scanties."

"What a purist! On my panties, then," she laughed, then added while looking slowly up at him. "Incidentally, Major, those were not my *chefs d'oeuvre,* just fancy enough to get run over in. What happened after I left?"

North gave her a liberally edited account.

"Then, my dear Major, I am more in your debt than ever," she declared, smoothing her very blonde hair. "How can I ever repay you? Most men would have made such a silly scene. You are unique. Do you know that?"

"Will you have something to drink?"

"Don't faint, but I'll say 'no thank you.' It's still too early," she explained, gracefully settling onto a low armchair which made the most of well-formed legs sheathed in expensive hosiery. "You see, what with getting back to Rio, I have much to do."

"For example?" Skillfully, he threw out the feeler.

"The carnival," Paula Harte said lightly. "Everyone in my club is supposed to appear as Arabian." Her smoky-blue eyes met and held his of clear gray-blue. "You should see my costume—what there is of it."

North barely suppressed a grimace as a barb of pain lanced at his side.

"I'd like to. Clothes may make the man, but with your charming sex, I wonder if the reverse isn't true? How did you know where to find me?" he demanded. "I am quite frankly curious."

"But surely you can guess?"

He steeled himself for a big, crucial gamble. If he guessed wrong, the status of his prestige with Paula would be irreparably damaged.

"Stuart Maitland."

The smoky-blue eyes met his with surprising directness. "Yes. Stu-art, of course. I hope you didn't think him indiscreet? You see, he trusts me implicitly."

"Obviously," murmured North, then lied pleasantly. "And I admire his judgment." Silently he added, "So much I'd like to break his damned-fool neck!"

He suffered some unpleasant moments as he tried to recall just how much he had last week disclosed to his subordinate. He knew now how a generalissimo must feel when an enemy force unexpectedly appears along his line of communications.

Slowly North's caller crossed her legs. "You have heard of our friendship from others?"

"No. Why?" the Intelligence officer asked and racked his imagination. Properly handled, Luis da Evaristo's confidential secretary *might* be converted into an invaluable ally. How to accomplish this? How?

"Our friendship is the scandal of the Itamaraty Palace," she announced with a touch of bitterness.

"Itamaraty Palace?" His brows rose. "You have me guessing."

"The Brazilian Foreign Office is there," smilingly she explained in low-pitched accents, and let her pale head sink back to rest on the chair. "They are, God alone knows why, displeased that Captain Maitland finds me attractive."

"They must be jealous of Maitland's good fortune," stated the dark-haired Intelligence officer. "Who could blame them? I am."

"I wonder?" she murmured and wrinkled her nose at him.

From a gray suede bag Paula produced a small case of gold and vermilion enamel. Slowly, she tapped a cigarette on the point of her fingernail.

"Why?"

"Because, from our first encounter, Major, you have intrigued and puzzled me. Not many men do," she added, as if to herself. "You are not curious. You have no nerves, it appears; yet I suspect you are not of a cold temperament."

He laughed, lit a match for her. "What makes you think that?"

"Last night in the compartment, most men would have tried to make love. Instead, you went to sleep. That was very ungallant," she complained.

"Years ago I learned to waste no time yearning for the unattainable."

Paula Harte laughed gently, drew a long puff on her cigarette.

"*Por Dios,* one would never have thought you such a philosopher. Besides, how can you be so sure about—about a woman?"

"One never should be," said he over the loud squawking of a pair of *araras*—macaws—in a courtyard below. "But possibly, as in the case of Benjamin Franklin and the beautiful baroness, I 'was waiting until winter, when the nights are longer.'"

"You make it impossible to take offense with you," Paula smiled, selecting a glowing maracujá blossom from a vase at her elbow and slowly twirling the flower between her fingers, "I have this morning learned some things about you, my dear Major."

"In Senhor da Evaristo's interest, of course?"

"It may be," Paula returned carefully, then amplified, "Perhaps a little about why you spent a week in São Paulo."

"You both flatter and astound me—Paula." He added the name deliberately, was pleased to note that she seemed far from annoyed.

"There is no flattery. I am Luis da Evaristo's most trusted private secretary. Yes, I am most intimate with his affairs," she amplified with a touch of pride.

Considering the quality of the Harte girl's clothes and jewelry, the possibility occurred that said intimacy might not be confined entirely to office hours. Absently, Paula brushed the flower across her lips. "Dom Luis is a very clever—and an ambitious—man."

"Will you have a drink?" Purposefully he repeated the suggestion. "A glass of water, maybe?"

"Yes. Some water, please. I am still quite heated."

When he arose and filled a glass from a carafe, she looked up quickly as she accepted the water and asked, "What do you think of Stu-art Maitland—Hugh?"

"He is very capable," North said truthfully enough, "one of the smartest young officers in our service, but just a trifle disingenuous, perhaps?"

"Yes, Stu-art is nice," Paula Harte drawled, bright lips rippling slowly back from even white teeth. "So fresh, so uncomplicated, so direct. One would never have to worry about trusting Stu-art."

"And that must be a great relief, I take it?"

The Harte girl smiled at the ceiling. "As you say, 'a great relief.'" She sat up frowning a trifle. "But Stu-art is so—so *lourd,* so serious about his duty, his sport. And, *Dios,* he makes love with so little finesse. Always he crushes my gowns, spoils a coiffure I have spent hours over." She sighed. "For myself, I prefer—"

Little crowsfeet appeared at the corners of North's eyes. "Someone like me?"

"You are both conceited and cruel." She affected to pout, but was really much amused. "And you have spoiled for me a pretty little speech."

"And I," North assured her with a smile hovering beneath his short military mustache, "prefer girls who keep their heads in an emergency. *Mon Dieu!* The cool way you waited for just the right instant to jerk that emergency cord calls for three deep bows in your direction, my dear."

Paula Harte uncrossed her legs, sat forward and said softly, "So you *were* awake."

"All of the time." To forget the dull pain stabbing at his side, North pulled out a short-stemmed pipe, studied his caller as he tamped in a load. "Really, Paula dear, with you in the same compartment, to sleep would be both ungallant—and impossible."

"Which could be taken two ways," she laughed and, amid a flurry of white skirts, arose. "However, I shall consider it a pretty speech and well worth—"

Suddenly she bent over the back of his chair and kissed him. As quickly his fingers closed over her wrist, prolonged the caress an instant. It was really quite a kiss.

"Thanks," grinned North. "It's nice to find an unexpected surprise so pleasant." He got up, wandered over to the door and with one eye on that enigmatic cake of soap, pretended to adjust the air conditioner. "By the way, Paula, just why were those hombres so interested in you?"

"An acquaintance of mine was killed—murdered," she explained simply. "I happened to have been with him earlier that afternoon on a matter of business. You see, Mr. Becker was shipping superintendent for the Americus plant." Her pink and white features contracted. "It was all most unfortunate."

"Could you guess as to why Mr. Becker might have been killed?"

"I think so, but I'm not sure, of course," came the hesitant reply. "Hugo Becker was never able to understand the Latin temperament," said Paula, looking out of the window. "I imagine Hugo hunted once too often on some jealous lover's preserve. His amusements, all too often, lay 'south of the sash,' as the North Americans say."

Quite without warning, he demanded, "Are you really half American?"

She treated him to a startled look that was inexplicably pathetic. "One sees, Hugh, that you, too, have been making inquiries."

"Haven't I already confessed that you interest me? And I hope you don't mind my calling you Paula."

"Have I not kissed you twice?" she reminded, regarding him steadily. "Yes, I suppose I am half American—North American, as people say down here. If Mamma had been different, I might have become a North American. It was too bad," Paula then added almost wistfully. "You have no idea, Hugh, what it means to be, in effect, without a country. The English, the Dutch, even the Rumanians love their land. It is bad to be an international mongrel like me."

She sighed, absently brushed a strand of pale hair from her cheek. "I have always remembered so well those things Mamma told me about her home. America must be wonderful. There is no fear, no secret police, no hatred there. Such a fine, rich and powerful country."

"You could become an American quite easily," North suggested. "Why don't you?"

She looked sharply at him. "By marriage, you mean?"

"Why not?" Deliberately he baited his hook. "I deduce that Stuart Maitland would—"

She made a small, eloquent gesture of impatience. "Stu-art is a dear boy, a very dear boy and he *is* handsome. He rides superbly, he is most generous, he dances divinely, and he plays tennis like a champion, but *Dios salvador!* beyond that—I am sure I would divorce him out of sheer boredom."

It was a pity, North reflected, that no dictaphone was recording this tête-à-tête.

Paula's dusky blue eyes swung from the flower to meet North's deep-set ones. "You will be at Mr. Standley's diner-dansant at Nictheroy this evening?"

"I hope so. Will you be there?"

"I may be. Senhor da Evaristo, having just come in from São

Paulo, will probably wish to dictate some letters during the trip over to the Club. He is a very busy man."

"Until later, then."

Paula Harte, with a singularly graceful gesture, bent to retrieve her wide-brimmed hat and for a fleeting instant North could visualize her in her girlhood. He was pleasantly surprised to detect a few freckles dotting the bridge of her nose.

Paula offered both her hands. "Perhaps, *muy amigo mío*, you would drop by for cocktails at my apartment, maybe tomorrow? Say half past six? I have an amusing little demon of a *curupião* bird who would put even Alesandro to shame in stirring up mischief. Imagine a bird that will not sleep except in a hammock and with a blanket over him?"

North laughed. "I take it in the leg, where do you?"

"No, really. I dare you to come and see for yourself." She put down her cigarette, sauntered over to a mirror and adjusted her hat with care. "My address is in the telephone directory."

"I shall try to," he murmured and covertly eased his shoulder holster to spare his hurt side.

"This has been a most entertaining—" she started to say, then broke off. "Oh, Hugh, I lost a bar of my favorite toilet soap in the compartment. I wonder if you came across it?"

"Why, yes," North said and let his gaze wander to the table beside the door. "I was wondering where it came from."

Paula crossed unhurriedly to the table. "It is scarcely for a man of your type. I am relieved. It is most difficult to procure Flor da Noite in soap form."

"Then I'm especially glad I found it." He smiled as, very calmly, Paula slipped into her bag the violet-tinted soap he had been handling when she had rung his buzzer.

Showdown

FERVENTLY Hugh North hoped that Maitland might not encounter his fiancée in the lobby. Her presence in the Copacabana Palace all too easily might lead to complicating—and inaccurate—implications. Better receive Stuart Maitland downstairs. In public, the Junior Military Attaché would be forced to keep a rein on what he said, and possibly what he might do.

Presently the phone rang. "Afternoon, Major," greeted Maitland's brisk young voice. "Shall I come up?"

"No, suppose we meet in the lounge bar? My room's hot and in an unholy mess."

Before quitting his suite, the Intelligence officer took care to conceal Paula's cake of soap in the depth of an urn supporting a thoroughly innocuous potted plant. Wrinkling his nose, he left the remaining bar of Flor da Noite in a drawer of the telephone table behind the book. Good God! If some of the boys could sniff his bedroom now!

"I'm mighty glad you phoned," Maitland arose, eagerly offered his hand. "We've been catching hell from the State Department over those radiograms. The Secretary of State is growing extremely uneasy. Had a couple of hot inquiries out of the Navy, too. They're keen for some kind of a report." The solidly built young fellow leaned forward, eagerness in every fiber of his being. "Have you found out anything? Anything at all?"

"No," North replied in a tone calculated to dampen the other's excitement. After casting a careful look about the nearly empty lounge bar, very gay with its carnival trappings, and making sure that no one else could hear a normally pitched conversation, he settled into a long chair and wished to God his side would stop hurting. "The groundwork in a case like this takes time, Captain."

"But," Maitland burst out, "there isn't time! Don't you know that that damned ship may make port *at any hour?* How can you—"

"Please keep your voice down," warned the Intelligence officer. Then as color mounted into Maitland's rugged countenance, he beckoned a waiter. "*Garçon!* Two whiskey-sodas. *Estou com pressa.*"

So this earnest-appearing young fellow had given out his address, had discussed the affair Americus? One thing that could throw North seriously off stride was to be not wholly sure of an assistant.

The Junior Military Attaché must have sensed that all was not as it should be. He remained uncomfortably straight on his chair with gaze fixed on the harbor. Yonder, a dull gray-painted armed merchantman of typically British design was threshing her serious and unromantic way out to sea. Like a smutty forefinger smoke from her squat funnel probed at the brilliantly azure heavens above Paqueta Island.

North inquired abruptly, "Do you know of anyone in the pro-Patriotista crowd who could be—well, approached? In such an immense organization there must be someone who can be bribed into selling out his pals."

Maitland fingered his big chin an instant, then faced his bronze-featured host sitting so coolly in the shade of a potted pinheiro tree. "I believe, sir, I could find someone like that."

North sensed what was coming and was sorry.

"You recall our conversation concerning Miss Harte?" Maitland began hesitantly, then, his color mounting, he went on with a rush. "Well, I—she, that is—she told me she has—er—once done intelligence work." Maitland brightened.

"Incidentally, sir, she knows a bit about the Americus matter."

North would have bet large sums on that fact, but kept tight rein on his now badly strained temper. Great God in heaven! Maitland must have been blabbing to his fiancée like a seventeen-year-old. The realization gave him a disconcertingly hollow feeling.

"She was very much interested and wanted to help me. She even warned me about a fellow named Becker. Said he was much too interested in that combination anti-tank anti-AA gun the Ordnance released—"

"And how did she know of that combination gun?"

"Why, I—I—well, I guess I must have mentioned it," Maitland admitted, flushing to the tip of his small crisp ears. "But Paula's all right."

An ominous chill crept into the Intelligence officer's voice. "Do you make a habit of discussing unquestionably secret and confidential government matters with a—a fiancée?"

Maitland's handsome, square-jawed features became drained of color. "Look here, Major, I'm damned if I like—"

"To the devil with what you like!" North's mouth suddenly thinned to a merciless slash. "Answer my question."

Maitland swallowed hard on nothing and his nostrils opened

and shut spasmodically like the gills of a stranded fish. "Yes. In a limited way I have discussed our suspicions of the Companhia Americus. But—" he looked North steadily in the eye —"*only* because I figured Paula could help us. Being in da Evaristo's confidence, she—"

"She has repeated every damned thing you told her!" came the acid interruption.

"No!" Going pale about the mouth, Maitland half arose. "She would not! I'd risk my career on that."

"You have risked it," was the Intelligence officer's grim observation. "And it's a pity. So far you've a splendid record— almost a brilliant one. I've checked, so I know. By what right did you give her my address?"

"She said she knew you," came the slow answer. Only with effort was Maitland keeping his voice steady. "She said she had met you on the train last night."

"Anyone could claim as much."

"That's so, but dammit, Major, I didn't mean any harm," Maitland declared desperately. "I'm as good an American as you, and I'd trust Paula with my life."

The pleasant sun-bathed terrace with its gaudy umbrellas, tall palms, tinkling fountain and gay parquet paving tilted a little before North's eyes. He felt unbearably hot, very angry.

"No matter what you think, you've no right to talk. In the UA-1 or the NKVD you'd find yourself shot for far less.

"Did Miss Harte describe how she left the train we were on?"

"Yes," came the sullen response.

"Do you know that she was trying hard to escape questioning in São Paulo?"

Triumph illumined Maitland's perspiring features. "Yes! She explained everything to my satisfaction."

"Your satisfaction, Maitland, is an inadequate yardstick," rapped the Intelligence officer.

The arrival of the drinks prevented some searing comments. How much, North conjectured, did this love-sick idiot know of Paula Harte's past?

When North spoke again, his voice held the quality of a knife drawn over a dry stone. "Whatever you believe of Miss Harte, Captain, you will under no circumstances discuss with her or give her the least information concerning my mission —or myself. Look here, you haven't mentioned those radiograms?"

"I guess I've been kind of dumb," Maitland replied slowly, "but I'm not that much of a fool."

"Do you really think she intends to marry you?"

The Military Attaché gaped. "Think? Why, I *know* she's going to. She's crazy about me, if that's any business of yours."

"It *is* a business of mine, Maitland. Anything even remotely connected with this assignment is."

"Why did you ask about her marrying me?"

"Because I think you're mistaken, Maitland."

For a long instant the solid young man in the panama suit sat rigid.

"I won't stand for this! You're trying to poison her in my eyes!"

"Calm down, Maitland."

"I won't listen."

"You will. Where do you suppose a private secretary finds money for such clothes? For such jewelry? On thirty or forty or even fifty a week? I warn you that Paula Harte is an accomplished—"

"Shut up!" A dreadful, deadly fury became kindled in Maitland's ruddy face. "I won't listen. I love her, my God, how I love her, and she is going to be my wife, understand? Nothing is ever going to prevent that. If you, or anyone else, ever says anything against Paula, I—I—"

"You'll likely make a worse fool of yourself than you are now. Now drop that sort of talk, Maitland. I know you're in love or I'd prefer charges for what you've just said. I've never stood for insubordination and I'm not beginning now."

The man across the table sat absolutely still except for a perceptible trembling. At length he drew a slow, shuddering breath.

"You're right, sir," he admitted frankly. "I am making a fool of myself because I'm sure of Paula, and that's that. But if—if anything ever went wrong, if I ever find that da Evaristo . . . I hate to think what I'd do," he added softly.

With a sense of sharp apprehension, North watched Stuart Maitland's chunky figure swing stiffly off across the terrace. Well, that was that. How could anybody be so confoundedly blind? So crazily under the influence of an ideal? Unless he saw the light and came to his senses Maitland would need close attention.

While catching his emotional breath and finishing his drink, the Intelligence officer let his eye wander unseeingly over an increasingly busy and sun-bathed terrace. In the background a native orchestra commenced to play a maxixe for the benefit of several light-hearted groups of tea dancers. One couple after another spun out on the dance floor, began to whirl and glide, all unaware that, in the background, was gathering a blast which might forever put a period to such carefree moments.

The more he thought about it, the surer Hugh North became that Paula Harte could, if she chose, disclose facts and plans that he needed badly to know about. For instance, who had arranged the diversion of supposedly exported munitions to various Brazilian states? What had become of those documents which, it was rumored, sealed a bargain between Luis da Evaristo and José Pujol?

One fact was obvious. Paula set material assets above all others. Um. A few thousands of dollars weren't a circumstance to the terrific sum Uncle Sam would have to pay if ever that freighter discharged its cargo of treachery and hate.

Hugh North paid his check and, after making sure that nobody seemed unduly interested in his movements, mounted to his room. Here his nostrils were once again titilated by the fragile fragrance of Flor da Noite.

After salvaging Paula Harte's original cake of soap from under the potted plant, Hugh North sought a desk near the window and placed the glistening, violet-tinted oval upon a piece of tissue paper. With the aid of a pocket lens, he critically examined every inch of the soap's surface. Upon it were the fingerprints of at least two, and maybe three, people.

It came as a relief, he found, to be working upon something concrete, and he forgot that steady burning in his side while holding to the light the water glass he had given to Paula. At least one set of imprints was already registered. Um. Yes. There were certainly two more sets of prints. One group was broad, short and distinguished by a reverse whorl on the thumb. The other was long and slim and there was a scar across the ball of the middle finger. To identify them would be to explain much.

Another discovery was the existence of a barely perceptible rough spot at one end of this glistening purple cake. Exercising care to preserve the fingerprints, North used the sharp, concave edge of the leather punch on his jackknife to work at the disturbed spot until he discovered an unmistakable line of cleavage. He felt his breath come quicker when the end of the punch grated against a hard substance.

Ten minutes of delicate manipulation freed what proved to be a tightly wrapped cylinder of thin white paper. This was secured by a length of blue-green silk. His fingers quivering, the Intelligence officer gingerly undid the bit of thread.

Then for some moments he sat motionless. With furrowed forehead he was considering the single line of writing.

BOLIVAR 27-18-22-6.

"Got it! by God!"

Relief welled up within Hugh North's being like a soothing spring. With the infectious rhythms of the dance orchestra below in his ears, he sought the phone and rang up J. P. Standley.

"Ever hear of a ship called the *Bolivar,* or which employs that name in some form or other?"

"God, yes!" came the discouragingly prompt reply. "Must be easy fifteen or twenty ships that use some part of old Simon's name. Among 'em is my own freighter, the *General Bolivar.* What's up?"

"Tell you later," North countered. "But will you work on that name in connection with the matter I spoke to you about? And say, J.P., if you can figure out any significance for the numerals '27-18-22-6' let me know *pronto.* They don't suggest anything right off hand, do they?"

"No, not off hand," the shipping man replied after a momentary hesitation. "Oh, while I think of it, my yacht, a green and black Diesel job, will be in the yacht basin that's just off the Praça 15 de Novembro. You can go aboard the *Miraflores* any time after half past six. Figure you might prefer crossing on her to catching a ferry."

Gratefully, North informed J. P. Standley that this was a very welcome suggestion.

"How's the party shaping up?" he asked and hung breathless on the reply.

"Da Evaristo, Setsukada and Count Altrocchi have all accepted," Standley chuckled. "Told you Aurora has what it takes to bring 'em a-running."

"Evidently. What about Dr. Rupp?"

"He told me he'd do his best to get there," Standley said deliberately. "I'm not sure, but I think he smelt a rat. By the way, your pal Maitland wants to bring along Luis da Evaristo's secretary—a Miss Harte. That okay?"

"Oh, quite," North murmured. "Quite."

Next, North rang up Lieutenant Nabuco, guardedly passed on the Bolivar information. The Brazilian Intelligence officer stated that he too had discovered a matter of deep interest. It would not do for the telephone. Major North would kindly arrange to grant him some time at Nictheroy?

Relieved that the affair was really beginning to take shape, Hugh North hunted up a slip of paper which closely matched that upon which the enigmatic message appeared. The forgery he executed was painstaking, skillful enough to have demanded the respect of an F.B.I. man. When he had done, the message read:

SAN MARTIN 27-18-22-7

It stood to reason there must be quite as many vessels named for José de San Martin as there were for Simon Bolivar. He even took care to reproduce the awkward granny knot which had secured the original message.

In the second of the substitute cakes of soap, he gouged out a hole just large and deep enough to accommodate the counterfeit. Next, from shavings the Intelligence officer worked up a paste which he applied to the moistened end of the substitute cake. After working the plug well in, he employed a razor blade to trim the end. He grinned when he found that absolutely no signs of cleavage remained.

Whistling cheerily, he put the counterfeit piece of soap into his desk drawer and locked it. The original cake and the water glass he reserved for a messenger Nabuco was sending. At Naval Intelligence Headquarters the development of those latent fingerprints might offer some significant revelations.

The Yacht "Miraflores"

A PARTICULARLY gleaming sunset was drawing an opalescent veil in the lee of the Dois Irmãos and was sketching blue-black shadow patterns behind the Corcovado, but on its peak the heroic statue to the Christo Redemptor remained bathed in a golden glory. The Pão de Assucar shone gray-green above the dark blue of the Bay of Guanabara.

Major Hugh North found no difficulty in recognizing Standley's yacht. The cabin cruiser, *Miraflores,* lay at her berth with brasswork fairly glowing and her paint work a triumph of unmarred glossiness. Seamen, neatly uniformed in white, were busy rolling up a tan-colored awning which, during the day, had shaded the deck.

As the Intelligence officer's spare figure bore down on the yacht's canvas-shrouded gangway, a pair of dark-faced officers appeared with startling suddenness and stood to salute. North suppressed a grin. If J. P. Standley wanted a guest to feel like an admiral boarding a friendly warship, it was all very well.

The senhor was most welcome aboard the yacht, the *Mira-flores,* the Captain declared. Would the estimable Major North please to order anything he might desire in the way of food or drink? No. The yacht had not been ordered to sail for another half hour—not until half past seven.

North received this information with gratitude. It would mean a great deal to catch precious moments of sleep. The hour's rest he had snatched at the Copacabana Palace had done miracles for his hurt side, but he could do with a bit more relaxation.

It was a real luxury thus to sink into an upholstered deck chair, to light his pipe and to lie watching a pair of lean, slate-gray Brazilian destroyers knife across the harbor in the direction of the Channel of Cotundoba and the South Atlantic. It lent him further satisfaction that these men-of-war were putting to sea in search of a vessel bearing, in part at least, the name of Bolivar. He closed his eyes and, in an instant, was enjoying a sleep so light that very little was required to break it.

How long he dozed on the *Miraflores'* afterdeck he had no idea, but eventually a sixth sense warned him of someone's intent inspection. Slender, effectively outlined against the yellow, green and red evening sky stood Aurora Morrow. A night breeze off the ocean modeled about her a filmy, long-skirted blue evening gown which could have originated only on Fifth Avenue; but possibly it had been created by some couturier on the Rua do Ouvidor.

"So-o-o, even a famous watchdog cat-naps?" she drawled, and the sunset touched fire to the brilliant color on her lips.

North arose and, inexplicably annoyed, bowed. "I'm a bit short on the shut-eye." Plague take this insolent chit! She was too smart by half.

At his tone her eyebrows expressed incredulous surprise. With an air of regal condescension the Morrow girl sauntered over to the rail, at the same time arranging a pale yellow shawl over her strapless evening gown.

"Don't mind me, Watchdog. Go right on sleeping, please," she invited and, with elaborate interest, considered the harbor now crowded with yachts out for an evening sail. Several self-important steamers in the coastwise trade were putting to sea, scattering dozens of piraguas, bumboats and fishing smacks. These went heeling about, their patched lateen sails orange, golden or brown in the sunset.

One *jangada,* the *Fé em Deus,* plowed by not a hundred feet away, its crew waving cheerfully even while devouring a huge platter of *empadinha de camarão.*

When one of the uniformed sailors ran ashore and commenced to cast off, North roused himself, felt the adhesive tape tug at his wound and sprinkle a dozen little barbs through his side.

"Aren't we waiting for Mr. Standley?"

"He was delayed in conference with a Mr. da Evaristo," explained the Morrow girl flinging herself carelessly onto a chair. Negligently she swung a bare, well-tanned ankle over one arm of her chair. Dull red-painted toenails peeped through her toeless blue and gilt leather slipper. "They'll be over soon, though, in J.P.'s flying boat," she announced with an air of elegant boredom.

Far too uninterested to exert himself, North made no conversation; merely watched the city rise, tower briefly above the *Miraflores'* stern, then commence to recede as countless thousands of lights began to blink into existence. For a while the roar of the traffic and the incessant honking of horns sounded overpoweringly loud. Off to port a municipal ferry, to a prodigal sounding of its whistle, was putting out from its dock at the foot of the Rua São José.

A steward in spotless white appeared, stood attentively. "*Desculpe-me,* is there anything desired?"

"You bet, Guiomar! I'm perishing for a daiquiri. And don't make it sour, either, or I'll raise merry hell," promised the girl, tapping her cigarette on a small gold case.

"Senhor?"

North smiled. "Whiskey and soda, please."

When the steward had disappeared, Aurora Morrow said over one bare glistening shoulder, "You disappoint me."

"What a pity. I was bent on affording you entertainment."

"Yes. I rather fancied you would order something complicated," she announced as if analysing a botanical specimen.

In faint amusement, North studied the girl's lovely, unnaturally immobile features. "Do I assume correctly that you aren't often mistaken?"

"Well, Watchdog, you're pretty mysterious, you know," she announced. "I haven't yet doped you out."

"Surely you don't come across people you can't—dope out?"

"Most people I meet I can diagnose pretty quickly," the Morrow girl told him airily.

"How very fortunate you are." Reluctantly, North emerged from his restful mood, tried to turn the moment to some purpose. "Do you happen to know a Dr. Rupp?"

"Who? Hermann the German? Oh sure, sure. He's supposed to be on J.P.'s loop tonight."

North suppressed a rising sense of irritation. "How would you diagnose him?"

If Aurora Morrow had a grain of serious thought in the exquisitely patrician brown head, it was most skillfully camouflaged.

"Oh, he's keen, even if he is heavy as lead before cocktails. Plays a good game of polo." She peered at him suddenly. "Say, you aren't the Hugh North who used to play back for the los Nanduces?"

"Guilty," he admitted with a faint smile.

"But why didn't you tell me?" she burst out, her languor departed. "I've seen you play. You were but wonderful. I saw your team win the Sands Point High Goal Tournament last year. You must know Lanny Pringle."

"Yes," North admitted without enthusiasm, "but we were speaking of Dr. Rupp."

"Oh, Hermann the German is very in the know about the trade between Brazil and almost every other country on earth," the Morrow girl went on. "To me it's all a big bore."

"I suppose so."

"You don't like Nazis, do you?"

"Not any part of them."

"Well, I call that narrow minded," she announced. "Some of them are perfectly angelic. Hermann is a dear and he dances the most divine *samba batucada.*"

North hitched himself up on his chair, aware that the yacht was speeding smoothly out into the bay past a rust-streaked ship with a Danish name but which was flying the American flag.

"*Samba batucada?*" North repeated.

For the first time interest animated Aurora Morrow's flaw-lessly made-up features. She hitched her wicker chair forward, cigarette dangling from her mouth.

"I guess you don't know there are two kinds of *samba;* the hot or *batucada samba,* as the Cariocans call it, which comes from South Brazil." Aurora Morrow actually smiled now that a daiquiri was deposited at her elbow. "Then there's the sweet, or *samba canção* that comes from up North. There's really no mistaking the two." She hesitated. "If you ever climbed off that high horse, I'll bet you could do a snazzy conga."

Despite himself, North grinned at her unconscious air of

patronage. "Who knows? In Cuba I used to do a pretty mean *danzon*. Go on," he invited, the smile still twitching at the corners of his mouth, "the more we Americans know about our neighbors the better."

She leaned so close that he could get a whiff of a perfume that would have aroused a stone monk. "At the Yacht Club tonight, what say we open their eyes?"

"Could be fun."

"Tell you what, we'll put that conceited Gino Altrocchi's nose out of joint."

A silence endured as the steward passed a platter of incredibly intricate hors d'oeuvres.

"Gino thinks he's quite one of the boys, you know," she said. "Quite the compleat fencer—if you get the drift."

North inclined his narrow dark head. "I get what you mean," he murmured, and relapsed into silence.

He could feel the girl's clear, pale eyes busy with him. Suddenly she asked, "Why don't you like me?"

He laughed, viewed her deliberately over his highball. "You think so because I don't babble all over the place over meeting the—let's see—the glamorous, wealthy and socially top drawer Aurora Morrow?"

"Oh, then you *have* heard of me?" she demanded with a return of her rotogravure page expression.

"Who could avoid it?" North demanded with perfect good nature. "Two years ago one couldn't read a paper, a magazine or a cigarette ad without seeing you framed against a zebra skin with a pair of stuffed and very eligible young bachelors to either side. They amounted to trade marks."

Blood poured into the slender pallor of Aurora Morrow's neck. "Really, you don't *have* to be so perfectly hateful."

North tinkled the ice in his glass, summoned a thin smile.

"My mistake. Thought your crowd's motto was, 'Nothing's sacred and anything for a laugh.'"

"Well—I—guess that's so; but what's the use of going around with a long face? Life's full of fun if you know how to get it."

"If you have earned it," he submitted. "Not five of that pub-crawling clutch of young wasters who were seen mugging about the night spots the last time I was in New York have ever earned a dime."

He stared out across the shining waters over which the sun was spreading a coverlet of rich crimson.

"You bright young things had better speed up your 'gather ye rosebuds' philosophy," he pointed out. "Before long there's not going to be very much unearned laughter."

"Croaked the Raven, 'Never more,'" observed Aurora in a cold, level voice. "You haven't a very exalted opinion of my generation."

"Not your generation, but your part of it—if you must have the truth," explained the lean, bronzed figure in the white dinner coat. "I've never had any intense admiration for glamour girls and the publicity hounds who run after them."

"Aren't you being pretty hard on us?"

"Possibly, but, strangely enough, I'm far from alone in my views. I suppose you know that your grandfather, Phineas Morrow, built a railroad system through the hottest, toughest part of the Southwest despite Apaches, thirst and crooked backing?"

Aurora Morrow's soft brown head inclined.

"And your own father, Andrew Morrow, founded the Tri-Continent Oil, then made the best Ambassador we'd ever sent to Italy up to that time. And then—"

"And then look at me," Aurora suggested slowly. "That's what you mean, isn't it?"

Had not North been so abstracted, so overwhelmingly aware of the magnitude of his responsibility, he would never have been so untactful as merely to shrug.

For many minutes Aurora Morrow sat staring out over the bay while the cabin cruiser churned speedily on, her lights beginning to duplicate themselves in the darkening water.

The *Miraflores* overtook a little excursion steamer all aglow with Chinese lanterns and throbbing to guitar music playing the ever-popular "Maria." From off the land came a sweet, musty smell suggesting a thousand miles of jungle and swamp in the Hinterland.

Her long page-boy bob swayed as the girl leaned forward and placed a fragile hand on his knee. "I wonder, Major, why nobody else ever put things just that way? Surprisingly enough, I—guess I rather like it, even if I don't admit that you're altogether right. My sort isn't really worthless. We've a terrific energy, even you will have to admit that—which seems to have —" she paused, fumbled— "to have gone into the rough."

She looked intently at the white-clad figure across the afterdeck. "Incidentally, I'll let you in on a family secret. Papa's estate has gone bust. Too many foreign holdings," Aurora explained. "The mines in France and Belgium have ceased to pay and the property in Italy and Germany has been confiscated. So it's a plain diet of prunes and spuds for the Morrows till the war ends—at least."

"That's hard lines."

"Father couldn't have foreseen all this, poor dear. He thought World War I would be the last."

North liked the way she stood up for her father.

"Tonight is my last night to howl," she explained, smiling a little apprehensively. "Right now, Major, you may not believe it but I'm worth little more than my clothes and some good furs which I hope to sell. That ought to keep me going until I can land a job."

"Land a job?" North demanded incredulously.

"Yes. I can't, I won't, live on J.P. any longer."

Suppressing his lively incredulity, North murmured, "Tell me about your side of Rio. What sort of places do you and Dr. Rupp go?"

She saw through his careless manner, said softly, "If you want to find out about Dr. Rupp, I'll get you the information. The same goes for Gino Altrocchi."

North smiled in the semi-darkness. "I'm interested to learn just how those gentlemen are concerned in ship movements these days. More specifically, if either of them is expecting a ship or even an important shipment."

" 'If either of them is expecting a ship or an important ship-ment,' " Aurora repeated carefully. "Gino ought to be easy. Just a matter of flattery and maybe a kiss or two, but Hermann the German—that, I mean to say, will take more doing." Her large, pale tawny-gray eyes sought his sun-darkened features. "How soon must you know?"

"The very first moment you think you've got something, you let me know at the Copacabana Palace." He spoke seriously even if he expected less than nothing to come of all this. "But, don't write and don't tell me anything you think important over the phone."

The girl's wide mouth parted in a natural, unaffected smile. "I say, Watchdog, this really is fun. Let's hoist a cocktail to to-night."

A Dark Hand Groping

AT THE German Yacht Club carnival decorations of yellow and blue and lavish festoons of electric lights glowed in splendid profusion. Across the little bay of San Fromasco and opposite the club glimmered red, green, yellow and blue lights. Out on the bay dozens of piraguas cruised about, their Chinese lanterns a-glowing with ever-shifting patterns of color. One heard nothing but talk about the impending carnival.

As Hugh North and Aurora Morrow left the stately old manor house which was now the club and crossed a wide terrace, a voice called, "I say there, Aurora!"

A sandy-haired young fellow of about thirty came hurrying up the terrace at a quick, slightly limping gait.

"Hi! there, Masibi. Pull any outside loops today?" greeted the Morrow girl, her lovely mask of indifference back in place.

"Not outside of Chez Julien's. What price the second dance? If it's a *maracatú,* I'll teach you some new passes I learned down in Santos."

"Can do. I feel just like a hot *maracatú* but if you teach me any more of those trollop's steps you picked up over in the Mangue, Tommy Andrews swears he'll break your goddamn neck for you," she added sweetly. "Major North," Aurora waved a languid, introductory hand, "meet Lieutenant-Colonel John Evelyn Andrew McCabe, better known as Masibi Jack in every bar from Panama to the Straits of Magellan."

North found himself shaking hands with an individual who long since had captured his interest. McCabe dressed, looked and talked like an Englishman, but still one sensed that he was not one.

The right side of the newcomer's face was a mass of shiny red and white scar tissue which suggested that he might have been hurled through a windshield at some not very distant time. He affected a small, carefully waxed mustache and lacked the first joint of the second and third fingers of his right hand.

"How d'you do?" he drawled as his rather small brown eyes took North in. Turning to Aurora, he said, "Well, see you later, Honeybear," and limped quickly and quietly away.

"There," Aurora said reflectively, "goes the soldier of fortune, modern edition."

"Why the nickname? Masibi is the name of a town in Bolivia, isn't it?"

As they started on down a wide flight of steps leading to the moonlit water, Aurora ducked her carefully coiffured head. "Go to the head, Watchdog. Jack says he was born of English parents but brought up in the Argentine. He's too thrilling and romantic for words. I guess he's flown for, or trained, a part of pretty nearly every air force south of Mexico."

"Why the nickname?"

"Gino Altrocchi told me that when Jack was flying for the Paraguayans in the Gran Chaco war he met up with a pair of Germans flying second-hand Fokkers. He got 'em both, but cracked up. Hence the limp and the rest of it."

"What's he doing nowadays?"

Aurora shrugged, resettled the pale yellow shawl over her bare shoulders. "He told me he's trying to have a drink in every bar in Rio, but I guess really he's awfully mad and resentful because the R.A.F. turned him down for an old crock. Jack must fly better than he plays roulette, or he'd never be here."

"An odd duck," North commented. "South America's full of broken-down flyers."

"I'm sure I heard a seaplane," Aurora said, "and I gather you'd prefer meeting Luis da Evaristo without too much of a cheering section on hand?"

North nodded.

It was curious that without ever having met Dom Luis da Evaristo, he should know so many details of the man's career, of his business and private affairs. North was aware, for instance, that da Evaristo's fortune stood on a par with those of the Crispis, the Guinles and the Matarazzos; that the da Evaristo interests extended from the busily smoking factories in São Paulo to vast coffee fazendas back of Bahia, and from thence into half-explored jungles in Pará where gaunt Indians drained wild rubber trees of their latex. The da Evaristos were one of the oldest, ablest and most respected clans in all the Brazilian Republic. A graduate of the Massachusetts Institute of Technology, Luis da Evaristo held a pilot's license and was an excellent wing shot. Unhappily married, he saw his wife much less often than he saw Paula Harte, for instance.

When North and his companion emerged upon a second and lower terrace, they saw a dull red amphibian drawing up to a landing stage. Two men and a woman in a white dress descended from the plane and crossed the landing stage. As they drew nearer, North recognized two of the trio: J. P. Standley and Paula Harte.

Aurora commented, "There's that Harte huzzy, Mr. da Evaristo's too, too private secretary. Very lovely, isn't she? She knows how to dress—and vice versa, or so I'm told," she added with studied sweetness. "They say, though, da Evaristo is tired of her and she's due for the grand bounce any day."

North yearned for time to pursue the subject, but already Standley was drawing near in company with a large individual whose dress shirt came glimmering up the steps. Luis da Evaristo was in fair physical shape, North estimated quickly and, from the way he handled himself, he looked as if he had once been a boxer or a lacrosse player. All in all he suggested immaculate grossness.

The presence of diamond shirt studs and a huge gold finger ring set with an unforgettably large emerald were the only things which would have distinguished Dom Luis from a successful American of similar age and position.

The Brazilian radiated vitality to a curious degree. Here was someone, one felt, for whom no undertaking was too bold, too difficult to attempt. He had an air of self-confidence and authority, his manner was charming, open and unaffected.

In his wake walked Paula Harte, more blondely beautiful than ever. There was, however, a preoccupation in her manner when she called, "Good evening, Miss Morrow. How are you, Major?"

"So you are the famous Major North of whom I heard in Singapore, in Cairo and everywhere else, it seems." Dom Luis' teeth flashed as he offered his hand. "This is a great moment for me. Good evening, Miss Morrow. You make the stars jealous of your beauty. Will you wear this insignificant flower?"

While North and Standley shook hands and Paula Harte stood looking on with a small, meaningless smile, Dom Luis offered a transparent box in which reposed one of the most extraordinary orchids North had ever beheld. Chiefly white, the flower was veined near the center with emerald-green and flecked with very tiny specks of ruby.

"But how exquisite!" Aurora Morrow murmured. "Ginny will go green with envy. Isn't it too, too—something, Miss Harte?"

"Oh, yes," Paula Harte agreed blandly, then added, "It is very like you, I think, Miss Morrow; rare and compelling of admiration. Do let me help pin it on."

"Prettily put," chuckled da Evaristo, and the diamonds in his shirt front blinked like miniature beacons when the group started up to the great glowing clubhouse where an orchestra had commenced to play an *embolada*.

Standley patted his niece's shoulder. "Keep at least one eye on Dom Luis, my dear. He's one of my most valuable clients. I want to introduce a friend of mine to Major North."

In the club's wholly deserted billiard room, Standley halted, turned, loaded to the gunwales with practicality.

"I've located five freighters which sound interesting," he announced producing a card from a small index file. "That's all

DUE	STEAMER	LINE	FROM	TO
Feb.				
23	*Bolivar Maru*	Osaka Shosen Kaisha	TENERIFFE	BAHIA
24	*Presidente Bolivar*	Comp. Chilena de Navigación	CAPE VERDE I.	CEARÁ
22	*Ciudad Bolivar*	Hispano-America	CADIZ	SANTOS
26	*Bolivar Liberator*	Lisbon-Brasileiro Companhia	LISBON	RIO
21	*Simon Bolivar*	Wesfal-Larsen Line	OPORTO	IGUAPE

there are to date and believe you me, I've checked in every direction."

"Thanks a thousand times." North glanced up from the neatly typewritten schedule. "May I keep this?"

"Sure. That's why I made it up," Standley grunted, irritably stroking thinning black hair. "Say, Hugh, I'm goddamned if I can make head or tail of those numerals."

Abruptly he shifted conversational gears without changing his tone. "I've put you up at the Gávea Golf Club, Hugh. It's handy and the greens are good. Sorry I can't play with you tomorrow but—Howdy, Gino, how's tricks?"

In the doorway had appeared a tall, well-fed man of about forty with a long angular face dominated by a thin, prominent nose, lively pale gray eyes and full-lipped mouth. In his buttonhole shone a brilliant little decoration rosette that accorded perfectly with the eyeglass glistening in his right eye.

"Ah, my dear Junius, I hope it *was* indeed you I saw pass," he greeted, putting down a short cigar and tossing a copy of *A Sentinella* onto a settee. "Such a divine inspiration, this party! I was prepared to perish of boredom, and Rio is so beastly hot on a night like this."

"Say, Gino, shake hands with my friend, Major North," Standley boomed. "He's a great guy. Figures to do some stag hunting in the interior."

The Italian bowed. "Such a pleasure, sir. If you would hunt the stag, I must write you a letter to my friend, Mateo Jungueiro. He is famous the world over. Yes, quite famous."

North expressed his appreciation and was interested to note that though Count Altrocchi affected a slim bracelet of solid gold links, his hand was muscular out of the ordinary.

"Come along, you fellows," Standley ordered. "Some pretty gals out front are eating their little hearts out for you."

"To find carnival upon us again is sheer delight," smiled Altrocchi. "You are fortunate, Major, to be here at this time of the year. Yes. Nowhere else will one discover such a spontaneous madness, so much music, such costumes and *mon Dieu!* what temptingly seductive women."

A moment later the three entered a large room—usually the casino—decorated with flags, bunting and thousands of flaming flowers. A dance floor loomed like a mahogany-hued island amid a white sea of sparkling table linen, silver and glassware. Already uniforms, brilliant evening gowns, dinner coats and the dark green and yellow livery of waiters were milling among the blossom-heaped tables.

"I guess that's our trough over there," Standley said. "There's young Maitland waiting."

At one side stood a long table decorated with clusters of pink and white orchids. To North's relief the Junior Military Attaché seemed perfectly at ease in a neat white dinner jacket that made the most of his broad shoulders and healthily bronzed complexion.

In a superbly designed white evening gown Paula Harte looked slimmer, younger than ever. Secured to Paula's shoulder by a huge platinum-and-diamond clip was an exotic blue flower which exactly matched her eyes. Perhaps unwisely, a heavy bracelet of sapphires and platinum gleamed on her left wrist.

Straight as a pillar and almost regal by comparison, Aurora Morrow stood beyond, deep in conversation with an Oriental, whom, on account of his stature, North at first mistook for a Mongolian. On second inspection this tall individual in well-tailored evening dress proved to be Japanese—probably from Aino, Kunashiri or one of the other northern islands.

The instant Aurora's companion faced about North at once

recognized him. That Ito Setsukada, the coffee broker, and Commander Baron Setsukada, former Naval Attaché to the Japanese Embassy in Washington, might be one and the same person had never even crossed his mind. The Japanese's recognition also was immediate.

"What a delightful surprise, my dear Hugh!" he cried as, heartily, they shook hands. "One hears you are major now. My congratulations."

Baron Setsukada spoke and acted like the Oxford graduate he was.

"Thanks, Ito. Your tennis game holding up these days?"

Setsukada's little black eyes twinkled as he turned to the patently impressed Morrow girl. "In 1937 Major North and I were lucky enough to win the Virginia State doubles championship together."

North smiled and patted the Japanese's shoulder. "Modestly, Baron Setsukada says nothing of the New England singles championship he won at Longwood."

"Please do not bore Miss Morrow with my insignificant accomplishments. Besides, I have grown a little old for singles," he laughed and ruefully touched stiff black hair that was going gray. "We shall have reminiscences later, eh?"

Only casually did North take notice of the arrival of Lieutenant Nabuco and Elena Camargo, a lively Brazilian girl with a voice like a brook and a face like a flower.

"When Ginny Carpenter and Conceição Morales show up, J.P.'s party will be nearly complete," Aurora confided, then added with a little frown, "Will you look at our genial host? Really, J.P. is impossible! He talks business day and night. Heavenly days! Hi, J.P., is this a dinner or a director's meeting?"

The shipping man stood, cocktail in hand, plunged in conversation with Count Altrocchi. Further on, Luis da Evaristo paid close attention to something Baron Setsukada was saying in an undertone. Abstractedly, the Brazilian kept chewing on the end of a long cigar.

In grim amusement North reflected that, within the radius of a few yards, were gathered a surprising number of individuals who, on the face of things, must be considered as deadly enemies. He'd have to look lively, sense every nuance in conversation. Yes, here was a rare gathering of Patriotista and pro-Axis bigwigs; occupants of other tables were staring, commenting. The group possibly was larger than he could cope with efficiently. He needed, however, to watch them together. Would Rupp appear?

As seldom before, a sense of apprehension began insistently to rasp at North's peace of mind. Of course, nothing would, or could, happen here in the ultra-conservative Yacht Club. Lieutenant Nabuco had fairly surrounded the clubhouse, yacht landing and service quarters with men who moved unobtrusively about, patiently admiring the really striking flower beds, formal gardens and a huge, uniquely designed aquarium densely populated by schools of gorgeously hued fishes.

"Better late than never, eh, Ginny?" Aurora greeted when Ginny Carpenter finally appeared, a frail wisp of a girl radiantly lovely in a full-skirted green evening gown. "You're practically on time only a good half hour late. Aren't we lucky? We've got a corner on men, actually two extras."

"Yo' uncle don't count," objected the Carpenter girl as she slipped a slim arm through Aurora's. "Ah know *him!* He'll be talkin' business to somebody all night, so we'll just about come out even. Tell me, Honey, who's that go'geous, nice lookin' man with the black hair and the short mustache?"

"Good eye," Aurora murmured. "Major North, I'm afraid you've made another conquest. Be kind to Ginny and always remember she's only a Southern magnolia blossom—with the technique of a pitcher plant," she added gently.

"Are you enjoying the cocktails, Miss Harte, or would you prefer a long drink?" Aurora cooed. "Don't you think Miss Harte's is a very apt name, Baron?"

The Japanese, who had been conversing in high good humor, apparently knew da Evaristo's secretary more than casually well. "I have held that belief ever since I met her last year in Belém. Are men blind?" he demanded of Hugh North. "Why has Miss Harte been allowed to remain single?"

"It all depends on what you mean by 'single,' Baron," Aurora murmured, turning away. "Captain Maitland, have a cocktail? You've been looking much too serious for carnival eve."

After a double round of cocktails further had thawed conversational ice, Aurora sought her place at the foot of a long table sparkling with glasses, silver and candles.

"Come on, J.P.," she begged. "No use ruining all our dinners on account of Hermann. The maitre d'hotel will be simply furious if those quail are overdone."

She motioned North to her right and put the girl called Elena between him and Nabuco. Then came Dr. Rupp's vacant chair and at the far end of that side a sweet-faced Brazilian girl named Conceição whom North had not even met. J. P. Standley sat at the far end of the table with feather-headed Ginny Carpenter sandwiched between Maitland and himself. Because of the shortage of girls, two men necessarily sat together on each side of the table. In one case, Maitland and da Evaristo; in the other, Dr. Rupp and Lieutenant Nabuco.

Either through malice or sheer carelessness, Aurora seated

Paula Harte to da Evaristo's right with Baron Setsukada on the other side.

While the guests were seating themselves, Ginny Carpenter tapped her glass and cried, "We've got to drink a toast or this won't be an honest-to-goodness dinner party. Any offers?"

"To Brazil," suggested Baron Setsukada, "our mutual friendly neighbor, and to my old friend Hugh North."

When they had finished the toast, North could have cheerfully drunk Ginny Carpenter's blood for, brightly, she called the length of the table, "Tell us, Major, are you *really* the white-haired boy of our Army Intelligence? Ah'm all of a twitter."

Luis da Evaristo

As THE dinner progressed, couples more frequently commenced to desert the table: Maitland and a rather unwilling Paula Harte, Altrocchi and Aurora, Standley and the girl called Conceição. Nabuco, North was glad to see, stayed put and furnished amusing small talk but maintained a quiet alertness which was very reassuring.

It was easy and natural for Hugh North to shift his seat to Maitland's empty chair beside da Evaristo. When he began by commenting on the excellence of the music, Dom Luis poised his cigar and the big emerald on his ring glowed like a flash of green fire.

"Is it not gay here tonight?" he inquired, fixing his gaze on North. "For me the rhythm of those different drums, the *cuica,* the *barrica* and the *omelê,* the lights, the laughter and the perfumes are like a soothing massage after a hard day's work."

"You have shipping problems?" North suggested.

"Eh?" da Evaristo's rather full features contracted and he looked hard at North. "What do you mean?"

"Mr. Standley said you were worried about the shipping of some merchandise," came the bland explanation.

"Oh—that," da Evaristo laughed shortly on a single note. "That was all right. Tell me," he lowered his voice and, under cover of a savage, noisy *maracatú,* said, "Why did you not try to see me in São Paulo?"

"You are a very busy man, senhor. Your time is precious."

His jet eyes apparently busy with the dancers, da Evaristo murmured, "I should not have been too busy to see you, Major. In fact, I rather hoped to have the pleasure of some conversations. I would have made your visit most interesting, perhaps."

Briefly North's gray-blue eyes flickered to da Evaristo's face, found it devoid of ulterior motive. He did note, however, that Nabuco was watching and so was Baron Setsukada, though he seemed absorbed in the girl Elena's rapid-fire conversation.

"Perhaps you return to São Paulo?"

"I don't know," smiled the Intelligence officer. "These days one's plans are necessarily indefinite."

"I shall be glad to fly you down, Major," Dom Luis offered, removing his frayed cigar. "I leave in two days."

"Very kind of you. If I go, I will call you."

Da Evaristo's rather prominent humid brown eyes flickered sidewise. "Suppose you call me. Here in Rio I can—er—make things interesting for you—very interesting. Ah, here is our friend Dr. Rupp, after all."

Da Evaristo's strong brown face seemed less carefree as he put down his wine glass and sat up.

Dr. Rupp was the last person in the world most people would have taken for an important Nazi agent. Bearing down on J. P. Standley's table was a pleasant-looking young-old man of about thirty-five. He was lean of body and his large features bore a careless and genuinely affable expression. The German's dark brown hair was wavy and not cut short, and no dueling scars disfigured a frankly attractive countenance. Only a slight scar running across the left brow and the lid drew attention to a remarkably good artificial eye.

"So sorry to be late, J.P.," he boomed. "Busy times at the office these days."

"Dr. Rupp," da Evaristo began, "is director-in-chief of the great Compania Estrella del Mar. They export everything you can imagine."

This Hugh North was grimly willing to concede. As he returned Dr. Rupp's easy bow and underwent a rapid inspection, North could not but marvel. In no way did this easy-mannered gentleman suggest the stiff, pompous and arrogant German diplomatists of the past. Yet if ever the Reich were to rule Brazil, Dr. Rupp would be principally to thank.

"Ah, yes. It is a privilege to meet the celebrated Major North. I saw him play polo once. I have never forgotten."

"And you, Doctor, I once saw winning a glider endurance contest in Bavaria."

Imperceptibly a tension made itself felt, such an instinctive hostility as seizes two shrewd and experienced antagonists of long standing.

"You are having a pleasant visit in Rio?" the German suggested, his one eye very bright.

"Very. It is so reminiscent of Paris—in the old days."

The German's thin lips tightened momentarily. "It is possible that the new Paris will some day be even more attractive."

"Ah, yes," North murmured. "Like the new London and the new Rotterdam?"

Steadily Dr. Rupp considered North as he smilingly conceded. "That, too, is possible, Major. In the natural order of things, much that is old must pass away—like old people."

"—And inferior races. Such, of course, have no right, no reasons for living."

Da Evaristo laughed a little too loudly and offered North a cigar.

"You really must try one of these."

"—And you, Luis, shall take one of mine," Dr. Rupp suggested. "Our friend McCabe gave me a handful in the bar."

"Better to keep them. They are excellent."

"No, Luis, I smoke only a little."

Aurora, flushed and lovely in her strapless gown, came hurrying up to the table with Baron Setsukada a step behind. "Well, Hermann, I thought you weren't going to show."

Dr. Rupp kissed the Morrow girl's hand, murmuring, "Not to dance with the loveliest young lady in Rio would be stupid, almost criminal."

"Whew!" She fanned herself with a menu. "Be a darling, someone, and pour me a drink. I'm perishing."

"Coming up!" Maitland hunted a fresh glass. Rupp selected a champagne bottle and started to fill glasses. To da Evaristo he said, "Luis, I think you have taken mine."

"What difference?" the Brazilian demanded with a wink. "They all will hold champagne."

Maitland stood gazing at the floor with a distinctly unhappy expression; the reason was perhaps because Paula Harte came swaying up to the table on Masibi Jack McCabe's arm.

"Hello, there, Dom Luis," the aviator nodded casually to da Evaristo. "Unexpected trip?"

"Yes," the munitions maker returned shortly. "What are *you* doing here?"

"Amusin' myself. Well, cheerio, old lad." And he limped away, waving to various acquaintances.

"There goes a grade-A heel," muttered the Junior Military

Attaché to North. "Down in Buenos Aires they claim McCabe would sell his sister into a bat-house if you met his price."

"A good flyer, though, I gather," murmured the Intelligence officer. "Keep an eye on Dom Luis," he added in an undertone. "He's got something on his mind."

"You bet I will, sir," Maitland replied with perhaps unnecessary emphasis. He seemed to have shaken off his depression of earlier in the evening.

"Anything else I can do?" he pleaded. "There's a fresh batch of inquiries in from Washington. They're fairly howling for action."

"I can't perform miracles."

"Making progress?"

"Some." If only he dared say, "Watch Paula every minute, try to hear everything she says. Don't trust her." But he couldn't.

There seemed nothing unusual in Paula's manner when she greeted Dr. Rupp except that she stood a little straighter.

"Good evening, Doctor. We were hoping you would get here."

"And I am glad that I did," the German laughed. "In the city, it is already noisy. Really, why do people go so utterly mad at carnival time? Such a childishness, all this noise-making."

"I had always believed you Germans to be fond of parades, of blaring bands," Nabuco suggested in polite surprise.

"Military parades are something different, you know," Rupp explained cheerfully. "They serve a useful purpose. But this carnival only encourages poor people to waste their savings on silly costumes."

"But, Doctor, what does it matter so long as they enjoy themselves?" Conceição demanded, reaching across the table for a champagne glass. "They have a right to pleasure, too."

"Exactly," Dom Luis agreed heartily. "What does it matter?" He gave North a gentle dig in the ribs that set the wound to aching afresh. "Let's go to the bar. This noise tires me."

"Oh, don't leave, Major," Ginny Carpenter pleaded and clutched his lapels. "Ah'm just dyin' for a rumba."

"I'll be back in a minute," North smiled, "but you'll have forgotten all about me."

"Not a chance!" she gurgled. "You make something tick inside me."

"I am forlorn," cut in Baron Setsukada. "Only just now Miss Carpenter declared *I* was inscrutable, fascinating and irresistible."

The German Yacht Club's bar was crowded but not nearly so noisy as its casino room. From the vantage of one end of the gleaming mahogany, da Evaristo inquired, "What will you have to drink? Name anything you like." He beckoned the barkeeper. "Bring that bottle of 1832 cognac."

"*Sim,* Senhor da Evaristo. *Com pressa.*"

The diamonds flashed as the munitions maker said, "Please, Major, you will come shooting with me next week? I know a magnificent spot. There are *tigres,* stags, ducks—"

"—And snakes?"

"Exactly. In Brazil we furnish the snakes free of charge."

It was evident that Dom Luis was enormously popular; every few moments men came up to shake hands, but as the cognac was served, there came a respite. Without changing his expression, the Brazilian observed, "Miss Harte tells me you met last night on the train from São Paulo?"

Last night! It seemed incredible that little more than twenty-four hours had elapsed since he had boarded the *Cruzeiro do Sul.*

"I found her an amusing and interesting companion," came North's wary comment.

Da Evaristo sighed. "She is—and very clever, too. Almost too clever. I—"

Just then Altrocchi came up. "Hallo there, Luis. Come and drink one of my famous cocktails," he invited. His gaze, however, was on North. "Really, Major, you must try one of my Lago di Como specials. The bartender at Cadenabbia gave me the secret."

Count Altrocchi had with him Elena, Lieutenant Nabuco's lovely little friend.

"Are they not exquisite?" she demanded in flawless French as Count Altrocchi began pouring a very pale pink drink from a well-frosted shaker.

"So lovely I'm afraid of them," smiled the Intelligence officer.

"No harm," laughed Altrocchi. "Even Senhorita Camargo is having her third."

"Thanks just the same," North smiled, "cocktails for my innards are sheer poison."

Elena Camargo gave a little squeak and extended first and fourth fingers as if to ward off the evil eye.

"Poison! Don't say such things."

"Why not?" The Italian shrugged. "How goes it, my dear? One man's meat is another man's poison?" He lifted his glass. "Well, an extra lively carnival to us all!"

Extra lively was right. Steadily, North's sense of apprehension grew. In his mind's eye he could visualize a low-lying, and probably very fast freighter, nosing steadily in towards the Brazilian coast, if she had not *already* discharged her cargo of treachery and death.

The more he dwelt on the disastrous coincidence of carnival

week and the *Bolivar's* arrival—she must, of course, be the *Bolivar*—the more breathless he felt. It was like being stranded on a broken levee and watching a flooded river eat steadily away at one's refuge. Bit by bit, an inexorable disaster was being hastened.

"Damn' good cocktail," Dom Luis was saying when Paula Harte sauntered in in company with Baron Setsukada. He sprang up. "Do you mind my stealing my secretary for a dance?"

The Japanese's teeth glistened. "If Miss Harte types as well as she dances, Luis, you are indeed the most fortunate of employers."

North's eye met Paula's, but now they were blank, uninformative. Her smile, as she accepted da Evaristo's arm, was mechanical, perhaps because Maitland at that minute appeared in obvious pursuit. His expression was not pleasant when he turned sharply on his heel and kept on as though nothing had chanced.

When the quartet returned, the ballroom was steadily becoming a scene of exhilarated confusion. Out on the terraces people were blowing horns as Americans do on New Year's Eve; in the town, bands were thumping and blaring away in that amazing moonlight which Brazilians boast exceeds the brilliance of the sun in England.

Dom Luis now was fairly bubbling with good humor. He stopped at McCabe's table, had a drink with him, and North distinctly saw the Brazilian covertly pinch Paula Harte on that portion of the anatomy which it is equally unwise to present to a friend or to an enemy. Next the munitions maker took a turn around the floor with Aurora, dancing with an extraordinary grace and agility.

"Still talking business?" he demanded presently of Standley, who had not budged from his chair. "Why don't you dance?"

"Saving my energy, Louey," smiled the host. "I quit the light fantastic when the turkey trot went out."

When da Evaristo began fumbling for a cigar and Setsukada offered him one from a handsome pigskin affair which held its contents in place with golden arms fashioned in a series of joined rings, North was surprised to notice, all at once, that the Brazilian was no longer wearing his massive gold and emerald ring.

Once more the music paused and dancers returned to their tables.

"Scott and Helena are going on," Aurora informed North. Then in an undertone, "You're right. Gino *is* expecting a shipment."

"From where?"

"Rio de Oro," Aurora whispered. "Is there such a place?"

"Yes. Spanish colony on West African coast. Good work, keep it up."

When he gave her fingers an approving pat, he was amazed to have her take his hand and hold it under the tablecloth. Aloud she continued, "Scott and Helena do caricature dancing —sort of like the Hartmans, only I think they're better."

The Intelligence officer found it amusing that in New York Brazilian dances were all the rage, while in Rio the reverse was true.

In that moment the lights blinked out and the dark glowed with hundreds of cigars and cigarettes until a spotlight silvered two supple young people in evening clothes. In the background a champagne cork came out.

Missing from the table, North noticed, were Maitland, Ginny Carpenter and Dr. Rupp. The rest were, with rapt attention, watching the dance team. Altrocchi and Nabuco were smoking cigars, but Dom Luis was too intent on a glass of champagne to light his perfecto.

North had momentarily directed his attention to the dance floor when da Evaristo abruptly put down first his wine glass and then his panatela. He heaved himself to his feet.

"I will return at once," he muttered, his mouth muffled in a handkerchief. "Fresh air—"

Considering the variety of liquors the munitions maker had drunk within the last hour, North deemed it was small wonder that Dom Luis felt a necessity for air.

North inclined towards Aurora's small, patrician head. "I'm going to see if he's all right."

"Okay. I'll talk to Hermann next." She gave his fingers a gentle pressure as he slipped so quietly out of his chair that no one except Standley saw him leave. The latter raised an inquisitive brow but remained still.

When Hugh North reached the lavatory, da Evaristo was not to be seen. Before a row of shining mirrors Dr. Rupp was briskly combing his hair. Captain Stuart Maitland, closer at hand, was busily cleaning his nails while whistling a popular *embolada*. He nodded pleasantly.

"Quite a blow-out, isn't it? I'd never have—" He broke off as Luis da Evaristo staggered out of a cabinet, his powerful features turned a hideous purple-red. Through bloated lips, he was emitting gasps and dreadful, inarticulate sounds. His eyeballs suddenly rolled upwards until only the whites showed, then with a strangled grunt the munitions maker collapsed onto the green and black tile floor and sprawled there, limbs jerking violently.

Captain Stuart Maitland had barely time to join North in bending over the stricken munitions magnate before Lieutenant Nabuco materialized from nowhere reinforced by two large and capable-looking individuals in ill-fitting dinner suits. Behind the plainclothesmen ran a pair of gray-green uniformed police. On Nabuco's order they quickly locked the lavatory door on its occupants.

"Must be a heart attack," Maitland suggested.

"Nonsense. Look at those lips!" Dr. Rupp glanced at North, then took the unconscious Brazilian's wrist. After an instant he fixed his one good eye on the group hovering expectantly above him. "Senhor da Evaristo seems to have eaten something poisonous."

"Send for an ambulance—stomach pump," snapped the Intelligence officer. "Quick!"

The German got slowly up from his knees, his clean-shaven features expressionless. "It is no use, Major. The pulse has stopped."

Central Army Hospital

IF DR. HERMANN RUPP held guilty knowledge of this affair, he was a consummate actor. But then, North warned himself, the Nazis had gone far because their agents *were* good actors; trusting neighbor states had discovered this to their despair.

Um. Why should Maitland have been in the lavatory when Luis da Evaristo came staggering in to die? A coincidence? Possibly. Yet, long years of experience had taught him to sniff at coincidence like an Englishman in a foreign restaurant. Maitland probably was quite trustworthy, yet the matter of Paula Harte remained.

As it was, that healthily tanned young fellow who was built so much like himself stood staring in horrified awe when Lieutenant Nabuco dropped a towel over the face now so distorted as to resemble the figment of some fantastic nightmare. The whole body, North noted, was gradually turning a loathsome purple-green.

He said to Maitland, "Go to the dining table, warn Standley to break the news and see that *nothing* now on the table is removed."

"Yes, sir." To be thus given orders roused Maitland from his trance. He looked relieved.

"Not even a napkin is to be touched. Lieutenant," he turned to Nabuco, "you will detail Captain Maitland two men?"

"Of course." Nabuco said in his clipped, efficient way, "Inspector Ramos of the State Police will be here very soon. A moment, Captain Maitland. Please inform Mr. Standley's party that they will be required to return to Rio for questioning."

That the Naval officer, too, was laboring under overwhelming responsibility was very obvious.

So it came about that, at two of the morning, an oddly cosmopolitan group of sad people in gay clothes appeared at that grim gray structure which, on the corner of the Rua dos Invalidos and the Rua da Relação, serves as the Central Police Station of Rio de Janeiro. One by one the guests made their depositions and posted bonds until only J. P. Standley, his niece and North remained.

"Say, Hugh," Standley demanded sotto voce, "does this *Bolivar* business have anything to do with—with poor Louey's getting knocked off? He was, wasn't he?"

"Da Evaristo was murdered, all right," came North's deliberate reply, "*unless* he committed suicide."

"Suicide, why?"

"Who knows? I only said it was possible."

"What about the *Bolivar?*" reiterated the shipping man.

The Intelligence officer's straight black brows met. "There's no proof yet—not even a lead. Still, there might be—"

"You'd better make up your mind," Standley advised. He had been very capable, very efficient ever since the tragedy had taken place. "In these latitudes the da Evaristos rate like the Rockefellers or Morgans back home. There'll surely be an unholy stink raised when the news breaks." He sighed. "This won't help my business standing any, goddamn it."

"Come along, and no arguments," Aurora murmured, lovely and as incongruously out of place in this bleak and grimly businesslike place as an orchid in a stokehold. As she passed an arm through North's and drew him aside, he was aware of a dry but stimulating perfume, of a certain correct nuance of mode in her appearance which Paula Harte could never possibly capture.

"I say, Watchdog, thought you might be interested in what I happened to see just before Senhor da Evaristo was—taken ill."

"Good gal," he smiled, "but I'm beginning to think it didn't just happen. Why weren't you watching the dancers?"

"Oh, I've seen them dozens of times. Well," she fixed him with her pale eyes and spoke slowly like a child trying to remember a recitation. "Senhor da Evaristo took a drink, then picked up his cigar. Um, let's see. Then he put it down quickly and gulped another drink." She paused, her lips a small scarlet circle. "I noticed because I think Miss Harte gave him her glass."

"You *think?*" North groaned inwardly. That was the devil of amateur assistance. "Can't you be *sure?*"

"Why—why, no." Aurora flushed to the roots of her still flawlessly arranged hair. "But I'm pretty sure. Anyway he drank. Is this being useful? I want to be, you know?"

"Very. What did da Evaristo do then?"

"He made a very queer face, remember? Then he got up and started out."

Lieutenant Nabuco, who had quietly come up from the assistant superintendent's brilliantly lit desk, asked, "Senhorita, you are reasonably certain it was Miss Harte's glass?"

Aurora bestowed on the slim young Brazilian one of her most efficient café society smiles.

"Why, yes. Miss Harte was on Mr. da Evaristo's right. I remember distinctly because she shoved her glass away from her and towards him when the dance team went on. Yes. I'm sure he took the glass in his right hand."

North looked about. From the drawn expressions of various officials, it was clear that this murder had come in the nature of a catastrophe. Everywhere telephones were busy, messengers went pelting down corridors and in the street a succession of automobiles coughed and roared away. Aurora Morrow seemed shaken out of her customary vague manner and was, for the benefit of Nabuco and a yellow-faced police clerk, answering a long stream of questions.

Still the impression persisted in North's mind that she was not telling the whole truth. Every now and then her gaze would flicker sidewise or she would light a fresh cigarette and glance at the row of Bertillon-system photographs affixed to a bulletin board.

"Really, Lieutenant," Aurora was saying, "I simply can't believe that, not three hours ago, I was dancing with Luis da Evaristo! He was so full of jokes, so merry—"

"—Merry?" Nabuco questioned. "You mean he acted *bêbado,* a little drunk perhaps?"

Definitely, Aurora Morrow shook her softly brown head, gathered her yellow shawl tighter about slender bare shoulders. "No, he wasn't the least bit stinko—just gay. Said he'd just got something off his mind—something very troublesome and that he felt well about it."

North asked, "He didn't mention or indicate what that was?"

Aurora hesitated. "No, but he said all Brazil would soon hear about it."

Something all Brazil would hear about? Um. A former fear returned to torment North. The *Bolivar* must already have landed! He went hot and cold by turns, then warned himself not to leap at conclusions.

"Did Dom Luis say anything else?"

"Yes. While we were dancing, he said he was going to go away for a while to visit some rubber estates his company had bought near Belém."

After a little while North suggested to Nabuco that Standley and his niece be permitted to leave.

The young Brazilian, putting down a steaming cup of coffee served by a uniformed servant, said, "But of course. They were not being detained. We are deeply indebted to you, Senhor Standley, for the use of your yacht and to you, Senhorita, for your good memory." Gallantly he added, "*A seus pés, se-nhorita.*"

Once the two Americans had departed, the Intelligence officers seated themselves. North filled his pipe. His side felt somewhat better. The Brazilian swallowed a cup of excellent coffee, folded his arms and heaved a sigh.

"I wonder *why* da Evaristo was killed," the Naval officer muttered as at the screens of the open windows a multitude of insects hurled themselves in futile persistence.

"Perhaps," North replied, "we can answer that when we learn *how* Luis da Evaristo died."

North settled back, eyed a faded ceiling spotted with sleeping flies. "When can an autopsy be performed? I think it is important that it be done as quickly as possible."

Nabuco nodded. Said he briskly, "The Superintendent has, at my request, already phoned to the coroner-in-chief, Dr. de

Nobrega. He said he will arrange to meet us at the Central Army Hospital as quickly as he can drive in from Ipanema."

"When it comes to getting necessary things done in a hurry," North commented with ready appreciation, "you're the shade of a rock in a weary land, Lieutenant."

"Mil agradecimentos." Nabuco flushed with pleasure and his teeth shone in the glare of the electric lights. "In Brazil these days, we are learning that tomorrow will not always wait for us."

North rubbed eyes that felt as if they had been fished from a New England boiled dinner. "I presume the table has been kept intact?"

"Exactly as it was; but I do not have hope of learning much from it," he shrugged. "Three different persons I observed gave the dead man a drink."

"Perhaps not. If so, we must work all the harder to learn *why* someone wished da Evaristo poisoned."

"But you yourself suggested a possibility of suicide?"

A twinkle shone in the American's eye. "For a purpose, and only as a possibility. By the way, when you had the body searched, were the valuables brought here?"

"Yes. I will send for them." His slight, white-clad figure arose, sped to a push button. "Why? Are you curious, Major?"

"I noticed that a ring da Evaristo had been wearing had disappeared. You could scarcely have failed to notice that gold and emerald ring?"

Nabuco looked crestfallen. "I noticed it, of course; but not that it was gone. I was very careless."

Presently a sleepy, walrus-mustached detective carried in a brown metal box of the sort similar to those employed in safety deposit vaults. From it Nabuco poured onto a sheet of clean, white paper the usual miscellany of objects found in a man's pocket. North noted fountain pen, key-ring, cigar case—very handsome one studded with large yellowish diamonds—and a well-filled pocketbook.

"Even for a millionaire that is much money," Nabuco murmured, peering round-eyed at well over a hundred contos of reis—ten thousand American dollars.

But of the gold and emerald ring there was no trace. Um. By cruelly racking his memory North was sure that da Evaristo had last been wearing it just before he had claimed his secretary from Baron Setsukada for a dance. Fifteen minutes later North had seen it gone.

With great care North examined the murdered man's effects, reserved his papers to the last. These included a private pilot's license and identification papers. There were also two unimportant letters and a partially completed cross-word puzzle clipped from some newspaper.

"The clothes," Nabuco suggested tersely, "are at the hospital. The ring might be concealed somewhere in them."

The American Intelligence officer roused himself and relit his pipe. "What was it you were going to tell me, by the bye?"

"*Ai!* In all this I have forgotten to say. Twice our radio stations picked up this afternoon a series of words from a ship not far off our coast. *A Nação depois a Patria.* They were repeated twice at intervals of twenty minutes."

"Means 'the nation, then the fatherland,' doesn't it?"

"Yes, just that. So they may mean nothing at all."

"Um-m, the words don't seem to say much at that. The nation, then the fatherland. Still, use of the word fatherland— Could Patria mean anything else?"

Nabuco shook his head. "No, it is the name of a newspaper. There are too many here."

"I see. Where was the ship?"

Nabuco spread almost femininely delicate hands. "We cannot tell. Then this evening our naval radio station at Rio Grande do Sul heard something I fear will puzzle you, Major. The call letters were B-O-L-I-V-A-R."

"Bolivar?" North sat bolt upright. "What did they say?"

The Intelligence officer passed over a slip of paper.

BOLIVAR 20-44-34-66

"A second was heard at eleven tonight. Here it is."

BOLIVAR 9-22-36-7-38

"Good God!" North groaned at this swift complication of a problem he had felt to be somewhat simplifying itself.

"We must not jump at any conclusions," he offered, after memorizing both radiograms. The more he thought about those three messages beginning with the word Bolivar, the more he wondered, especially since the call letter corresponded to that on the encoded scrap of paper inside of Paula Harte's now famous bar of soap.

"Cross-word puzzles are such a waste of time," Nabuco remarked, fingering the papers among da Evaristo's effects. "But they amuse. Sometimes some good ones appear in *O Braziliero*."

"I wish I had time for them," North returned. "I wonder that da Evaristo did."

"Merely another form of mental relaxation—like the theater and murder mysteries," the Brazilian suggested.

At that moment the telephone bell began to jangle with spiteful, insistent trills.

"That will be Dr. de Nobrega," Nabuco predicted.

The coroner-in-chief, from the Central Army Hospital, conveyed his most distinguished respects to the celebrated

Major North and stated that, as a special dispensation, he would conduct an immediate autopsy. The Minister of Justice apparently had been busy, now that Luis da Evaristo had been assassinated.

It was with deepening alarm that North watched the façade of the great Central Army Hospital loom up, all pale silver and jet shadows, in the moonlight. In that structure the problem presented by 304 G-2b might find its answer. It was depressing to abandon the balmy, sweet-scented tropical night for an atmosphere of ether, disinfectants and suffering.

In silence North and the Brazilian Naval officer followed a worried-looking interne down a succession of pale-green painted, dim and resounding corridors. A sick man in some ward to the right was groaning "Maria! Maria! Ai, Maria!" slowly, hopelessly.

Occasionally, nursing sisters in wide, white caps and voluminous gray skirts appeared and disappeared like embodied ghosts. With every step Hugh North's heart sank lower.

As the heels of the party clicked along a suddenly brilliantly illuminated corridor leading to the autopsy room, Hugh North commanded his jangled nerves to obedience, forced himself to shake off a deadening sense of fatigue. Outside the autopsy room quite a knot of officials had gathered. Most of them bore the marks of rudely disturbed slumber written large across their faces.

The Chief of Detectives and the elaborately uniformed Superintendents of the Metropolitan and State Police forces stood in the foreground hotly arguing some point. The background was fairly swarming with reporters. There was desperation in their eagerness. Very clearly, various city editors had dispatched their minions with instructions to get the da Evaristo story at no matter what cost.

"That is Judge Alguir, Minister of Justice." Nabuco indicated a vigorous old man with a head like a Roman senator. His bright pink cheeks glistened silvery from a day's beard.

Dr. Paulo de Nobrega proved to be a rotund, but solemn individual with a grayish torpedo beard. Big eyes, brown-black like a spaniel's, peered from behind thick-lensed spectacles.

Conversing dazedly with Judge Alguir was a well-dressed young man who, at first glance, must be Dom João, Luis da Evaristo's brother.

"Ask anything you will, any amount of work, your Excellency," cried João da Evaristo. "My family will not rest until the cowards who did this are made to pay."

Cowards? Why the plural? North wondered.

Dr. de Nobrega spoke in hurried undertones, explained to the new arrivals, "Without the permission of the new head of the family, we could not otherwise undertake this autopsy until some court so ordered. May I present Dom João da Evaristo?"

North offered his hand, feeling desperately out of place in his wrinkled white linen evening clothes among all these deeply stricken people.

"I wish it had been possible for us to have met under pleasanter circumstances, senhor," North murmured. "I hesitate to—"

João da Evaristo roused himself, made a decisive motion with his hand and turned reddened eyes on the lean-faced American. "If it is for the good of the State, we cannot permit an instant's hesitation, Major. I am overwhelmed. I had expected Luis to come to my home when he returned from Nictheroy."

"Did he say so late this evening?" North demanded.

A surprised murmur circulated the group when Dom João inclined his smooth black-haired head. "Yes. But how did you know?"

"I didn't," came the quiet reply. "Do I gather that he wanted to tell you something of great importance?"

"Yes. Exactly that."

In the background the reporters were scribbling furiously. Nabuco, now heavily out-ranked, looked at once worried and hopeful.

"Luis sounded so happy I wondered if he had been drinking too much," the murdered man's brother continued and his shoulders rose in a little shrug. "I regret to say that Luis and I have not been quite so intimate this last year as previously." Dom João looked very unhappy. "You see, Major, Luis favors, even backs, Pujol and his Patriotistas, while I—" the younger brother's voice deepened, rose with indignation until the corridor resounded—"hold them to be a pack of vicious, self-seeking traitors—wretched Quislings, do you understand? They would betray the Republic to that Spaniard, Pujol."

The athletic figure looked steadily about the semicircle of uniformed and white-gowned figures. "It is in my mind that Luis had decided—" he choked, broke off. "That is all. You may proceed with—with—the—the inquiry." João da Evaristo buried a quivering face in his hands and turned away.

"Come, João." Another and still younger member of the family put an arm about his shoulders, guided him into a nearby office.

At Judge Alguir's command the reporters, protesting vehemently, were herded down the corridor and out of sight. Lesser officials hustled off. It was not every day a great millionaire was murdered.

The autopsy room proved to be modern and well lit with

rows of seats climbing amphitheater-like above the operating floor. Draped in a sheet, the dead man's body lay ready on a white-enameled operating table. The two superintendents of police, Judge Alguir and Nabuco took seats in the first tier of benches. Hugh North, Dr. de Nobrega and a colleague, one Dr. Ramalho, remained on the operating floor.

North now wished he had part of that Scotch highball he had left behind at the German Yacht Club. First and last he must have beheld several hundred corpses, some of them horribly mangled. Yet never had he rid himself of an awe at that phenomenon of death. Greatly he envied such unimaginative souls as could crack grisly jokes over some peculiarity of a cadaver, or even indulge in gruesome pranks.

When the preliminary investigation began, North watched intently. At the back of his mind an incomplete memory was stirring. Sometime, somewhere in the past he was sure he had seen a body which closely resembled this peculiarly colored and abnormally swollen corpse. But *where? When?* Try as he would, he could not recall.

"This, gentlemen, is a most unusual case," Dr. de Nobrega announced, "but I believe we shall have small difficulty in identifying the type of poison employed."

"And why so, my dear Paulo?" challenged Dr. Ramalho acidly.

"The very swiftness of the toxic action limits our field, my dear Guiomar," de Nobrega snapped. "We may dismiss such poisons as arsenic, phosphorus, mercury, aconite, strychnine, phenol or chloral."

Luis da Evaristo's body, a little flabby about the waist but otherwise muscular and well tanned, lay helpless under the glaring blue-white operating lights. The edges of teeth in the half-opened mouth glinted, created gruesome little highlights.

North watched the two doctors pursue their examination. Then, faced by a paradox, he scrutinized every inch of the dead millionaire's skin.

Finally he straightened and inquired, "Gentlemen, we are agreed that Senhor da Evaristo met death by poisoning, are we not?"

The two medical men inclined their heads. "Nothing else could have brought about death with such symptoms," muttered Dr. de Nobrega.

"Nor with such swiftness," added the gaunt, mournful-looking Dr. Ramalho.

The coroner-in-chief joined bushy gray brows, spoke a trifle pompously. "The nature of this poison does not immediately suggest itself." He turned to Nabuco. "Lieutenant, you have stated that the deceased drank liquors with several people?"

"With at least six persons," Nabuco instantly replied. "One wonders—"

"It is very clear," cut in Dr. Ramalho, "that someone spilled prussic acid into the deceased person's glass."

"Someone at the table, eh, Doctor?" North suggested. "The poison was rapid."

"Exactly."

"But why, my dear Guiomar, do you suggest prussic acid?"

"One cannot otherwise consider the amazingly swollen condition of the mouth, my dear Paulo."

Dr. de Nobrega shook his iron-gray head. "And you, Major, what is your opinion on the point? I see you also have noted that there is no odor of prussic acid."

Out of politeness North pretended to deliberate. "Gentlemen, why are we so satisfied that it must be something the patient *drank* which killed him?"

This caused a stir among the bright buttons glimmering

in the background. The Chief of Detectives stood up in the amphitheater, leaned forward.

"*Desculpe-me*," he said in a hoarse, low-pitched voice. "But to me it appears you have to deal with a poisoning of the blood. No? In Amazonas once—"

Dr. Ramalho glared. "My dear sir, it is we who are conducting this inquiry. Kindly reserve any remarks until the conclusion of this autopsy."

North, however, nodded in the speaker's direction and gave Nabuco a look which prompted him to shift to a seat beside the crestfallen Chief of Detectives.

Dr. de Nobrega, directing a cold look at his colleague, observed, "Senhor Andreza is correct. The symptoms do indicate a toxin introduced into the blood stream rather than into the digestive tract."

"Nonsense!" snorted Ramalho. "Sheer nonsense, my dear Paulo. To poison the blood stream one must have a wound. Eh? Now where is the wound? Though I have examined the cadaver from head to foot, I have found not even a scratch." He glared across the body lying naked, so tortured, so pitifully revealed. "I challenge you to show me a wound! Yes, it is a digestive poison we must seek!"

A brief silence fell in the chill, white-painted amphitheater. The odor of disinfectants seemed ever stronger; that and the sour, musty odor of death. The witnesses scuffed their feet, looked nervously at each other. Outside an ambulance bell could be heard clanging loud, louder.

North mustered a small smile and turned to de Nobrega. "May I borrow a dentist's mirror and light?"

Round-eyed, both doctors considered him an instant before Ramalho obliged. "What is on your mind, Major?"

"I quite agree," the Intelligence officer replied deliberately, "that there is no trace of a cut, incision or abrasion on the exterior of da Evaristo's body. However—"

His voice faded as he bent over the dead man's gargoylesque head. It was so swollen that its eyes were concealed beneath great shiny folds of purple-green flesh. And to think that this was all which remained of him who had come laughing up from Standley's amphibian, of the bonvivant with whom he, himself, had been drinking and joking not five hours ago, of the excellent dancer who whirled Paula Harte and then Aurora Morrow through a gay *caTereTê*.

"I came across a somewhat similar case once," he apologized while rolling up his sleeves, "else I should not venture to conduct even a cursory examination in the presence of two so celebrated medical men."

Setting his teeth, the Intelligence officer first separated the dead man's lips, then called for forceps to keep the mouth well open. Everyone leaned forward as North commenced to play his dentist's light into the dead man's mouth. It proved so swollen, however, that Dr. de Nobrega found it necessary to hold the lips back with clips.

Faint odors of brandy and cigar smoke reached North's nose as, very slowly, he circulated his light over the tongue, then employed the little circular mirror to examine the roof of the mouth. All at once he straightened.

"Gentlemen, what do you see there?"

The two white-clad figures bent low.

"See where?" Dr. Ramalho's manner was testy. "I observe nothing."

"There, just back of the right incisor," insisted the dark-haired American. "There is a small purple-red ring in the gum. It appears to have been punctured."

"I see it now," admitted Dr. de Nobrega.

"Doctor, I wonder if you can sound that puncture? Its depth may be of great importance."

Presently the coroner-in-chief announced, "The incision is shallow, not more than a quarter of an inch in depth."

"You see? I was right!" boomed the Chief of Detectives, his great mustache quivering. "Dom Luis *was* poisoned! Yes. With a *curare,* a vegetable poison! The Indios of the Yapura and Caieira Rivers use it in war."

Suddenly North remembered the case of Senator Babcock. "Senhor Andreza," he suggested, "no doubt refers to *antiaris toxicana.* That is so, is it not, Senhor?"

The Chief of Detectives beamed broadly. *"Sim, sim!"*

"Of course *strychnos tiute* might also do the trick," North added as, absently, he tested his hurt side. The wound was throbbing painfully once more but it bothered him not half so much as the realization that time was flowing stanchlessly away.

Judge Alguir arose, descended gravely to the operating pit. He turned clear gray eyes on North. "If what you say is true, Major North, and this poison was introduced into the deceased's blood stream, *how was this accomplished?"*

14

"A Woman Is Only a Woman, But—"

QUERIED the Superintendent of Metropolitan Police, "Did Senhor da Evaristo drink of anything containing cherries or olives?"

"Yes," North replied, rolling down his sleeves. "I saw him drink a cocktail containing a cherry."

"With whom, please?" Nabuco demanded softly.

"With Count Gino Altrocchi."

The eyes of the witnesses flickered questioningly. They had sensed the implication, all right.

"Why, senhor, do you ask that?" demanded Judge Alguir.

"Because, your Excellency, it would be possible for a murderer to place within such a cherry or olive some sharp object covered with the *antiaris.*"

The Superintendent of the State Police stood up, gold buttons gleaming and his starched khaki uniform pale in the bright lights. "Tell us, Lieutenant Nabuco, is it not possible that the murderer administered this poison through food?"

Nabuco informed his questioner that this was impossible. Only glasses had been on J. P. Standley's table for many minutes preceding the millionaire's collapse—and the poison had acted very swiftly.

138

Dr. Ramalho suggested, with an acid look at his colleague, "Possibly, your Excellency, our North American friend has found an explanation?"

During several moments Hugh North had been recalling details of the evening concerning Luis da Evaristo. His arrival at the landing stage, his jewelry—ah, *there* was a bit of unfinished business!—his mannerisms, his habit of clapping friends on the back, his nervous smoking. North had just arrived at this recollection when Dr. Ramalho put his query.

He plucked up a scalpel and indicated one of several small, dark brown triangles of tobacco adhering to the dead man's tongue. Carefully he removed as large a piece as he could find, placed it in his notebook and looked up. Said he soberly, "I think, but mind you, I am not *sure,* that Luis da Evaristo was poisoned by means of a cigar."

Amid a penetrating silence disturbed only by the distant groans of patients down the hall, North asked, "Some of you no doubt will recall the manner in which Senhor da Evaristo smoked?"

"Why, yes, nervously. Always he was chewing the end—" de Nobrega broke off short. "Ah! I see! The poison was lodged in the butt of the cigar. When Dom Luis chewed, a needle or something sharp punctured his gum."

"But that is fiendish!" growled Judge Alguir. "Who would do such a thing?"

North said, "Only someone very familiar with his habits."

"A search—a very careful one—will be made for the cigar which Dom Luis held when he was taken ill," Lieutenant Nabuco promised.

"I wonder if you will find it?" the dark-haired Intelligence officer murmured. "Perhaps. But I am not inclined to underestimate the intelligence of the killer."

"Who could have given him that cigar?" Nabuco demanded anxiously. "Somebody at our table?"

"That is a subject for further meditation," North smiled. Cheek-bones more pronounced than ever, he bowed first to the Minister of Justice, then to the rest of the group.

"I think," said he, "if you will meet me at seven this morning, Lieutenant, we will have had time to digest our findings and can compare notes."

Pourparlers

NOT in many a year had Hugh North felt so thoroughly fatigued. His eyes felt like brandied cherries and his skin was dry and hot. He sat back on the cushions of the Chief of Detective's car and tried to relax. Long since he had discovered it was bad business to flail a jaded intelligence too long.

Even at this ungodly hour the city was far from sound asleep. Back in the Praça Onze, drums were still muttering and rumbling and several night bars were crammed with outlandishly costumed merrymakers already priming themselves for the morrow.

He found it fine to be alone, to be watching a succession of handsome moonlit buildings flash past. A land breeze, as gently soothing as the hand of a trained nurse, had sprung up and was wafting seawards the languorous odors of a hundred million tropical blossoms.

Incongruities he had discovered long ago were more or less accurate points of departure—the incongruous seldom is logical or ordinary. Da Evaristo's ring and that cross-word puzzle, for instance? But no, he mustn't think about the case.

Yes, it was pleasanter to recall the subconsciously arrogant loveliness of Aurora Morrow, Paula Harte's memorable legs and breast, the beauty of Guanabara Bay and the way a school of porpoises, all coated with phosphorescence, had frolicked alongside the *Miraflores* during her tragic return trip.

Almost before the Intelligence officer was aware of it, the police car stood panting before the Copacabana Palace and his policeman-chauffeur was holding open the door, murmuring, "*Se faz favor, senhor?*"

North immediately sought his suite on the fifth floor, but his perceptions were so dulled that he failed completely to notice a reek of cigarette smoke until he had closed his door. Though his sitting room was in darkness, he could see, by the moonlight, someone seated in a deep armchair by a window which overlooked the sea. He recovered instantly, freed his automatic before he greeted.

"Enjoying the view, Paula?"

Slowly she turned her pale head when he switched on a low table light. "You are not surprised. You expected me?"

"Not so much you, my dear, as your partner."

"My partner?" She uncrossed her legs, sat up a little and looked hard at him. "Why do you say such a thing?"

"Because—well, because of several things."

"Really, Hugh dear, you have gone crazy," she drawled. "Not that you have not had cause—"

He lit a cigarette and went to stand over her. Lord, she was appealing in her low-cut and very smart white evening gown. Why the devil hadn't she long since found that second, carefully counterfeited cake of Flor da Noite and gone on her way? Maybe she wasn't as clever as she seemed?

"Really," he yawned, "I wish you hadn't come around tonight. I'm dead for sleep."

"Now don't be cross," Paula begged. "Remember I have just

joined the great army of the unemployed." She got up, poured herself a highball from a bottle on the mantelpiece. "That was a horrible business at the Yacht Club. Has any progress been made?"

"Pour me a small one, too. Progress? Well, none to speak of." He dropped into a chair facing her. Long ago he had transferred the .32 into his right-hand pocket.

Paula moved very gracefully, her full skirt undulating about legs trim in the sheerest of flesh-tinted stockings. She had used a flame-colored lipstick and was as well made up as usual, yet it was clear she, too, was far from fresh, and worried, badly so.

She summoned an artificial smile as she raised her glass. "Well, *salud y pesetas, amigo*. I think we both need this drink. Incidentally, there's nobody here but me, and what *did* give you the idea I have a partner?"

"Though you're a rather efficient young woman, Paula, I still don't believe you shot the shipping manager of the Companhia Americus. Besides, there is a little story told by fingerprints."

Startled eyes, their pupils very large because of the dim light, swung to meet his. She flushed.

"Fingerprints? Oh, that piece of soap, I suppose?"

"Possibly."

"It was about that I came to talk. Do you mind?" Paula Harte queried. "This dress always was too tight." She eased a celluloid zipper on the side of her gown. "I must have put on a couple of pounds in São Paulo."

"Make yourself comfortable," sighed the Intelligence officer. "I'm going to put my feet up."

"Oh, Hugh," she demanded almost plaintively. "Why *do* things have to be the way they are?"

"You look very well as you are."

Suddenly, Paula sprang up and went over to perch on the arm of his chair. Her fingers rippled across his forehead. They were cool, he noticed, and capable.

"*Muy querido,* you look so weary I could cry."

"Don't. Suppose you give me a kiss instead."

"Oh, Hugh, why do—why *can't* I have someone like you to respect, to love?"

He swept her suddenly onto his lap, held her there. She remained quite still, with her platinum-pale head resting bright and fragrant beneath his chin.

She began to talk half to him, half to herself in a quiet, surprisingly gentle tone. "Hugh, can you understand what it means to be quite alone in the world?"

"Perhaps I do," North suggested.

"I wonder," Paula sighed. "You see, you are a man and men seldom understand the ignoble subterfuges, the sly practices women have to employ to—well, to achieve that security. A man reaches it by direct methods. Please . . . kiss me. I—I need it."

"What of Stuart Maitland?"

He felt her slender figure contract a little. She said coldly, "We have already discussed that, Hugh. Besides, tonight we had a quarrel, a serious one. He accused me of things I forgive, but cannot forget." She continued without looking up, "Hugh, I am in a terrible predicament. One that may even cost me my life."

"Oh, nonsense." He eased her weight away from his hurt side, but found it remarkably pleasant to feel the soft pressure of her body against him.

"No, really," Paula said quietly. "I have chanced to learn something that many people wish to know. It is dangerous knowledge."

He set her gently but firmly on her feet. "When you begin talking like that, my dear," came his dry comment, "it's high time you sat in the other chair."

"You are nobody's fool," she laughed as she crossed to the other armchair.

She swung her legs over one arm and kicked off her slippers. After pulling the toes of her stockings, she heaved a little sigh and sat back.

"Go on," North invited.

"Before I do, will you tell me whether Luis—er, Senhor da Evaristo died without making a statement?"

North hesitated, then told the truth.

"Thank you," Paula Harte said and, reaching to the table beside her, plucked up a cigarette and lit it.

"You said you had problems," North reminded with deceptive casualness.

"Yes," said she, speaking in brisk, matter-of-fact accents. "I possess information that should be worth many hundred thousands of dollars."

"I wonder if you do?"

She looked at him from under her lashes. "Darling, if you think I failed to find that piece of paper in the soap, you are mistaken."

"You found it, then?"

"Of course. In the flower urn. That was not a very original place to conceal it. No. What I know has not to do with that."

A sense of furious exasperation swept through him. How fantastic to know that, locked within the shapely head directly opposite, were certain facts he must learn. Force would not serve as a successful key. It was clear now that, as he had suspected, Paula Harte knew something of the inner workings of the Americus concern. How much, was yet another matter.

This amazing young woman undoubtedly was a past-master in the art of bluff.

Faced by as neat a problem as he had ever encountered, he thought hard, gravely raised his highball.

"To you, my dear. In the course of a largely misspent life, I have been privileged to know some very clever women, but the late Luis da Evaristo's secretary ranks near the top."

"Only *near* the top?" she chided, swinging her legs and tinkling the ice in her glass. "Come now, darling, how many girls of twenty-seven have you known who've won what I have—all on their own?"

"Couldn't say," North said. "You have been extremely smart. Still, you do want more, don't you?"

The girl in the chair opposite sat quite still. "Yes. I want someone smarter than myself to take over the running of my life. I grow a bit tired of scheming, working, and—" she looked hard at him—"I want a country. Since this war I have been realizing more and more what it means to be—well, an international chameleon—like a White Russian."

"But you have a passport."

"Yes, only that, though," she replied peering out at the moonlit sea. "There is no doubt that Chile is a fine country, but it is not mine, any more than is Brazil, or—" she made a little face—"the United States."

"Nevertheless, you *are* half American," North reminded. "There are things that could be done to—well, to speed your naturalization."

"Could you—" she began eagerly, then checked herself.

"What's the matter?" the Intelligence officer demanded.

"Only that I have first to consider my personal problems; I must move quickly, too."

She arose, commenced to pace back and forth, looking surprisingly short in her shoeless feet.

"No, Hugh. What I know should be worth a million dollars." Paula Harte paused in the center of the French gray carpet. "I will 'tell all,' as your columnists say, to whatever government, or person, will deposit to my account five hundred thousand dollars."

North whistled. Imagine cabling Washington for credit of half a million! The Department would indulge in assorted and spectacular cat-fits. Yet why shouldn't that sum be forthcoming instantly? The very men who would think nothing of supporting a bill to spend a hundred times that on a dreadnaught would howl to high heaven before they'd appropriate a fraction of that amount to forestall a catastrophe which, if ever it came to pass, would cost the United States billions. A very characteristic tragic lack of perspective.

"You may be able to get that much," he smiled, "but I sincerely doubt it."

"*I* don't," Paula replied serenely. "I know of two groups who will fight to publish *or to suppress* what I know."

North found a pipe, commenced to repack its bowl. "Paula, this is a very dangerous game you're contemplating. I suppose you know that cartridges are cheap?"

"I am not afraid," Paula announced with an assurance that North could not but admire. "If anything happens to me, the information will be published. I am no trusting schoolgirl. Possibly you have noticed?"

With those words a light, vivid and dramatic as a Very flare bursting on a starless night, lit the gloomy aspect of North's hopes.

Said he quietly, "Among cruel, degrading and hazardous professions, that of a free-lance espionage agent ranks high. An

Intelligence officer at least is working for his government and receives a certain amount of backing. Say what you will, there's an odd satisfaction to be found in working for others. I wouldn't hold out for that half million." He leaned forward, laid a hand on one silken knee.

"Why not?"

"Because my government will pay you a quarter of a million, and we will see about your being granted American citizenship in a hurry. Your mother's having been American will help."

"Really, Hugh?"

"I'm entirely serious, my dear."

She sped over to him, slid her arms about his neck and held lips near his as she whispered, "I will think on what you have just said, darling. Tell me. You—you would perhaps think better of me if—if—?"

For answer he gathered her close.

"I, too, have conditions," said he gently, "but first let me—"

He broke off short, froze into immobility as from the background a guttural voice rasped, "You will raise your hands, step apart and stand quite still, please. It iss safer so."

The Callers

AN ICY hand seemed gradually to close its fingers over Hugh North's heart, draining it of life. If ever deadly purpose had been expressed in a human voice, it was in that command. There was no way of describing the essential menace contained in those few words.

Paula Harte, too, must have realized it. Slowly, her face setting itself in rigid but not unattractive lines, she moved away. Her eyes had become huge and deeply shadowed. If she were not as startled and upset as himself, he had another guess coming. Still—

In a mirror North made out two rather short individuals wearing blue silk handkerchiefs tied over their faces. They were standing just inside the bedroom door and each of them was leveling a Luger automatic pistol of a caliber large enough to command respect—nothing like that ridiculous miniature gun Paula had half revealed aboard the *Cruzeiro do Sul*.

Immediately, North deduced how they had entered. As in many hotels, the various rooms and suites had connecting doors, in the interests of convenience and as a precaution against fire. Moreover, to an experienced lockpicker, the average hotel door lock called for hardly a moment's consideration.

One man was costumed as a sailor, the other as a green-uniformed cavalryman with bright red frogs laced across his thick chest. North groaned inwardly.

The taller of the two men, he in the cavalry costume, moved quickly, quietly into the sitting room and made a hurried inspection of the coat closet, then of the space behind the sofa. His lithe speed reminded North of a leopard on the prowl. Said he at last, "To interrupt so tender a scene iss a pity, but we are in a hurry."

"You have just come in?" North demanded so quickly that the other replied before he meant to.

"Yes. We have much to do."

Groping desperately for a ruse, he heard Paula heave a tiny sigh of relief that the conversation of the last fifteen minutes had not been overheard.

Quite pale by the light of the table lamp, she demanded, "Well, senhores, what is it you want?"

"Vun gold und emerald ring," grunted the shorter man in accents suggesting Scandinavian origin. "Ven da Evaristo reach' Club he vore ring. You remember, Mees Harte?"

"Yes, I remember it," she replied very steadily but moved not a muscle, kept her dark blue eyes fixed on North. "Senhor da Evaristo wore it very often. Why?"

"Yust before he die, da Evaristo no have got ring any more."

"Well?"

The taller intruder snarled, "One of you two has that ring. Give it immediately or you will be killed. I warn you, I am in a great hurry."

In the pre-dawn night someone touched off a string of firecrackers which set a thousand reports echoing and reëchoing along a hundred quiet streets. Above the dark blue handkerchief, the speaker's menacing blue eyes flickered between North and Paula Harte. A sense of impending doom grew so strong that perspiration sprang out on the Intelligence officer's high brown forehead.

"Come. Hand it over. I will not wait longer," he snapped.

"Don't shoot. You are looking in the wrong place," the Intelligence officer declared in a voice that quivered like an overstrained cable. Lord, but the muzzle of that Luger looked huge as the end of a flour barrel. "All da Evaristo's personal effects are in the keeping of the police department."

Vehemently, the sailor shook his head. "Dot ring iss not among dem. Ve haff certain information."

Um. So there had been a potential Quisling among the high officials present at the autopsy? As nothing else, this realization brought home the difficulty of the job before him.

The taller man reminded, "In a minute now, you will be killed. We have no time to argue."

"But for God's sake, man, be reasonable," North burst out. "How am I to give you what I simply haven't got? What makes you so sure I have that ring?"

"In close conversation with da Evaristo you were seen just before he died," the cavalryman said, moving slowly forward. A broad red stripe descending his breeches lost itself in a highly polished riding boot.

"So were others. Why pick on us?"

The short blond man also moved closer, his little, bright blue eyes deadly intense. "Mees Harte iss secretary. *Ja,* Gustaf, I t'ink she is der one."

"It is possible you are right, Fölke. I think we shall shoot."

"You'll only raise a hue and cry," North argued. "Search us if you want. We will promise to keep still."

The terrorist called Gustaf knew his stuff, all right. He kept his automatic trained on North's eyes. It is psychologically far more disconcerting to stare down the bore of a threatening firearm than to see it pointed at one's heart.

When Fölke bore down on Paula Harte, she fell back an involuntary step before the mortal threat he presented.

"Come, the ring. Where is it?"

"I don't know, you fool. I haven't got it. I know nothing—"

Fölke's shoulders hunched suddenly under his sailor's blouse. There came a resounding crack. Slapped very hard indeed, Paula Harte went staggering sidewise; emitted a curious breathless cry, like that of a small animal driven into a corner. Hand pressed to her cheek, she swayed, more than a little dazed. Her long bobbed hair had fallen over her face.

"You can k-kill me but you'll not f-find the ring."

"*Find,* eh?" the man called Fölke grunted. "So here it must be hidden!"

"No, no!" Paula whimpered as her tormentor gripped her arm, twisted it savagely. "Oh-h, no, for God's sake—" There sounded the soft snarling of ripped fabric. "Please, *o Dios, por piedad, no me queme así,* don't torture me. I cannot tell you where—"

"Let her be, Fölke, while I search this one."

To North Gustaf snapped, "Allow your jacket to slip to the ground. If you even reach towards that pistol in your pocket—"

"I won't," North promised grimly, his eyes riveted on the intruder's stiff brown hair. If he came just a foot or so closer, a sudden sidewise slap at that Luger might accomplish much.

As he shed his coat, North saw four livid finger marks taking shape, marring Paula Harte's pink and white complexion. Though tears stood in her eyes, he suspected they were those of impotent rage, not of fright. Otherwise, Paula stood rigid under the threat of the sailor's pistol.

"Turn your pockets inside out, one hand at a time," Gustaf directed.

Hugh North emptied his pockets and thanked God nothing of a leading nature was in them.

They made him strip off his socks, expose the cuffs of his trousers; and they even searched the waistband of his shorts. When they discovered the dull brown stained compress secured to North's side, Gustaf grunted and Paula took on a very curious expression.

"So? And where did you earn that?" Gustaf demanded. The sight of the wound seemed to him disconcerting.

"My barber made a mistake," North assured them with disarming frankness. "Thought I was his wife's boy friend."

"So?" Gustaf said. "Well, that ring certainly is not upon him."

"Thanks, I was a bit warm before," North observed dryly, but felt a trifle absurd barefooted and wearing only his dinner coat trousers.

"Sit down. Keep closed your mouth." The man in cavalry uniform again proved his experience in such matters by moving around behind North's chair. Here, presumably he held his weapon at the base of the Intelligence officer's skull. Only a fool stands before a prisoner and anywhere near within arm's reach.

Fölke put down his pistol and searched the whole suite with impressive skill, haste and thoroughness. Then his chunky figure bore down on the girl in white.

"You. Bend over!"

When, suddenly, she obeyed, the terrorist's hand, bony and

covered with a heavy growth of blond fuzz, briefly probed through the base of Paula Harte's blonde hair.

"Swedes make clumsy hairdressers," she muttered, looking very small against the French-gray walls. The bright tinting on her lips stood out garishly against the pallor of her features.

Ignoring the remark, Fölke bent carefully to examine Paula's discarded slippers.

"I seldom wear rings on my toes," she pointed out to North's amusement. There, by God, stood a girl in a million, morals or no morals.

"Do you mind if I put on my slippers? Having them off makes me feel so undressed."

Even Fölke uttered a guttural laugh. "*Ja.* Put them on." Then a moment later, "Now you vill take off dot dress."

"I will not!"

"No? Den *I* vill."

The man in the sailor costume suddenly gripped the front of Paula's evening gown, gave it such a savage yank that the fabric parted and Paula reeled, stood exposed in a daintily embroidered slip. Fölke certainly did a thorough job of searching. The slip went and, perhaps needlessly, brassiere and stockings. A moment later, Paula Harte would have been unable to conceal even so much as a thread. Perfectly proportioned as any nude goddess the old Greek Phidias ever wrought in stone, Paula Harte remained quite still, an expression of frozen disdain on her features.

There was not a thing North could do. Not with that Luger at the back of his skull. Perforce he saw all that happened.

"May I put my slip back on?" Paula demanded in a quivering voice.

Fölke fell back, picked up his pistol. "*Ja.* But you make vun pretty picture so. Eh, Gustaf?"

"Look here," North objected suddenly. "You've made your search. Now can't you leave us alone? After all, we have been very patient."

"'So are the dead," Fölke growled, pushing Paula's chair over so that it rested beside North's. He motioned the girl to seat herself; when she had done so, he circled back of her chair, too.

"You very hard will think while I count ten," the man, Gustaf, said.

North felt the muzzle of the automatic come to rest against the base of his skull. That was the way the Spanish had executed each other during the Revolution. His stomach writhed. Even a .22 would quite effectively blow out the back of a man's skull.

"If me you cannot satisfy where that ring is, then, Herr Oberst, more firecrackers celebrating the carnival in this room will explode."

The end of the long, long trail was now in sight, North reflected. At long last. His mind flitted back over the unpeaceful career he had pursued; back through Rumania to Hungary, Egypt, Hawaii, China and dozens of other lands in which he had stood face to face with the Dark Angel. Alas, that the gears of his mind seemed stripped by fatigue.

All he could think of was, "Perhaps da Evaristo gave it as a gift?" It seemed plausible. Maitland had seemed to think so, all right.

"Not dot ring," Fölke corrected savagely.

Gustaf cleared his throat. "One, two—"

Clad only in her slip, Paula Harte sat stiffly on her chair, lips ghastly beneath what little lipstick remained on them.

North said, "You don't think we'd be such fools as to throw away our lives. Of course, Dom Luis gave it—"

"Six, seven, eight—"

Paula's hands beat suddenly on her chair's upholstered arms. "No! Please. Major North has reminded me!"

"So? Speak up quickly." The studied calm of a surgeon in the midst of an intricate, perhaps fatal, operation was in Gustaf's tone.

"I am certain Luis had his ring when he danced with me, because I felt it when he—he squeezed my hand."

"Who next did da Evaristo dance with? Quickly, now."

North felt his breath halt half way to his lungs. This play had better be good. If it *was* a bluff—well, it would be the last Paula Harte would ever attempt.

"It was Miss Aurora Morrow."

"Mees Morrow?" Fölke echoed. "So!"

Indecision appeared in the manner of the two terrorists. They must have exchanged glances though neither North nor Paula could see.

"Yes," Gustaf muttered. "A possibility. You remember what *he* said?"

Fölke said, "Let us kill dem. Neffer haff I killed anyvun so beautiful. Not even in Poland."

"No. Someone might downstairs be suspicious." Gustaf's tone was authoritative. "I go now. I the lights will turn out. Sometime Fölke, too, will go, but do not turn your heads before twenty minutes. Fölke has not missed in years."

Carnival—Sunday Morning

OF COURSE, the telephone wire in North's suite had been severed, so he had had to take time to descend innumerable flights of stairs before he could rouse a sleepy operator. How far Gustaf might have got by now there could be no telling.

Because already Rio was in the mood of its greatest day of the year, he got through to the Standley residence after a delay of many minutes. More time was lost while some servant summoned J. P. Standley. He sounded cross and only half awake.

"What the roaring bells of hell d'you mean rousing—"

"This is North. Hugh North. Where's Aurora?"

"Oh. It's you. Aurora? The hell with Aurora! Damned brat's a regular night owl."

"Wake up and make sense, J.P. This is no joke. Where *is* she?" North insisted.

Immediately the shipping man's tone became altered. "Sorry, Hugh. I'm only half awake. Anything I can do?"

"Only keep on trying to find Aurora."

"Okay. What then?"

"Tell her to get to Police Headquarters *pronto* and to stay there, *no matter what happens,* until I see her."

If that wouldn't beat the Dutch! Aurora out pub-crawling after a night like this. She must have the constitution of a marine.

"Say, Hugh, what in hell's all this urgency about?"

"Can't tell you over the phone. I'm not fooling. I'll call back later."

He next put a call to Naval Intelligence Headquarters, was gratified to find that alert young Lieutenant Nabuco still very much on the job.

"Ah, so good of you to call. What—eh?" He listened carefully to North's account of the visit of the terrorists. *"Deus!* Sailor costumes are a milreis the hundred. *Sim.* I will send out searchers at once. Yes. To every bufete, cocktail bar and bistro. This is most difficult, unfortunate; Miss Morrow is North American."

The Brazilian's tone conveyed a far sharper anxiety than his words.

When Hugh North regained his room, Paula Harte had disappeared, but sketched on the mirror of his bureau in lipstick was the outline of a pierced heart and the words,

"My apartment tomorrow, cocktails. Important!!"

Taking the precaution this time to prop chair backs under all door knobs opening to the outside, Hugh North changed the dressing on his hurt side. It still looked inflamed but no worse than before. This done, the Intelligence officer dropped on the couch and, hoping against hope that Aurora Morrow had, by good luck or good management, escaped the gentle attentions of Gustaf and friend, plunged at once into a slumber which resembled unconsciousness rather than sleep.

After what seemed like a very few instants, a loud and insistent rapping roused North in time to see the sun thrusting its burnished red disc out of a glassy Atlantic. Wide awake in a split second and feeling definitely refreshed, he sought the door.

"Good morning, Major," came Ramon Nabuco's familiar accents. "I have with me a complete report of the autopsy findings."

"Come in.

"You've found Miss Morrow?" North demanded anxiously.

The Brazilian's face darkened and he bit his lip. "I regret to report we have had no success in that direction. Mr. Standley is growing most concerned. Of course, she will soon be discovered, but—" he shrugged— "this accursed carnival. So many of my men are on leave and the police are on special assignments. It is most unfortunate."

Unfortunate was right, North mused as he began to dress. Like a rising gale his apprehensions increased at the sound of much loud band music floating up from the Avenida Atlantica. Everywhere auto sirens and horns wailed insistently, and somewhere bells were clanging with a maddening insistence.

Nabuco must have read his thoughts. "This affair of the freighter has been well timed," said he heavily. "Why is Miss Morrow in such danger?"

"Although I'm not by any means positive, I believe Luis da Evaristo gave her—to keep safe for him—a ring."

"Obviously, this ring must be of some great significance," Nabuco observed as if to himself.

"Obviously, but to whom? Answer that and we're on our way to a better understanding."

"Have you any theory?"

"Only a theory," North said, sitting in shorts and socks on

the edge of his sofa. Slowly he ran his fingers through crisp black hair in need of combing.

"And that is?"

"Consider the company at dinner, Lieutenant. Immediately, we can dismiss as suspect—well, whom would you say?"

The Brazilian lit a cigarette, commenced to pace up and down.

"Mr. Standley, Miss Carpenter, Miss Morrow, Senhoritas Camargo and Morales," Nabuco said rapidly.

"You don't include Maitland?" North demanded, his respect for the Naval officer rising still further.

"No. I think he was greatly jealous of Senhor da Evaristo." He paused. "The woman, Harte, is—well, too informed. No?"

"Dangerously so. And as a group, that leaves—?"

"Rupp, Altrocchi and the Japanese. Of them, whom do you suspect?"

"None, until we can study the dinner table and make an analysis of tobacco particles," North said. He paused, fingering his chin and making a small rasping noise among the dark bristles sprouting there. "That is some indication."

"But why should *they* kill da Evaristo? He was so very pro-Patriotista, which also means pro-Axis."

Louder still grew the clamor below. From a back window could be seen an endless line of brightly clad humanity surging back and forth across the Avenida.

North said slowly as he rose prepared to freshen up, "Three bits of conversation make me wonder about that."

"That da Evaristo was pro-Axis?"

"Exactly. He hinted to me that he had much to tell. He told his anti-Patriotista brother that he had come to a decision that would restore their friendship; he told Miss Morrow he had just had a great weight lifted." From the bathroom the Intelli-

gence officer talked more rapidly as the idea developed. "Yes.
I think Luis da Evaristo was pro-Patriotista but so definitely
against Axis influence that he was ready to break with Pujol.
Does that seem too impossible?"

"No! No!" Nabuco burst out. "It is most reasonable. *Bom!*
Now I shall set men to watch Rupp and the others."

"The important thing is first to find Miss Morrow. The people back of Fölke, and Gustaf will cut her throat the instant
they think it advisable."

"You were right, Major. It was *antiaris toxicana* that killed
Dom Luis. There was much alcohol in his stomach, but no
trace of poison." He paused outside the bathroom door. "I have
been trying to form a theory about the cigar smokers, but it is
difficult. I, myself, was smoking, so was the Japanese, so was
Altrocchi—about Dr. Rupp I am not sure."

"He smoked one cigar," North muttered through his lather.
"But for the moment, there are more serious considerations.
Da Evaristo is dead, and certainly the murderer must be
tracked down, so keep after the question of the tobacco. It will
form a valuable pointer, though such evidence won't convict
the killer. For the moment, it is far more important, I think, to
learn *why* he was murdered."

"Do you imagine he knew of those radiograms from your
agent 304 G-2b?"

"Possibly." North plunged his face into a steaming towel.
"But I feel increasingly sure that certain activities of the Americus Company, the Estrella del Mar Company, and the arrival
of that freighter are intertwined."

Wiping his hands, the Intelligence officer emerged, as down
the corridor outside raced a group of people yelling and blowing horns as if their lives depended on it. What a nice sane

atmosphere in which to solve the most critical problem of his career!

"Lieutenant, I wonder if you can secure for me a copy of each of the newspapers published in Rio?"

Laughing, Nabuco threw up his hands. "*Ai, minha mãe!* Do you know how many there are?"

"A dozen at least, I suppose."

"More than twice that. Twenty-seven in all, so how many copies do you require?"

"If you have to hunt back six months," the American Intelligence officer said, "I want you to find which paper it was that printed the cross-word puzzle found on Luis da Evaristo's body."

Lieutenant Nabuco appeared dubious. "This will exhaust valuable time, Major. You are quite convinced the effort is worth it?"

North interrupted the knotting of a powder-gray tie. "Tell me, could you guess which newspapers might be in Pujol's pay?"

Quickly the Brazilian replied, "There are the *Nova Ordem* and the *O Continente*."

North shook his narrow black head. "I don't mean obvious propaganda sheets. What papers with a real circulation might be *secretly* controlled?"

Suddenly, he recalled an impression of Altrocchi, sartorially perfect and jadedly aloof, entering the German Yacht Club's card room complete with cigar and newspaper. Which had the latter been? His refreshed mind responded.

"What about *A Sentinella*?"

"You must be mistaken," Nabuco replied with polite doubt. "The editorial policy of *A Sentinella* is strongly pro-government."

"Is it widely read?"

"Oh, yes. Almost like your *New York Times*. Its syndicated features appear everywhere in Brazil."

"Can you name one or two?"

"Yes, *A Nação* in São Paulo, *O Universo* in Recife and *O Patriota* in Belém."

"Who owns *A Sentinella*?"

"Why, Dom João da Evaristo among others—all good republicans. Dom João quarreled with Luis over the latter's pro-Pujol sentiments. That is why I am inclined to be so doubtful."

"The idea was only an inspiration," North confessed. "Still I wish you would investigate a little, see whether the word 'Bolivar' might have any special significance in *A Sentinella*."

Nabuco's narrow black brows shot up in graphic astonishment. "But—but Major, the steamer? Do you not still believe the Bolivar messages have to do with this steamer we seek?"

"Definitely," came the enigmatic response. "But not in the fashion I first thought. Our Axis lads aren't to be underestimated, so there is no point in overlooking any bets."

The suite's phone, having been repaired, began insistently to ring and presently J. P. Standley's deep voice came over the wire.

"Well, Hugh, you can set your mind at rest. That screw-ball niece of mine spent the night at Ginny Carpenter's. Ginny had invited a gang of hell-raisers in their carnival club to come in for early breakfast."

"What did you tell her?"

"I warned her to stay at Ginny's," the shipping man stated. "But Aurora is more independent than a gob on shore leave. Always has been."

The Heel

FOR many minutes after Lieutenant Nabuco's trim, slight figure had departed down the corridor, Hugh North sat still, earnestly attempting to shape a course of action. Time now was as rubies and fine gold and, once lost, could not be recovered.

In which direction should he gamble his precious and fast-dwindling reserve of hours? It gave him the shakes when he thought of that still exasperatingly unidentified ship plowing inexorably nearer and nearer to some Brazilian port.

There were, he decided, two principal problems urgently demanding his attention: the matter of the Bolivar messages and the curious disappearance of Luis da Evaristo's ring.

Louder, and more insistently, swelled a varied din outside. Cowbells tonked, cymbals shivered and thousands of raucous horns brayed. Below, the tight-mouthed onlooker could see varicolored paper streamers arching across the sidewalk and into overcrowded cars. Clouds of confetti were being tossed from apartment house windows. From a hundred wrought-iron guarded balconies flags, bunting and bright shawls were fluttering, reflecting the fresh morning sunlight.

Following an inspiration born of considerable reflection and observation, North summoned the valet, a flat little man who looked as if he had been stepped on in childhood.

Said he, "I wish a costume."

"That will be very difficult to obtain, senhor. The carnival has begun."

North insisted. "I want one if it costs two contos."

"Yes, sir. Has senhor any preference?"

"Decidedly. I wish a green military uniform, preferably a cavalryman's."

"That should be very easy," the valet smiled.

"Why?"

"Last autumn *The Congress Waltzes* was presented at the Opera. Nearly the entire cast wore them."

Quickly the valet took North's measurements, promised immediate results. Two contos of reis were not to be come across every day; indeed not!

Sedately, North breakfasted in his room on coffee, *abacates* and *fios de ovos*—threads of eggs cooked with sugar and coconut. Um. Before this sun went down he proposed to learn a good deal about the Estrella del Mar Company. Its multiple tentacles, it seemed, stretched to the most remote provinces of Brazil—ostensibly to promote trade!

Taking the precaution to have his .32 handy in a fold of his napkin, he summoned his waiter to clear the table. Probably there was no justification for such wariness for, thanks to Lieutenant Nabuco's insistence, there would be no further calls from unidentified strangers—costume or no costume.

In that dead-end corridor which led to the Intelligence officer's suite two porters with searching eyes and powerful shoulders methodically, endlessly, strapped and then unstrapped a set of valises. It was comforting that a delivery boy from the costumers had a difficult time in gaining admittance.

Thanks to the valet's precautions the uniform fitted reasonably well. It was, to say the least, theatrical; very dark green with yellow braid frogs and patent leather boots of dashing design. Completing the outfit was a busby of black astrakhan lamb sporting a yellow tab and a rakish black and white osprey plume which, added to a sabretasche, made of the longlegged Intelligence officer a figure right out of one of Meissonier's canvases.

It was curious, North reflected as he hooked up the tunic, that, although he had served in the United States Army since 1916, he had worn its uniform but seldom.

Rather amused at the whole business, Hugh North considered the extent of his make-up, for, in place of masks, always hot and unsatisfactory, a great majority of celebrants in Rio sensibly preferred liberal applications of grease paint, false hair and other forms of make-up. Somewhat of an expert, the Intelligence officer skillfully thickened his brows, enlarged his eyes by extending their corners, darkened the white patches at his temples and, with the aid of collodion, adorned his chin with a neat and very dashing torpedo beard.

By the judicious use of a lining pencil he altered his expression. When he inserted an eyeglass over his left eye, the effect was truly startling. Grinning, he surveyed the lean, faintly sardonic figure copying his movements in a full-length mirror.

"Ich habe die Ehre, Hertzogin," he declared and bowed from the waist like the veriest Prussian Junker.

He straightened self-consciously when, in the corridor, he heard a girl's voice objecting. "Stand aside, I tell you and don't you dare to touch me! I'm in a hurry."

To North's ineffable relief he recognized Aurora Morrow's coolly detached accents.

When he flung open his door it was to find Aurora, wearing that same colorful Bahiana costume he had seen in the offices of the Standley Steamship Company. She had made herself up with very dark tan make-up and her lips had been widened to a discreetly negroid thickness. Right now she was breathing quickly and looking down her nose at the two badly puzzled porters barring her progress.

"Hugh," she demanded, "won't you call off these incredible fellows? They are being dull and very obstinate."

"Yes. Kindly let the lady pass," he instructed the two porters who immediately stiffened to unporter-like attention.

"A thousand pardons, senhorita, but orders we received." They broke into broad white smiles and stepped aside.

Only then Aurora turned, got a good look at North. "My God, you look just like Rupert of Hentzau!"

"But come to rescue you, my dear," he laughed, closing the door behind her.

"Nice start for a busy day, eh what?" Aurora murmured. "Any coffee left in that thermos?"

"Plenty. Help yourself. But first—"

"You want to know about that ring?"

The bloody fool! Hadn't she a grain of sense? Couldn't she realize that this was no scavenger hunt or game of that sort?

"You don't mind waiting until I finish my coffee?"

"Don't be an idiot!" he burst out, but grinned instantly. Exasperating as she was, it wouldn't do to antagonize this curious young woman.

"You said I have been a fool all my life," Aurora reminded, demurely seating herself while he poured her coffee. "So I'll stick to the role just long enough to justify your august opinion."

There was nothing he could do but grind mental teeth—and be patient. When, for a second time, her hand crept down to rub her knee, he saw it bore a dull red bruise.

"Where'd you collect that?"

Through a mouthful of roll and coffee, Aurora replied carelessly, "Taxi driver tried to get fresh."

"How do you mean, 'fresh'?"

"I guess he'd been leaning into a mug of *cachaça* a bit too often. When I told him to drive me over here—"

"Against orders," North interrupted severely.

"Since when has Major North been giving me orders?" Aurora stared challengingly over her cup. As quickly she changed her manner. "Please skip that, Watchdog. I forgot. Well, as I was telling you, I gave the driver this address—I made J.P. tell me where you were. When the taxi-man tried to drive into the Jardim Botanico, I told him to turn into the Avenida Epitacio Pessoa. Well, all he did was to shake his stupid head and put on speed."

Aurora frowned at the recollection. "There was such a mob on the street I thought he hadn't heard me, so I repeated what I'd said. I didn't like it when he kept on, so I—"

"So you what?" North demanded thoughtfully.

Aurora added exactly three drops of cream to her coffee, stirred it and then looked up brightly.

"Why, I took off my slipper and socked him on the back of the head with its heel."

North choked slightly on his astonishment. "You *what?*"

"I guess I bopped him, Hugh," came the airy admission. "When I want to go to a place, I want to go there."

"All right, you bopped him. Then what happened?"

"Since he was but definitely kayoed, the taxi barged off the road and into a tree. Hence the bruised knee. It isn't bad, is it?" she demanded, twitching up her yellow and red pleated skirt and exhibiting a dull red lump.

"With careful nursing you'll live," North smiled. "What then?"

"Oh, when a crowd gathered, I mingled with it and simply got another taxi. You wouldn't want me kidnapped—or would you?" she added doubtfully.

"Not with that ring on you."

"Thanks for them few kind words, Watchdog. You're just too, too gallant this morning." Then a throaty chuckle escaped the girl in the barbarically colorful costume. "That's one on you!"

"One what?"

"I was smart enough to leave poor Luis' ring behind."

"*What!* You haven't got it?"

"Uh-huh," Aurora replied coolly. "That is yes, and no."

"For God's sake, girl, talk English. Make sense! This is no joke."

She sobered instantly. "No, Hugh, it isn't. I was too smart for them. From the way Luis acted, I guess there was something pretty queer about that ring."

"Good God, girl, where have you left it?"

"With Ginny Carpenter, of course," came the calm reply. "Ginny's sound, even if she acts wacky."

"Where is it?"

"Locked in her bureau drawer. Among her panties and whatnots."

"A bureau drawer? Oh, my Lord!" He began buckling the holster onto his sword belt. "Come on. Wipe the egg off your chin and get moving."

"But, Watchdog, I'll be no good till I've had my cigarette," Aurora drawled, her eyes pathetically rounded.

"The devil with your cigarette," he rapped with a flick of anger. "This isn't charades we're playing."

She jumped right up, set straight the basket of brightly-colored artificial fruit stitched to her bright blue turban.

"Oh, Hugh, did I do wrong? I *was* trying to be careful."

"I suppose leaving the ring was about the most sensible thing you could do with it. Especially in view of what happened. Two bits, the driver you socked wore a green uniform?"

She nodded. "Yes. But however did you guess?"

"Green seems a popular color this carnival."

"But," Aurora protested, "that's not right. The official colors this year are blue and yellow."

As they hurried out of the suite, North shifted the guards inside, instructed them to admit no one during his absence but to answer the phone and to trace all calls. On emerging onto the crowded, sun-drenched Avenida Atlantica, they were irresistibly engulfed by a maelstrom of the carnival. Even at this early hour bars everywhere were overflowing.

Chiefly in blue and yellow, Greek nymphs, Pierrettes, Amazons, Columbines, Egyptian Ouled-Naïls, ballet dancers and women wearing a thousand and one garishly effective native costumes were mingling with acrobats, gauchos, Roman soldiers, lion tamers, Aztec Indians, soldiers, devils, clowns and field marshals. Farther, a great swarm of persons cavorted about in huge and utterly grotesque papier-maché caricature heads and torsos.

"Hurry, hurry! There's not a second to lose!" an infernal voice kept yelling in the back of North's mind. Hurry? Impossible. This was one day when "hurry" was a word unknown —along with "worry," "reason" and "work."

All sidewalks were jammed to overflowing, and dozens of children and their dogs pursued slowly rolling automobiles groaning under tremendous loads of crazily attired humanity. Everywhere confetti flew and people from their balconies sang *emboladas* as they hurled gaily colored paper streamers at the cars.

"Don't close your eyes," Aurora cried when a trapeze artist, gorgeous in blue tights and yellow loincloth, dashed up leveling a little metal atomizer. He squirted it at North and his companion and sent in their direction a fine spray reeking of gardenias mingled with ether.

"*Até amanhã!*" he shouted.

Involuntarily, North shut his eyes and for an agonized second he feared the worst. But, almost instantly, the burning sensation vanished. Already the trapeze artist had turned his *lança-perfume* at a reveler made up as a ridiculous, pot-bellied policeman.

Groups of mulattoes, uniformly costumed as Tritons, were singing in competition with other carnival clubs.

"That is one of the official songs for this year," Aurora explained as they ducked a shower of confetti and scrambled into a taxi driven by an Italian who was obviously very proud of his Micky Mouse costume.

Hugh North fell a prey to deadly apprehensions as the cab commenced its trip along the Avenida Atlantica in the direction of the Gávea suburb. Its progress was infuriatingly deliberate for, time and time again, celebrants blocked the street by locking arms or doing the *cordão*, a crazy form of snake dance.

"Can't you get more speed?" North begged with anxiety gnawing rat-like at his mind. "Twenty milreis if you get us to Gávea in a real hurry."

"Hurry? *Corpo di Baccho!*" The Italian waved expressive hands. "Signor, one must not hurry on carnival day."

"Olé-e—"

A pretty mulatto had sprung on the running board to kiss the chauffeur on the end of his nose. Chortling, he stopped his taxi and started in pursuit as she fled giggling. Immediately, people swarmed all over the cab's body.

"Smile, damn you, smile!" sang Aurora and waved cheerfully as a four-piece band began to parade around and around the stranded taxicab.

"*Pinhão, Pinhão, Pinhão! Oi! Pinhão Correu!*" chanted the revelers.

All traffic had halted so nothing was to be gained by a change of taxis.

Shaking inwardly, the Intelligence officer perforce watched a carnival club go through a short play, something very similar to an animated Punch and Judy.

"Isn't this *something?*" Aurora demanded, her features alight. Jumping up, she blew a kiss to the gallant gendarme who rescued Punchinella from the advances of a very villainous Punch.

Everywhere the doors of homes stood open, people wandered in and out singing, dancing and playing *cavaquinhos, reco-recas,* accordions and other musical instruments. Time and time again impromptu bands would form, parade a block or two, only to separate in order to become absorbed by other units.

Eventually the chauffeur returned waving a bottle of red wine, and wearing a yellow rose over one ear. A trip which should have required not more than twenty minutes wasted three priceless quarters of an hour.

"Watchdog, we are here!" Aurora announced, jumping out. "Believe it or not. By the bye, Ginny's got a beaut of a hangover. Claims it's got four sharp corners and is trimmed with unborn elephant fur."

North, in no mood for further delay, had hard work to keep from racing up the front steps.

"Hi, Aurora! Where you been? Pub-crawling already?"

Two or three young people in costumes resembling Aurora's came swaying out onto a lawn shaded by a magnificent jaca tree.

"Yep. Boys 'n gals, this elegant gent I found in a very elegant quandary, second floor front. May I present the Baron—" She turned. "Say Mister, what *is* your name?"

It was a really magnificent twirl North gave to his amplified mustaches. "I am Baron von und, zu ober und unter, hin und aus der Ostbanhoff!"

"Come on in, 'Raura. Teddy's just mixed a batch of blue mother-in-laws."

"With a name like that, you need at least a couple of drinks," advised a dark-haired Bahiana who greeted them at the door, perspiring gently under her grease paint. "Honey, who's this? My, ain't he *handsome!*"

North readjusted his monocle and chucked Ginny under the chin, produced a coin. "So pretty a speech deserves ten pfennigs. My good wench, I will see you at moonrise."

Ginny swept an awkward curtsey, affecting embarrassment. "Oh, thank you, *mein Herr*. You are very, very generous." She switched accents. "Maw she says Ah shouldn't ever go to the planters' big houses."

"And if I should give you a hundred marks?"

"Why, Boss man, you be talkin' sense," Ginny drawled. She slipped her arm through North's. "Now come on, Baron, I want you to try a blue mother-in-law cocktail. They sho' do look like hell, but they taste simply divine!"

"Hello, old lad!" North felt a slap on his back. He turned and, despite blacking and other Bahiana make-up, recognized Masibi Jack McCabe. "Fancy meeting you here!"

"Real party, isn't it?"

"Rath-er!" drawled the aviator. "Hardly knew you. Look like a real, saber-clanking Boche." He glanced about, lowered his voice. "Nasty mess last night, eh what?"

"It was all of that," North replied cautiously.

McCabe came closer. "You have seen Miss Harte recently?"

"No. Why?"

The flyer shrugged, looked really concerned. "I'm worried about her. If they were out to scrag her boss, don't you know, they might—"

"Carry on a step further? Yes. It's possible," North replied and began polishing his eyeglass.

As a group of guests came charging up, he assumed his foreign accent and passed the monocle to McCabe.

"Show me how to wear this, *mein Herr*," he pleaded. "It iss only you English know how."

McCabe was obliging as Ginny came up bearing two glasses filled with a bluish-tinted cocktail which, as far as North was concerned, was only slightly preferable to embalming fluid.

"That monocle in blackface," Ginny remarked, "sho' is original. You've got it all greasy, silly."

"Sorry," apologized the flyer.

"It's all right," North said, "it won't take a minute to clean it," and he took out his handkerchief.

Aurora tugged at his arm. "Come along, Watchdog." Then to Ginny, "I've got to catch a seam in Hugh's uniform coat. Be a good gal and show me your sewing kit."

Ginny stared a little, "My, but we sho' are gettin' domestic all at once."

With Dom Luis' ring filling his thoughts and with heart quickening, North followed the two girls into a hallway done in cool light green.

"I say, Major," McCabe called. "You can't shanghai the two prettiest girls here. Not cricket." His darkened face grotesque, he came limping along.

North said quickly sotto voce to Ginny, "That ring Aurora gave you. Please give it to me as quickly and quietly as you can."

"Ring?" Ginny trilled, turning her pretty painted face. "Laws, such excitement over a bit of jewlery. Mr. da Evaristo's secretary came to get it about half an hour ago."

"Who's got a ring?" McCabe queried pleasantly. "You getting engaged, Ginny?"

"No such luck fo' little me," Ginny sighed, taking a gulp of her cocktail. "I'm goin' to be an old maid, I reckon."

"–With an Emerald Ring"

HUGH NORTH recovered from the impact of Ginny Carpenter's stupidity a split second later. Damn! The girl's naturally high voice, magnified innumerable times by cocktails, must have penetrated the smoke-filled living room where a gorgeous and very tall Samurai warrior was rather expertly performing sleight-of-hand tricks.

North squeezed the hostess' arm, whispered savagely as Aurora snatched playfully at McCabe's calabash drinking bottle, "Quiet, please, on that subject."

Ginny Carpenter batted limpid, cornflower-blue eyes. "So sorry. Truly I am. Excuse me, Major."

Aurora, turning, said sweetly, "If ever I go looking for a damned fool, Ginny, I'll know just where to start."

North sighed, reluctantly accepted the setback. "How about that sewing?"

Masibi Jack emitted a rather alcoholic laugh. "Ginny," he said, "le's go back to the bunch. As you sew, so shall you reap —or is it rape?"

"Reap, honey," Ginny cooed. "My, you sho'ly are buildin' up a bun."

McCabe nodded mechanically, flung an arm around her.

"Virginia, my pet. I yearn for you. You react on me like spun honey, warm white velvet and two martinis on an empty stomach."

"Why, Misto' McCabe! How *very* nice of you," Ginny cooed, her lovely bacchanalian mouth provocatively up-tilted. "I do believe you could write poetry—beautiful poetry."

"To further inspiration I shall go pluck us a bouquet of blue mother-in-laws."

When, solemn as a hanging judge, McCabe wandered back towards the living room, North stuffed his handkerchief, eyeglass and all into a breast pocket.

Aurora fixed her friend with a small smile that was somehow infinitely insulting. "Darling?"

"Yes, Honey?"

"Did you ever realize that if someone gave you half a brain, you'd still have half a brain?"

Ginny Carpenter's vivid little mouth drooped into a pathetic crescent. "But Sugah, how was I to know? Aftah all, everybody knows Miss Harte is Mr. da Evaristo's own very extra private secretary. You tol' me so yo'self."

North cut in, "Please, Miss Carpenter, what did Paula Harte say when she arrived here?"

Ginny cocked a small brown head to one side, stared into her half-empty glass and considered.

"Well, now I reckon I can remember. Yes. Miss Harte said Dom João told her to come ovah to fetch his brother's ring. Co'se I reckoned it was all right to give it to her. If it wasn't," Ginny demanded brightly, "how could Dom João know the ring was here?"

"Dom João probably didn't even know it was missing,"

North said slowly. "Well, the harm's done. Let's get out of here, Aurora."

The Morrow girl started and her vividly painted features lit. "You—you want *me* to go along? You really mean it?"

"Yes. If you really wish to—lend a hand."

He needed her wit, her obvious familiarity with the city and its ways as an ally. Besides, during carnival, a single person always presented a ready target for revelers of the opposite sex.

Baron Setsukada looked up as they entered the living room and smiled through the gray-blue haze of cigarette smoke. "Good morning, Hugh. You cannot be planning to leave us so soon?"

North shook hands, lied convincingly. "The Lord forbid! Aurora and I are just slipping down to the corner store. She needs some filler for her *lança.*"

"That is well," the Japanese murmured as he drew North to one side. "I am wondering if—has any progress been made?"

"Progress?"

"Yes. On solving the lamentable murder of our poor friend, Dom Luis?" His oblique jet eyes openly questioned North.

North's yellow braid epaulettes gleamed to his shrug. "I was hoping *you* could give me news about it. What has happened?"

Setsukada bit a precise semicircle from the little cake he was holding, then said, "I am told the police are furiously at work, but I have heard nothing beyond that."

Setsukada's smooth brown brow furrowed itself. "How horrible is this world becoming, Hugh. Every day there is murder done by decent men that their nations may—" He broke off as Aurora drew near amid a persistent throng of admirers.

She caught at North's arm. "Come on, Watchdog, we've got to get started before we can come back."

"Where are we going?" Aurora demanded as quickly as they were out of ear shot.

"To grab a cab."

"My car's in a garage just around the corner," she offered. "We might make better time if I drove you."

"Splendid. And you won't get out and play?"

"Not without you, Watchdog," she smiled.

Presently Aurora appeared driving a smart dark green club coupé.

He said as she drove out of the garage, "Aurora, it's only fair that I warn you."

"Don't, or I'll be hurt," she objected quietly. "I'm having the time of my life."

"Maybe. But I don't think you understand that while you're with me, you stand a good chance of collecting a slug in some part of that very attractive anatomy of yours. You see, my dear, I'm mixed up in a mess where everything and anything goes. Suppose you just drive me to the entrance of the Estrada do Redemptor—"

"I'm tagging right along with you," Aurora announced firmly. "There seem to be precious few people you can be sure of around town."

"I am not fooling," North insisted as he got in, his busby plume fluttering gallantly in a hot breeze off the land. "You really can get hurt; in fact are very likely to."

Aurora Morrow fixed her eyes upon him so intently he noticed little golden lights in their depths.

"I got to thinking last night," said she slowly, "about those cracks you made about me and my crowd when we were on J.P.'s boat. We may be café society lights, wacky, rude and selfish; but I don't think we're worthless. You may be right, but wait and see. When our country really does get in a jam,

I'm betting that most of the playboys will drop everything to help. Look at those suede-shoe English lads. The R.A.F.'s full of them."

"I hope you're right," was North's dubious reply.

Presently, Aurora turned her turbaned head. "Is it *kosher* to ask what we're going to do? Needn't answer lest you want, you know."

She accelerated, threaded an expert course through a group of Negro celebrants gathered around a beer barrel and chant-ing some wild song from up Bahia way.

"I intend to call on a friend on the Estrada do Redemptor." He remained evasive. "Don't suppose they'll be in, but you never can tell on a day like this."

Number 1081 proved to be a large, expensive and yet con-servative-appearing apartment house with the usual ornate white façade, window boxes and dark blue sun blinds.

"Please wait in the car," he directed as Aurora brought the coupé to a halt.

Deeming it wise to resume his role, North feigned far higher spirits than were his, and swaggering in, clapped the *recepção* on the back.

"Greetings, O Keeper of the Keys. I seek a queen of great beauty," he announced with bibulous gravity.

"And do we not all, senhor?" The *recepção*, a bald, fat little fellow, beamed, brought out a formidable-appearing bottle. "To the carnival, senhor, drink deep. Today there is no care, no sorrow!"

He splashed half a glass of vermouth. North accepted it, seated himself on the desk.

"My friend, you are a genius in the art of fine living. There is no doubt of that. Tell me, is there a rarer queen of beauty than the luscious, the glorious, the exquisite Senhorita Harte?"

"There is none fit even to hold her mirror." The *recepção* bowed almost double, then kissing his fingers, raised the bottle. "To the ever adored Senhorita Harte! *Deus!* My friend, you are already the third to call on her within the hour."

"Third?"

The little man rolled liquid, dog-like brown eyes. *"Sim.* There have already been inquiring a *bahiana,* and a Japanese —I spit on his soul. Senhor, I do not like, I do not trust these yellow men."

"But is the senhorita in?" There was no need to counterfeit eagerness, North discovered.

Plump hands shot far apart and the *recepção* sighed. "Alas, senhor. Early this morning senhorita went out. Beautiful as a goddess, she put the sun to shame. Ah, *Deus, Deus!* Such a figure, such hair!"

North left the *recepção* enumerating Paula's charms, for all the world like a train caller announcing stations.

"No luck?" Aurora queried.

"No luck. Think we'll get on to brother João's."

North obeyed a sudden hunch, asked first to be driven to the United States Embassy. Without making his identity known, he inquired of the doorman whether Captain Maitland was there. He was told no, that unaccountably the Junior Military Attaché had failed to appear this morning. Also, the doorman implied that his Excellency, the Ambassador, was nothing if not put out about it.

Odd. Odd. What could have befallen Stuart Maitland, or prompted him to go A.W.O.L. on this of all days? There remained no other course now than to seek enlightenment from Luis da Evaristo's brother, Dom João.

A block from the Embassy a curious thing happened. Aurora had slowed to let a file of dancers prance by, gravely wagging demonic cardboard heads and jumping up and down to the frenzied hammering of a great *omelê* drum when, from amid a literal storm of yellow and green confetti, loomed a figure. He rapped sharply on the coupé's window.

North's hand shot to the automatic on the seat beside him when he noted that the stranger was garbed in a flashy green dragoon's uniform with a glaring red plastron and red epaulettes. What the unknown really looked like would be impossible to tell. Besides glasses over hard gray eyes, he was wearing a cardboard nose which would have put that of Cyrano de Bergerac to shame.

Half guessing what impended, North cranked down his window far enough to permit conversation.

"*Ich bin Koerner aus Recife,*" the dragoon announced in a guttural voice.

"*Gut. Ich bin Riefenstahl aus Rio Grande do Sul,*" North chanced in quick, accentless German. "*Wie gehts?*"

"*Wir fertig sind.* We are ready. Has there been any change in the orders?" demanded the Fifth Columnist over a sudden blare of trombones playing from the summit of a huge float depicting the discovery of flight.

"Why do you ask?"

"The sentinel has said nothing since last night," explained the broad-shouldered man outside.

North sat very straight, glared suspiciously a moment before rasping, "Should be more discreet, Herr Koerner. Where are your people meeting?"

The man on the running board glanced mechanically over his shoulder. "We do not yet know, *mein Herr.* One presumes they will appear as usual this afternoon."

He wrinkled his nose at a circle of dancers gamboling around a clump of magnificent jacaranda trees.

"Du lieber Gott! What a joke to turn a machine gun on such fools. I wait with difficulty."

"It would be most amusing," North agreed mechanically. "You have your guns ready?"

The fellow's heavy features lit. "*Ja.* And every man a marksman to teach these mongrels respect for our *Wehrmacht.* Well, Herr Riefenstahl, I must go on. *Auf wiedersehen.*"

"Can't we drive you anywhere?" Aurora demanded in remarkably good German.

"Your pardon, Fraulein," the other said with sudden suspicion in his tone. "I have my work to do as you have yours."

"But surely we will meet later?" she trained her most devastating smile on this curly-haired ruffian in green and red. "You have made me wish it."

The dragoon smirked under his paint. "*So?* Where then shall it be?"

Instantly, North nudged her, laid five fingers on the seat beside his companion.

"Five o'clock," Aurora murmured, leaning far over towards Herr Koerner. "At the Assyrio we shall drink to—our leader. You know the Assyrio?"

"*Ja,* Fraulein. At five *punkt.*" Then in a low voice he added fiercely, "*Heil Hitler!*"

With a curt nod he turned, went capering rather clumsily away as a *rancho* or carnival club of Negroes came prancing down the street, each man holding onto a gilded rope to keep formation about a group of what Aurora described as *candomblés,* or witch doctors, fantastically arrayed. A band was valiantly playing "Favella," and a group of half-grown boys ran about lavishing coins of silvered paper on the crowd.

"You rate full marks," North patted Aurora's hand on the wheel. "Where did you learn German?"

"Oh, Mamma and I spent two winters in Garmisch-Parten-kirchen. I think she was in love with a Bavarian Alpinist at that time."

Very shortly the imposing gateposts of the da Evaristo estates appeared and a shining asphalt driveway coiled off through a green-gold tunnel formed by the branches of many handsome mulatos and figueiras bravas. It appeared that the brothers, Luis and João, occupied identical homes set less than a hundred yards apart.

These proved to be huge, handsome structures of pale brown stucco, designed in the old Portuguese colonial style. They lay among formal gardens glowing with hundreds of exotic tropical plants. Despite an enormous funereal wreath hung at the entrance to the driveway and another at the front door of the left-hand mansion, parties of celebrants were swarming over the beautifully kept grounds.

It required all of North's tact and persistence to penetrate a cordon of private detectives encircling both houses. In the home of the murdered man, Venetian blinds on the ground floor were closed and there was a general air of suspended animation.

Before the residence of Dom João da Evaristo, however, the driveway was fairly choked by government and imposing-looking private cars. Further, a steady stream of messengers, couriers and officials came and went.

"Nice and quiet here," Aurora remarked as she parked in a wide, graveled courtyard. "The murder seems to have stirred quite a rumpus."

"If someone poisoned Edsel Ford, there might be quite a rumpus, too," North pointed out.

After some delay the two, feeling foolish and uncomfortable in their carnival regalia, were ushered into a library which seemed gratefully dark and quiet after the sunny tumult of the street.

"I wonder why it's socially caviar to say 'my foot hurts', but simply god-awful to say 'my feet hurt'?" sighed Aurora, easing her sandals of gilded kid.

North had commenced to pat his tunic in search of a package of cigarettes when suddenly he stopped and took out his handkerchief.

As he started for the library door, North said abstractedly, "I'm going to talk to one of those detective Johnnies outside."

"What's up?"

"Got something I need to send down to a friend at the Naval Intelligence Bureau."

A moment later, the Intelligence officer was confiding the carefully folded handkerchief containing his eyeglass to a yellow-faced individual who much more resembled a bandit than a detective.

"*Sim,* senhor, prints will be developed with all speed," the fellow murmured and glided from the hall just as voices were heard on the stairs. "I shall personally speak to Lieutenant Nabuco."

The Intelligence officer's heart skipped at least three beats when he recognized one of those voices. He made haste back to the library.

"Aren't you the busiest Watchdog ever?" Aurora drawled from behind a monsoon of Egyptian cigarette smoke. "Don't you ever rest? I'm beginning to wonder if you're entirely mortal."

"It's you, my dear, who suggest a visit from the gods," smiled the Intelligence officer.

"Shush." Smiling, she reached up to brush North's cheek

with her fingers when the voices on the stairs grew loud enough to penetrate the library.

An expression of distaste marred Aurora's painted lips. "Damn! Can't I ever be rid of that Harte wench?"

"*I'd* prefer not to be," said he, truthfully enough.

"All men are fools," snapped Aurora Morrow. "And you disappoint me. Such an obvious—"

She broke off her discourse as Paula Harte in a severe, dove-gray business suit entered on the arm of Dom João. North now had opportunity better to appraise the murdered man's slightly younger brother. Dom João was slighter of build, better looking in a heavy, dark way and had a grim, jutting chin that suggested obstinacy. Right now his eyes were swollen and he was extremely ill at ease.

"Miss Harte, you have been the soul of kindness," he was saying. "Especially at such a time, more than ever one appreciates such—"

He started as the two occupants of the library arose.

"Why, Major, this is a surprise of the greatest. And my dear Miss Morrow. I kiss your feet. I am so glad to welcome you both." But one could tell he wasn't pleased by the costumes.

Paula Harte's self-assurance was absolutely flawless as she flung a delicate double-barbed gibe. "Good morning, Miss Morrow. How very well your costume becomes you!"

Aurora drew herself up as a dowager hailed by a street Arab.

"And how well yours becomes you," she returned coolly. "You really should wear it quite often, my dear."

Paula flushed at the implication.

"By the bye," Aurora continued, "by what right did you follow me to Miss Carpenter's home?"

Dom João stared a little. Paula treated the other girl to a sweetly poisonous smile.

"Since you were not at home, Miss Morrow, I reasoned out that that was where you had taken my employer's property."

"He *asked* me to keep it!"

"No doubt," came the quick reply. "But my friend, Major North, wished it to be preserved with care."

"*Your* friend!" Aurora blazed.

"Yes. My friend," came the equable reply. "I decided to find it for him. You see, he was tired," she added blandly. "After all, it was half past four of this morning."

Aurora spun about, her face rigid beneath its paint. "Hugh, she's lying, isn't she? You weren't with her last night?"

"I was," he admitted lightly, "in fact, one might say that I was seeing quite a lot of her."

Aurora hesitated, for once looked completely out of her depth. Dom João stood looking on in amazement; to him all this was meaningless.

"What have you done with that ring?" the Morrow girl demanded icily as Paula Harte airily pushed straight a small straw hat. "If you've—"

"The ring?" Dom João broke in. "Oh, it is here. Miss Harte has just given it to me." He fished in a pocket, then held out his hand.

It was the famous ring all right, North decided. There could be no mistaking that huge, glowing emerald and its massive gold mounting.

Weird Combinations

SAID Major Hugh North to the tall young Brazilian, "One hesitates to intrude at a time like this but it is important that we talk privately, Senhor da Evaristo. I trust you—"

A wave of Dom João's long-fingered hand cut short North's apology. "Anything and everything in my house is entirely at your disposal, Major. Ladies, a thousand sincere apologies. Excuse us."

"Please take as long as you wish, Dom João," urged Aurora, avoiding North's eye. She was still appearing mighty annoyed and perplexed over Paula Harte's none too subtle implication.

North couldn't suppress a smile at the vision of two young women stalking to opposite ends of the library, each wrapped in monumental dignity. João da Evaristo, walking quickly and silently, led his guest down a seemingly endless corridor on the second floor until at last he paused before a handsomely carved door.

"My own study," he explained, facing this wiry figure so very debonnaire in the green and yellow hussar uniform. "We will be comfortable here, Major, and quite private. I do not fully understand what you are about, but I am assured it is for the good of Brazil—and the regime Vargas. That is so?"

"Quite so," came the quiet reassurance.

Dom João seated himself, leaned forward eagerly and, looking much younger, said, "Then I am most eager to help. The Minister of Foreign Affairs has called me on the telephone asking your whereabouts. So also has your Embassy. They appeared most agitated."

They had good reason to be, thought North, but did not say so.

"Senhor, I would like very much to examine your brother's ring."

In silence, Dom João passed it over. The ornament was fashioned of red gold with a design in which two pythons fought and strained. Tiny rubies gleamed to mark the eyes of one and minute diamonds glittered to indicate those of the other. The fangs of both fancifully gripped the emerald's setting. This bit of work purported to represent the conventionalized aureole of a sun. Within these divergent golden rays a big emerald glowed with a verdant intensity which was wholly fascinating. Nearly unflawed, the jewel must have been worth many thousand contos of reis.

Slowly, North revolved the ring. When he shook it, a faint smile lit Dom João's sensitive, pale brown features. He held out his hand for the ornament.

"Please, Major, let me save you time," he suggested. "I have one similar. Dom Luis and I exchanged such rings some years ago, when business had been good." He smiled. "Please to watch."

North held his breath as Dom João braced thumb and forefinger against one of the golden rays emanating from the ring's setting. When he had given the emerald a double turn, both stone and mounting came free, disclosing carefully cut threads on a shallow stem. Revealed to the Intelligence officer's gaze was a tiny compartment in the body of the ring.

"So?" North breathed as he recognized within this a minute strip of onion-skin paper. His breath came with a little hissing sound.

"Dom João, do you happen to know what is on that paper?"

Highlights glistened on João da Evaristo's carefully smoothed hair when he jerked a nod. "Yes, Major. I know without looking. It is a series of numbers."

Numbers? Recollections of "Bolivar," the 304 G-2b messages flickered across the screen of North's imagination. Was this the key? Fervently he prayed so.

"In my brother's house," came the Brazilian's slow accents, "there is a wall safe. Each month Dom Luis has the combination to it changed." He suppressed a little smile. "We every one of us keep a few secrets from the world, do we not?"

The Intelligence officer used the point of a pin to free the little roll of paper.

"True enough, only some of us keep those secrets better than others."

"Poor Luis had more than most. Naturally, it was impossible for him always to recall a combination so frequently changed."

"Oh, I see," North muttered. "Dom Luis merely wrote down the new numbers and hid them in his ring where he would always have them handy?"

"Yes. An admirably simple arrangement, no?"

"Admirably," North said, as a great many perplexities evaporated.

It suddenly became sparklingly clear why Luis da Evaristo had been prompted to entrust this ring to a comparative stranger. Belatedly, the munitions maker must have become convinced of a lively personal danger. Um. What particular act or word had warned him? Who had bestowed upon him that cigar and its ingenious deadly device? Common sense argued that in that wall safe must lie secrets dangerous enough to cause Luis da Evaristo to die a hideous death.

His hopes began to paint the future with the bright hues of optimism. Perhaps in the next few moments he would find a knife with which to cut this Gordian knot of tangled clues, half-understood motives and intricate personalities.

It was hard to maintain a calm exterior. Had he not worked, reasoned, fought hard for this chance to balk the inevitable ruin of a friendly all-important neighbor?

In his mind's eye he could again see Herr Koerner and thousands of others of his ilk inexorably marshaling their fellow Fifth Columnists, mounting their machine guns, spreading their lies, awaiting the word, *"Los!"*

How near now to the Brazilian coast was cruising that inoffensive and prosaic-appearing freighter? Near. Critically near or there wouldn't be so many green carnival uniforms in Rio. Black hats, gray trousers, dark blue coats plus suddenly produced armbands had been the uniform in Holland. Green here.

Finally Hugh North recalled himself to the present.

"Was it not considerate of Miss Harte to fetch me this ring?" Dom João demanded. "Such loyalty to an employer is unusual in these days." He sighed. "Luis was very much attached to his secretary."

North felt prompted to inquire, in that case, why it was to Miss Morrow, not Paula Harte, that Luis da Evaristo had entrusted his ring? But there was nothing to be gained and, after all, Paula Harte had done the honorable thing. There was no denying that—for the present, at least.

Carefully, the Intelligence officer unrolled the strip and found typewritten on it what certainly seemed to be the combination for some safe.

Aware of an excited thumping of his heart, North suggested evenly, "Suppose we go at once to your brother's residence?"

Dom João hesitated.

"You recall what the Foreign Minister said?"

"Very well, indeed. Yes. We shall go at once. A gallery connects our homes. It curves around the rear of the hill upon which these houses are built."

Somber activity ruled and the odors of countless flowers pervaded the home of the murdered munitions maker. Servants with downcast eyes tiptoed about and many black-robed priests came and went.

A majordomo, bent and yellowed with age, began to sniffle at the sight of Dom João. "Ah, Dom João, what an evil, what an accursed day is this!" he gurgled as he opened the glass-paneled gallery door.

They followed him through a living room very redolent of the joy of living, and presently arrived in an efficient-appearing private office. Here filing cabinets loomed everywhere like miniature skyscrapers. There were a dictaphone and a pair of typewriters in addition to an adding machine. Maps, graphs and cases for blueprints filled the wall space surrounding a handsome desk of brass and teakwood. Surprisingly, an enlarged snapshot of Paula Harte in riding clothes remained on the desk.

With innate tact, North suggested that Dom João open the

safe. For the life of him he couldn't guess where it might be concealed.

The younger da Evaristo nodded heavily and went over to lift out the lowest drawer of a filing cabinet. This he laid aside and stood back disclosing a dial knob let flush into the floor. His reddened eyes swung to the martial figure in green and yellow.

"Major, will you be so good as to call off the numbers?"

As the other prepared to kneel, the Intelligence officer inquired abruptly, "Am I right, senhor, in guessing that your brother had recently had a change of heart concerning the Patriotista movement?"

"You are a very shrewd man, Major. I wonder how you knew? He swore to me he had informed no one in Rio of his decision."

Dom João caught his breath and little knives flashed at the depths of his eyes. "He confided to me last night when I met him at the airport that he had been deceived, had been made a fool of. Pujol he had always believed to be working for the true good of Brazil. That is my only consolation today."

Dom João's color rose. He talked with mounting rapidity and looked just a trifle self-satisfied.

"I have reasoned many times with Luis. Finally, when he learned that Pujol, that accursed Judas, only was preparing to open a road for foreign conquest, Luis was sickened, furious. To me Luis admitted his mistake, also his desire to atone for it."

"Did he mention the people with whom he dealt?"

The young Brazilian made an angry, impotent gesture. "*Deus,* no!" he said. "There was no time for details at that moment, Major. He would have given me all the facts last night on his return from the German Yacht Club. Poor, poor

Luis." The brother's eyes commenced to fill. He turned his back. "Please to call the combinations?"

" 'Right 17 to left 11,' " North called. " 'Right 52, left 6, left 27.' "

He stared down upon the broad white-clad back of João da Evaristo. It was sweat-marked at the shoulders. A breathless moment endured—became interminable as the younger da Evaristo tried, pulled, then jerked at the knob. Angrily, he spun the dial.

"We must have made some mistake, Major. Do you mind repeating?"

There was no mistake. The safe would not open to this combination.

North stared out at a garden subdivided into blue, yellow and red patterns, inquired in bitterly level tones, "Did Miss Harte visit in this house?"

"I do not know." João da Evaristo pressed one of a series of buttons. "I will find out. She only sought me a few moments before you arrived."

Presently the ancient majordomo appeared.

Sim, senhor, the senhorita Harte had appeared to present condolences. *Sim,* she had come to the office to find certain papers belonging to the Companhia Americus. She had been desolated over the irreparable loss of Dom Luis.

"You utter fool! You monkey! You, you Portuguese!" The Brazilian's jangled nerves flared and the majordomo flung up a warding hand.

"*Desculpe-me,* Dom João. *Não compreendo.* When Dom Luis was alive, we servants had orders that Senhorita Harte was always to come and go as she wished."

Swiftly North's glittering hopes went crashing, tumbling into the cesspool of confusion.

He sighed. "Of course. Well, let's go and question Miss Harte. Our confidence in Miss Harte, senhor, seems to have been a trifle premature. It is obvious she knew of the ring and its use."

João da Evaristo glowered. "The damned, sweet-speaking *puta!* Playing on my sorrow, my sympathy. So sweetly she returns the ring—after stealing—God knows what! Come. We will find her at once."

North raised a quizzical brow, helped himself to a cigarette from the box on the desk.

"If we find Miss Harte still in your home, I will be greatly surprised."

"Bolivar"

"BUT I do not understand. Why should Miss Harte have gone like this?" Dom João burst out bewilderedly.

Hugh North itched in his subconscious mind but had no idea of where to scratch as he remarked, "Having almost certainly—er—preëmpted certain of your brother's private and confidential documents, she would hardly wait around. Especially when it was discovered that she has altered either the safe's combination or the numbers opening it."

Dom João glared across the library where Aurora Morrow was demurely rearranging her turban before a mirror. There was a sort of cat-plus-canary look about her, North thought.

"You are sure Miss Harte has stolen documents of value?" demanded the Brazilian. "If she has—"

"She has," North told him. "I'd bet my bottom dollar on that. But it mayn't be just papers. It could be plans, formulas, models—"

"But where would—where could she take them?"

North shrugged, noted how Aurora's smile had deepened. "Rio is a large city, senhor. You are more likely to know than I. You will have to excuse me. This is a serious setback."

Dom João nodded. "I shall take my own steps to apprehend this—this thief!" and he almost rushed from the room.

Aurora who, with too elaborate an interest, was now surveying a brilliant collection of tropical fish, glanced up as North, very grim now in his hussar's uniform, came striding over.

"Back on the merry-go-round?" she queried. "So your little blonde playmate ran out on you, Watchdog?"

"Seems so. Come, let's get a move on."

He broke off as the front door swung back and silhouetted the erect, athletic figure of Dr. Hermann Rupp against a bright rectangle of sunlight. A step behind him came Count Altrocchi. Both men wore cutaways, top hats and carried portfolios under their arms.

The German recognized North immediately despite makeup and carnival regalia. When Dr. Rupp grasped the implication of North's wearing a green uniform, a surge of furious color mounted his muscular neck.

"Mein Gott!" The words, propelled by sharp surprise, were barely audible.

His companion paled, swallowed hard on nothing ere he bowed.

"A pleasant surprise, Major, to find you here. But why in costume? It seems hardly *de rigueur.*"

"We came thus at Dom João's request," North lied blandly.

"Yes," Aurora put in. "He phoned my uncle's home—broke up a nice little crap game, too."

"Ah?"

The manner of both men remained unruffled.

"Ah, how very lovely you look in your costume, Aurora."

Dr. Rupp summoned a rather wooden smile, offered his hand and shook hers with a naïve heartiness which would have done credit to a Rotarian from Kansas. There was none of the hand-kissing, heel-kicking Prussian about him.

"By the way, just what are you boys doing here?" Aurora demanded.

"We have come to extend our condolences to Dom João."

"Damned decent of you," North said. "You were business friends, I take it?"

"Yes." Dr. Rupp answered him sharply, kept his eyes on the green uniform. In his look a crouching storm seemed gathering to spring. He seemed at once furious and dangerously disconcerted. "One hears the most intriguing tales about you, and your extraordinary cleverness, Major North."

"Flattery, Doctor, or sheer unadulterated nonsense."

Dr. Rupp snorted, turned to Aurora, "One sees now, dear lady, why you were named Aurora."

Altrocchi's thin features relaxed their mask of weary cynicism.

"Being German, Hermann has understated the case. Today your beauty would cause the Goddess of the Dawn to envy."

"If I'm named for any goddess of the dawn—" Aurora's laugh unrolled like a bright satin ribbon—"I suspect it was because Mamma guessed I would grow up to be a night owl like herself."

Aurora waved the cigarette the Italian had lit for her. "Say, Gino, how's about you and Hermann joining Hugh here and me at the Gávea Golf Club this p.m.? City's getting too damned noisy for words."

Altrocchi, with one eye on his companion, said eagerly, "But yes, dear lady. At what time?"

Dr. Rupp laughed shortly. "But of course. Major North is a man I have long wished to know. You will really be there?"

"Of course he will," Aurora promised airily. "I want to show him off before that hateful Judy Chamberlain—she's the biggest lion hunter in all Rio. I'll be going into my dance about five, boys, so come early. I've forgotten more about a *maracatú* than most of the local pros."

She flashed the somber figures on the steps a smile, slid her arm through North's. "Come on, Watchdog, let's toddle and find Teddy before he goes down for the count."

Very casually, Altrocchi called, "I say, Aurora. Have you seen Miss Harte anywhere today?"

Dr. Rupp cut him short. "Poor Luis' secretary knows where to lay hands on certain business papers. They concern a shipment for the Compania Estrella del Mar, my import-export firm—a shipment of perishable goods. Time is valuable. You understand?"

"Oh, sure."

North said, "I haven't had the pleasure of seeing Miss Harte since last night. Have you, Aurora?"

"No," said she in a flat voice. "And I don't want to. Come along."

As they neared her car, Aurora gave his hand a small squeeze, chuckled. "My God! I'd never dare marry anybody who can think so quick and who lies with such a straight face!"

"You're not a half-bad actress yourself," North countered, smiling down into the sweet symmetry of her face. "That phony bid to the Gavea Golf Club was an aces-up performance. I wish I could express my enthusiasm more adequately."

She stopped the car at the entrance to the Rua Barbosa. "Why don't you? It's carnival time."

"Who said I was bright?" North demanded and, with Rupp and Altrocchi looking on baffled from the background, he kissed Miss Aurora Morrow briefly but not without effective-ness.

"Um-m," Aurora murmured, replacing her lipstick. "For a sample, not bad—not bad at all."

Hugh North thought hard as the car gathered speed. He entertained no illusions that Dr. Rupp would misinterpret either his presence at the home of Dom João or his choice of a green hussar uniform.

What wretched bad luck that he and Aurora had not left Dom João ten minutes earlier! Damn. He had slipped badly in granting Paula Harte opportunity to walk so calmly out of the scene.

To find her promised to be the very devil of a job—one at which he might very well fail altogether.

"Oh, by the way," Aurora's voice intruded on his rumina-tions as a cacaphony caused by competing bands swelled louder. "A while back I took a bit of a liberty."

"Don't dramatize," North laughed. "You've been taking them your whole life."

The girl guided her car around a group of children watch-ing a performing dog do tricks, and said, "I put words into your mouth, dear Watchdog. That's one thing I've never done before."

His chief sense of well-being departed as he tried to clarify a vagueness in her expression.

"What do you mean?"

Her turban fluttered gaily as she turned her head and gave him an oddly serious glance. "I have always wondered what girls like the Blonde Baggage do with themselves during day-light hours."

"So what?"

"Remember that detective with a big mole on his nose?

The one that tried to give you the bum's rush when you wanted to go into Dom João's house?"

"Yes, I remember ticking him off."

Aurora Morrow pressed hard on her horn to clear a trio of guitarists from her path, murmured, "Well, I told him *you* said he was to—er—shadow the B. B."

"Words fail me," North said, reveling in a warm influx of optimism.

"Did I do wrong?" she demanded anxiously. "I figured you might be curious, too."

"Don't be an idiot!" He kissed her on the cheek. "You're wonderful! You're an angel! You're the ultimate bright button!" Suddenly he broke off. "Where did you tell him to report?"

A small secret smile plucked at Aurora Morrow's brilliant and pleasantly curved lips. "That brings up another—er— liberty. You'll be horrified, I expect."

"Go on."

"This will sound like a proposition," she warned. "And I'm not so hot in that field."

"*Will* you get on with it?"

She considered him warily an instant before she said, "Well, Hugh, I thought it would be kind of constructive fun—" her next words came out with a rush— "for us to take a suite at the Hotel Avenida."

"What!"

"Yes, dear. You see, it seemed to me there's been a lot too much traffic up to your digs at the Copacabana."

"Why?"

"Why else would you have had to have those guards outside?"

"Good Lord, girl, do you realize what you are suggesting?"

"No, but I think it might be interesting to find out." She straightened on the seat with a supple movement of narrow hips. "Don't look so horrified. You know I'm right. The Axis boys didn't look so pleased just now.

"Besides," she added in her cool, confident voice, "I told the detective with the mole to report to Mr. West at the Avenida. You can't do everything, Hugh, so I intend to try out for the 'friend, guide and philosopher' role—with a dash of light housekeeping thrown in."

There could be no doubt that Aurora's reasoning was sound. Entirely too many people had knowledge of his whereabouts and, through the mischance of the encounter with Rupp and Altrocchi, the future promised to darken a great deal before there was any chance of improvement.

"Very well. I'll register. But you, my dear Infant, are not going to park there."

"Why not?"

"Because for one thing, I've been duck hunting with J. P. Standley and I know how mighty handy he is with a shotgun."

She laughed, shook her head. "He'd be glad to be shut of me."

"But what about clothes?" North protested weakly, for the idea was really beginning to appeal. "The shops are closed."

"This costume plus some fixings I'll highjack from the chambermaid will have to do."

Suddenly it struck North how utterly grotesque it was to be playing a game of deadly seriousness all rigged out in fancy costumes and grease paint. When a corner telephone booth hove into sight, the Intelligence officer indicated it. "Makee stop."

"Going to call up the B.B.?" she demanded.

"Who?"

"The blonde bitch—Paula."

"No. You know I don't know where she'd be."

"Okay. Just wanted to make sure."

While calling Nabuco's number, he felt tempted to murder a group of semi-drunken revelers who, seeing him at the phone, began to blow horns and sing outside. When Aurora thoughtfully turned on her car's radio, they went over to serenade her, drenched her with their *lança-perfumes.*

The first chance he got, North decided, he'd better get out of this rig, though the costume granted him the advantage of a very handy pistol holster.

Lieutenant Ramon Nabuco controlled his voice, yet excitement leaked through his tone like rain through a cheap poncho. Would Major North be kind enough to come at once to his home? Yes? Good. Senhora Nabuco, his mother, would offer a midday meal; a poor one, no doubt, but filling. Yes. Senhora Nabuco lived on the Rua Monte Luiz, number 116.

That, like most of his countrymen, Lieutenant Nabuco had been belittling his possessions was very evident. While not large, the Nabuco home stood very white, neat and serene amid a grove of paineiras. Senhora Nabuco proved to be fragile, white-haired and charming. She made much over Aurora.

Because the old lady spoke no English, conversation was carried on in French during a most ample luncheon consisting of *sopa de abóbora, feijão preto,* a delicious concoction of black beans, pork, beef, spice and mandioca flour. For dessert there were *fruta de conde*—custard-apples sun-ripened and very delicious—washed down with a cool soft drink made from a native tree bark. It was called *guaraná.*

For North, this interlude offered a seriously required breathing spell. He sat back, impressed by Aurora's evident knowledge of local matters, her deftness in guiding the conversation to include Senhora Nabuco.

Soon the old lady's little emerald earrings were flashing and her tiny hands, blue-veined and parchment-hued, became active. Her thin laugh crackled almost continuously. Clad in black and seated against the background of an old yellow-brown wall on which many very friendly lagarto lizards darted, she presented an unforgettable picture of dignified old age.

"These are busy times," the wrinkled old lady said. "One son, Campo, I have in the aviation. He is far away in Recife. Another, José, is with the customs service at Santos, and so I hope to keep my baby near me." She beamed on her son while brushing a vivid butterfly from a plate of *goiabada*.

"Mamma is a great one to complain," laughed Ramon Nabuco. "She says I never come home."

"One cannot conceive how such a neglect becomes possible," North said politely, and at the same time raised an eyebrow.

Nabuco saw and arose a moment later. "By your leave, Mamma. There is something to be discussed. *A seus pés, senhorita.*"

North, his face freed of paint, bowed also.

"Don't hurry, Hugh. I'm having the grandest time."

He felt strangely moved by the gravely solicitous look Aurora gave him. Seen amid the sunlit flowers of the Nabuco porch, she was, in her brilliant costume, a sight to touch tinder to the spark of any man's emotions.

On a small terrace overlooking a garden pool that fairly blazed with Victoria Regia lilies and half a dozen varieties of water hyacinths, the slim young Brazilian lit North's cigar, then his own. They seated themselves on comfortable rattan chairs.

Politely, North waited for his collaborator to start talking.

Nabuco said suddenly, "I have learned of the circumstance of the ring."

"From whom?" North inquired. With a pair of jewel-bright humming birds feeding on an agapanto plant not two yards away, it was difficult to concentrate on a struggle the outcome of which might soon cause the shedding of much blood.

Again the vision of Herr Koerner's brutal blond head at the car window reoccurred.

"*Wir fertig sind,*" he had announced hungrily. Yes, ready to drench this beautiful, care-free city with blood, ready to spray its streets with machine gun and shell fire.

"From Dom João. I asked him."

"Shall we come to that later?" North suggested. "What I am really anxious over is information about those newspapers. You have learned something?"

Energetically, the slight figure in spotless white nodded its head.

"*Sim.* Concerning the puzzle we have discovered a good deal."

North felt prompted to embrace this energetic and efficient young man. "You have discovered the identity of Bolivar?"

"*Sim,*" Nabuco's teeth glistened. "This Bolivar is a skillful professional creator of cross-word puzzles. No man, but a French woman." Nabuco consulted a notebook. "She resides on the Rua Condido Benicio."

Though a dove—Nabuco called it a *pomba cola*—came fluttering down to explore the tile flooring of the terrace, North paid it no attention.

"This is fine work, Lieutenant. Please continue."

Flattered by the North American's enthusiasm, Nabuco studied his notes. "Inquiry reveals that puzzles by this Bolivar have been widely syndicated—at least to all the capitals of our principal states such as Pará, Pernambuco, Bahia, Minas Geraes, São Paulo, Santa Catharina and such."

North pursed his lips, peered unseeingly into space. "Then I seem to have been right? 'Bolivar' had nothing *directly* to do with ships."

The Brazilian said, "You were shrewd to sense that so early." Jumping up, he went inside and returned carrying a light table, a pad of paper and a pencil. "I have here that puzzle which you removed from the body of Luis da Evaristo."

"Good. When was it printed?"

"Two days ago, the day that you, da Evaristo and the woman, Harte, quitted São Paulo," came the prompt information. "Here it appeared in *A Sentinella*. You were right about that, also."

The singing of a caged bird in the garden sounded very loud as North recalled the message found in that cake of soap. How did it go? 27-18-22-6? Yes. That was it.

"Will you look up word number twenty-seven horizontal? If that fails, try the same word number vertical."

"A moment, please." The Brazilian Intelligence officer's lips twitched as he talked silently to himself.

"The definition is 'an errand.'"

"Um. A task? No. A sending? No." He hesitated. "Would the Portuguese word for mission fit?"

"*Missão?* Yes. Yes." Excitedly, Nabuco scribbled down the word. "Next number please?"

"Twenty-two."

"Horizontally, the definition is 'fourth day.'"

"Um. The fourth day? That would be Tuesday," North muttered intently. "Would that fit?"

"*Sim! Sim!*"

"Tuesday. And today is Sunday!"

"Now we are learning things."

"But not fast enough," North growled.

The voices of servants, making merry in the kitchen of an adjoining villa, invaded the veranda as the two men sat intent on their apparently trivial task. A little later they straightened, caught up cold cigars and studied a message which read:

MISSION ARRIVE TUESDAY PREPARE

"This would seem to suggest that the vessel you are hunting is expected on Tuesday?"

North shrugged.

"It might—but there are many kinds of mission, Lieutenant." He relit and drew several puffs on his cigar, to the annoyance of a gorgeous butterfly which had begun to flutter over the card table.

"Who can have sent this?"

"Somebody with a shrewd brain," North murmured as if to himself. "Maybe Pujol, maybe Rupp, maybe somebody aboard the ship. Again, it could be someone wirelessing from Berlin, giving orders to those in the know."

Nabuco passed a perplexed hand over his eyes.

"I am very stupid, Major, for it is not yet entirely clear. This radio-Bolivar business."

A low chuckle burst from North. "It's none too clear to me, either. Yet I suspect it works something like this. First, the big boss of this *putsch* decides what's to be done and composes his orders. For example: 'Green uniforms will be worn.' He gives this to an aide who scrambles the order of the words and instructs Bolivar to prepare a puzzle in which all those words appear."

"That is clear, Major. What next?"

"When the puzzle is completed, Bolivar then turns it in to

his—or her, you say—chief. He then locates the necessary words in the key puzzle and copies the numbers as they then appear. The correct sequence thus becomes of the greatest importance." North smiled. "The number sequences are then distributed by radio, mail, word-of-mouth. All the faithful have to do is to look up the right puzzle to get their instructions. It is superbly simple."

"I see. Naturally, only the most general instructions could so be sent."

"Naturally. But there would be priceless hints given." North flashed a smile. "You see, this is almost identical to Fifth Column methods in Holland, Norway and Denmark."

"What of those other two radiograms?" Nabuco demanded eagerly. "The ones that were picked up yesterday night? I can put some cryptographers to work."

The man in hussar uniform hesitated. "It will do no harm, but I suspect the corresponding puzzles will not yet have been printed."

"That is so," Nabuco admitted, emitting a small sigh. "What, then, do you propose?"

North flicked his ash over the rail. "Shall we drop in on Mademoiselle 'Bolivar'? It might prove a very instructive visit."

Under the Thumb

Because it was still the hottest part of the day the celebration had slacked perceptibly. Soaked with perspiration, hungry, and exhausted by antics sustained for several hours, a vast majority of the revelers had deserted the littered streets of Rio in search of hospitable taverns, restaurants and the homes of friends.

Consequently, Lieutenant Nabuco made good time. He had insisted on driving his own car and on leaving Aurora Morrow to refresh herself amid the dim coolness of the Nabuco home.

"Incidentally," North reminded, "you forgot to mention Miss Bolivar's name."

"It is Ernestine Berthier," Nabuco supplied. "She is twenty-nine years of age and single."

"How long has Mlle. Berthier lived in Rio?"

"That I have been attempting to discover," Nabuco replied, overtaking a *bonde* filled to overflowing with noisy, variously costumed celebrants. "But she cannot have been here above a year."

"In what kind of place does she live?"

"A third-rate hotel, the Hotel of the Two Hemispheres. The neighborhood is not of the best."

Already they were entering a poorer neighborhood where goats, dogs and semi-naked children roamed at large and macaws and parrots screeched in every doorway. Over several doorways hung a curious device—that of a human fist with the thumb protruding between the first and second fingers.

Such *figas* were for good luck, Nabuco explained, as were also the occasional rams' horns mounted on poles.

The noise of the city here was very different. Wooden sandals clattered and clacked over greasy cobbles, hawkers bawled out their wares and dozens of dealers in pets came swarming out of every patch of shade.

"You seem thoughtful, my friend," the Brazilian observed presently.

"Yes. I was wondering where I could buy a package of bright orange, or bright green, envelopes?"

"In God's name, why?"

North chuckled, "I will demonstrate, not lecture."

By dint of a considerable detour, a stationer's shop was discovered; and North solemnly purchased a package of glaring yellow envelopes.

Still wondering what could have happened to Stuart Maitland, Hugh North enclosed a single sheet of blank paper and addressed an envelope to Mlle. Ernestine Berthier. Half a block from her address the American Intelligence officer bestowed a few milreis on an urchin and told him to deliver said letter to the hotel's reception desk.

"I am wondering," North murmured, "why that name sounds so familiar? I'm sure I've heard of Ernestine Berthier before."

"And I am still wondering why you choose to address her a blank sheet of paper in a yellow envelope."

"You'll see in a minute."

When North and his companion entered a distinctly dingy lobby, a slatternly clerk at the desk did not even look up. As North had fondly hoped, it was quite unnecessary to inquire the number of Mlle. Berthier's room. His bright yellow envelope had been tucked into compartment 3E.

Nabuco showed his admiration as, quite unchallenged, they commenced to climb a stair. "Splendid. There was no need for inquiry, no risk of alarming the object of our interest. I shall remember that."

A gentle rap on number 3E's dirty gray panels produced no response beyond a furtive sound behind the door. Nabuco, alert and ready for any eventuality, rapped again, then called in high-pitched Portuguese, "A telegram for Senhorita."

"You may pass it beneath the door," sighed a small, uncertain voice.

Nabuco got around that. "*Mil perdões,* but my receipt book must be signed. It is too thick."

When there followed a clicking sound North prayed that no anti-burglar chain might restrain the door. He applied his weight smoothly, firmly against it.

"Oh, *Mon Dieu!*" a woman gasped as both men stepped within a fair-sized one room apartment.

A quick glance about lent North the impression of dreary stagnation. There was a picture of a man in a French artillery uniform with a rosette of crepe attached to its frame. An untidy bureau supported a certificate which gave the clue to Mlle. Berthier's identity. It was an award of the Prix Goncourt.

An odor of stale food hung in the air and the blinds, half drawn, emphasized the gloomy atmosphere. A table-desk and one whole wall of the room were covered with Portuguese, German and French dictionaries and bundles of papers. Yellowing stacks of newspapers rose like a low breastwork to waist height.

"Please, Messieurs. I—I have done nothing wrong. What is the meaning of this?" panted this plain-looking little woman. Apparently she had been roused from a nap. Her feet were tucked into badly scuffed slippers and she was clutching about her a dark red wrapper of cheap cotton which must certainly have served its owner long, if not well.

Mlle. Berthier's hands and chin began to tremble as Nabuco re-locked the door and nervously she dabbed at dull, stringy hair that might once have been a beautiful golden-brown.

North bowed and in French which had not grown rusty through recent disuse said, "Please not to disquiet yourself, Mlle. Berthier. We deplore this intrusion. We have only to ask you—"

The woman caught up a pair of steel-rimmed spectacles, put them before a lined face that retained traces of beauty and spirituality. She retreated slowly. "From me you shall learn nothing, absolutely nothing. So go, please, go at once."

"We have not come only to leave, senhorita. Here is my authority."

Nabuco produced a metal badge. It was pitiful to see how this faded literary genius positively cringed before an emblem of authority—before even a comic opera uniform.

"I know nothing," she gasped in French heavily tinged with the accent of Normandy. "I have committed no crime. Please do not harm me."

Reassuring as possible was North's tone as he said, "Your pardon if I disagree, Mademoiselle. A lady clever enough to win the famous Prix Goncourt and to compose the fascinating puzzles of Bolivar *must* know something."

Mlle. Berthier's thin form began shaking more violently and her eyes grew round with terror as she backed across the room towards a disordered bed.

"No! No! You do not understand. In God's mercy, leave me alone."

Involuntarily, she glanced at her desk when North started forward. He paused, studied a scratch pad, noted that upon it appeared a long list of words in German. Near it lay blank cross-word graphs indicating that she had been intending to set to work before long.

With the skill of long experience North set about to re-assure the patently terrified writer. He recalled her literary triumphs, the honors accorded her. But she remained hunched upon her bed, fists clenched on her knees and kept shaking her head.

"That was in another world—a lost world," she quavered.

That Mlle. Berthier's attitude typified that of her nation crossed North's mind. She seemed stunned, broken and utterly hopeless.

"We do not wish to learn much," the Intelligence officer murmured, offering her a cigarette. "Merely the name of the person or persons from whom you receive your instructions."

The woman lifted a pallid, bruised-looking face. "I do not know, Monsieur. I do not dare to know."

Nabuco, from the background, spoke quietly, "Can you indicate his nationality?"

"I do not know."

Aware that nothing was to be gained from pursuing this course, North hesitated. Mlle. Berthier would respond only to the kind of arguments to which she had been so obviously subjected.

"Very well. This gentleman is going to arrest you on a charge of conspiring against the security of the State. You will go to prison."

The reaction was violent. Mlle. Berthier began to sob, joined pallid hands in supplication. "*Non! Non!* I can endure nothing more."

"Then answer, my friend," Nabuco rasped.

"When did you last receive Dr. Rupp?" North demanded.

The reddened eyes wavered. "But Monsieur, of this Dr. Rupp I have never heard." She raised her head in a weak gesture of despair. "You may as well leave, Messieurs. You will learn nothing from me." She bit her lip. "I cannot—I *dare* not—speak."

Intimately familiar with the Haushofer technique, North suggested, "If you love your family—"

The woman's face quivered as if a raw nerve had been iced. "*If* I love them! *Seigneur Dieu,* what am I not suffering to free them?"

North thought fast. This woman was a Normande. What concentration camps were known to be in Normandy?

"They are prisoners at Caen?"

"No—no. In Rouen. The worst of all!"

The dreary room became a pit of silence peopled with wax figures. At length Nabuco suggested, "You do not like this work?"

Dull despair was eloquent in the shaking of Mlle. Berthier's head. "It is a long time since I have done anything I wished."

An alternative suggested itself and North said, "You could use money? A great deal of money?"

The reddened, weak-looking eyes swung up to meet his

glance, but Mlle. Berthier relapsed into apathy. "No, not even money will do any good. I—I—must do what I am told and say nothing. That is their only hope."

"Guards can be bribed; even SS men or Black Guards," North persisted. "Mademoiselle, in order that that world you once knew may return, I beg you to help us."

"Messieurs, believe me. I would speak if it were only myself who would suffer," the woman mumbled with a smile of infinite sadness. "Yet how can I doom, to God knows what fate, my mother, two brothers and a sister?"

"Their sacrifice might save many thousands of lives," pointed out Nabuco. Among the shadows his white-clad figure seemed slighter than ever.

An ugly, stubborn look came to dominate the flaccid features of the French woman. "Let the rest of the world take care of itself. My family is at stake."

North felt prompted to point out that just this attitude, repeated a thousandfold, had brought the Third Republic crashing down into an ignoble, dishonorable defeat.

"At least tell us this," Nabuco pleaded in his light, pleasant voice. "Have you sent out a puzzle today?"

The unhappy woman turned sidewise on the bed and lay flat, sobbing violently. She gave him a look full of agony.

"Oh, I dare not. I dare not! *Pitié. Je vous en prie!* You lack any idea of the threats, of the terrible things that would follow."

It was a peculiar form of defeat, this, North recognized. Violence would accomplish nothing, bribery less, an appeal to patriotism less yet.

"Very well, Mademoiselle, since you seem determined not to aid us, we will go," North told her gently. "We understand

and respect your grief. On your part you must promise to say nothing of our visit."

Mlle. Berthier sat up, removed her glasses and mopped her nose. "If you have asked for my apartment they will know. I will have to admit it."

"On my honor, no one knows," North declared and explained the ruse of the envelope.

Mlle. Berthier got up, ran to the door. "I will say nothing. I promise it. Now go! Please go! If *they*—" What a world of hatred she injected into that single word— "were to suspect what you have guessed—that you know so much—"

She grabbed at North's hand and, before he suspected her intent, kissed it. "I pray for your success."

Nabuco hesitated, selected a card from his notebook. "If you should find you need protection—if anything should happen, I—here is my address."

It was only when they regained the sunlit sidewalk and breathed fresh air again that they realized how dark and stale had been apartment 3E.

A touring car liberally festooned with black and yellow crepe streamers rolled by, and a pretty girl called out the Brazilian's name. Nabuco waved energetically.

"Senhorita Berthier must once have been as happy as that," sighed North's companion. "What do you think we should do?"

For some moments, North made no reply, merely stood watching some buzzards rocking in the hot blue heavens high above Rio.

His cheek-bones became momentarily prominent as he said, "I'm afraid I am forced to take a very cruel step."

"Cruel? You?" Nabuco smiled. "But that is unthinkable."

"Not when the good of the United States is involved," was

North's grave statement. He followed Nabuco into a little coffee shop.

North's companion gave him a quick look. "You intend to threaten the French woman?"

"No, not her," North said, settling into a little wicker chair and drumming with his fingers on the smooth marble top of a little table. "Because I lack time I must ask you to look up the biographical sketch I am sure you will find in *Contemporary Continental Authors*. It's published by an English firm."

"Yes. And then?"

"Learn the exact names of her family—the mother, brothers and sister."

Nabuco blinked as a detachment of mounted police went clip-clopping by, the head stalls of their horses bright with flowers. More blossoms had been thrust into the riders' caps or into the front of their tunics.

"Do I foresee that, most tragically, Mlle. Berthier's entire family has been exterminated by a British bomb?"

"You are quite right. But you must be extra careful, Lieutenant, to carry conviction, or we are in a worse fix than ever. Paper, form, the handwriting, stamps and all, must be perfect counterfeits."

"You know I am all of an eagerness to be of help, Major, but—" He shrugged, spread his slim, almost feminine hands.

North said, "Surely you have in your service people who can forge postmarks, who would know the nature of forms used to notify civilians of deaths in German occupied territory?"

"At other times, yes," came the unhappy reply, "but this accursed carnival." He shrugged. "I will do my very best and—" He checked himself for, bearing down on their table, came what appeared to be a *bonde* conductor.

He seated himself at a nearby table, then turned, faced Nabuco and waited.

"Well, Carvalho. What is it?"

The new arrival shifted his seat to North's table. "The tobacco, senhor tenente. We have found a cigar of the same leaf as that particle given the chemist."

In a flash returned visions of Luis da Evaristo at Standley's dinner, of the glittering table, of Aurora vague, flippant, cartooning her emotions and everyone else's.

The detective, with the air of a deep-dyed conspirator, produced a small wooden box, opened it.

"What do you make of this, Major?"

North with a toothpick lifted out the none-too-pleasant-smelling evidence and scanned it with great interest. It was, to all intents and purposes—save one—an ordinary half-smoked cigar. That exception was the presence of two circular impressions faintly etched on one side of the cigar.

The Intelligence officer riffled through the cards in his mental filing cabinet, came to one and stopped. He knew now who had prepared that lethal perfecto—and was both surprised and shocked.

"See what you make of it," he invited.

But Nabuco was impatient to be at his assignment and gave the stub only a very casual inspection.

At the Nabuco home Aurora Morrow appeared, declared herself greatly refreshed. Her make-up had been repaired and her hair re-dressed beneath its outlandish basket of imitation fruit.

"Oh, Hugh, why *did* you take so long? I've been—well, I

guess I've been worrying." Both her hands went out to him as he strode into the Nabuco drawing room.

"Couldn't be helped, my dear. And now, let's get going. There's plenty to be done."

"Go where?"

Lights twinkled at the back of North's gray-blue eyes. "Home. And do not spare the horsepower."

"Home?"

"Can you have forgotten that light housekeeping?"

Aurora blushed, recovered promptly. "Yes, m'lord."

When they arrived beside the packed and jammed sidewalk before the Hotel Avenida, Aurora suggested, "Watchdog, suppose you sit in the car? Let me do the registering. Allee same time I catch look-see about lobby."

A sudden rush of conscience to the heart made him protest.

"Look here, Aurora, you really can't do this. There's your reputation."

"Plenty of people, including Winchell, Sobol and Lyons, have tossed innuendos at it," she announced cheerily, "but it's still in working condition. You know very well, Hugh North, you *need* somebody like—like me. I *have* been useful, haven't I?"

"Indispensable, my dear. But—"

"To hell with it. I say it's spinach. You know you can't go back to your own hotel, and I've already told that mole-faced detective to report here. You know, the one I sicked on your friend the B.B." A nasty edge entered her tone as she added, "I suppose you're panting to see her again?"

"No dirty cracks now," North grinned. "I am. And how! While you're at it, Infant, suppose you have the management send up—say, what is your particular tipple?"

"Moët et Chandon, 1928," came the prompt response. "Vervier '32 isn't to be sneezed at, though." She gave him a curious half-tender, half-mocking smile. "By the way, how much does Uncle Sam allow us for quarters?"

"Tell you later, but don't stint," North replied. "On your way, Chiquita. I've got to consult a solemn guy by the name of Prescott about money matters."

He did so from a public telephone booth while Aurora Morrow unlocked the luggage deck and, bold as brass, disappeared into the Hotel Avenida a stride or two behind a broadly grinning porter.

Due to the carnival it required quite a while to complete a connection but, eventually, North succeeded.

"My God, man, where *have* you been?" Profound agitation was loud in the First Secretary's voice.

"Round about. Why?"

"We have been hearing rumors, very serious rumors of political unrest in—" Prescott's voice hesitated— "in Minas Geraes, Maranhão and Pará. For God's sake, *what* have you learned about that infernal freighter? Tell me anything you can. For what it's worth."

The man in the telephone booth heaved a small sigh. "I hate to pass on unsubstantiated information. I figure she will make port somewhere in Brazil some time on Tuesday."

"Some time? Somewhere?" came the exasperated queries. "God above! What have you been doing all this time, Major?"

"Playing gin-rummy," came the bitter response.

Silence. Then, "Sorry, Major. I'd hoped you'd have more news. Don't you know her name?"

"I wish to God I did; but if I have any luck, I should be able to tell you before sunrise tomorrow."

"Tomorrow? My God, tomorrow's Monday! If this ship's due on Tuesday—"

"If we'd a decent Intelligence service down here—" he started to say, but didn't. "Mr. Prescott?"

"Yes, Major?"

"Inside the next few hours I may need two hundred and fifty thousand dollars in ready cash."

"A quarter million—what?"

"Dollars. American; not Chinese or Mexican."

"Man alive, do you realize you ask the impossible?" Edward Prescott sounded outraged, almost insulted.

"I ask a cheap price for peace in Brazil."

"But, but—they'd have assorted cat-fits in Washington if we asked for a half of that. After all, the Military Intelligence allotment isn't—"

"You needn't remind me." His nerves were jangled and right now North granted them relief. To hell with those cookie-pushing, protocol-kissing diplomats. They never stuck their precious necks out. They had never felt that dreadful dry puckering of the stomach which only mortal fear can produce.

"You can tell them this. A quarter million is needed, and it's *got* to be made available! I'm counting on you to see that that cash is ready by five o'clock this afternoon."

The other gasped. "You can't really mean that?"

"Can't I? Listen, Prescott. I have never been in more deadly earnest than now. That quarter million I ask *may* be the best investment the government has ever made. Good Lord, man," North's weary nerves spoke. "After all, that's hardly the price of a couple of heavy bombers."

There was a pause, the sound of muffled conversation. "I'll see what I can do," Prescott said, "and by the way, where did you send Maitland?"

"He hasn't made an effort to reach me. God knows why, and I've needed him for a thousand reasons."

"The hell you say!" Prescott blurted.

"The hell I say!"

"But that isn't like him. Did you say anything to him? He's always been dependable."

"Has he?" North was rude for one of the few times in his life. If this wasn't just like a top-hatted diplomat! First give a man hell, and then no support.

"If that money isn't made available, I disclaim any responsibility in this case. It's simply got to be ready."

Before the First Secretary could offer further objection, North hung up the receiver and strode out of the booth. A chunkily built individual in a green and black grenadier uniform slunk aside and mingled with the crowd.

Because of this North kept on past the Hotel Avenida. Sure enough, there was the grenadier hurrying along, his neck craned. He was at once a very inexpert shadow and a nuisance, to be disposed of with all speed.

Selecting the all-but deserted entrance to a huge office building, the Intelligence officer slackened his pace until the shadow was stumping along but a few paces behind. Putting on a sudden burst of speed, he darted towards a revolving door. Once inside its panels, he delayed until the shadow entered the section behind, then revolved the door around until he stood free. At that instant, he whirled, jammed a screwdriver blade on his jackknife under the edge of the door. A vigorous kick drove home the improvised wedge and prevented the revolving door from moving either forward or back.

For the life of him, Hugh North couldn't resist the temptation of solemnly thumbing his nose at the Fifth Columnist who, livid with impotent rage, was hurling himself frantically at the immovable door.

Quite alone, North proceeded to enter the Hotel Avenida.

On the Joys of Light Housekeeping

AURORA MORROW was unpacking the bag brought from her car.

"Oh, hello, dear. Be done in a jiffy," she called from the closet of the very comfortable suite she had engaged. *"Some* phone calls you put in! You've been nearly half an hour."

That she had not been wasting time was evident. Cigarettes and flowers had been distributed. A short rank of most appetizing-looking bottles stood on the sideboard ready for service. She had even taken the precaution to prop a chair under the door knob leading into the next apartment.

"Thorough," North smiled as he closed the door behind him and locked it.

"Please put the key into your pocket," Aurora begged. "When the villian has a gal at his mercy, that's the thing to do."

"Who has who at whose mercy?" he laughed and commenced to unhook his yellow-frogged tunic. "Whew, it's hot."

"Um-m. As someone said, the climate of Rio is divine—six months of midsummer followed by six months of hot weather."

"Be a good wench, will you phone down to the kitchen?"

"Good heavens, Watchdog! You're not still hungry? You simply stuffed at the Nabucos'."

"I want a complete chef's uniform. This," he indicated the hussar's uniform, "is getting too hot for comfort—in more ways than one!"

Her eyes narrowed and her casual manner departed. "Then they made another pass at you?"

"Only a mild one."

"Oh-h, Hugh. I'm worried, worried sick over what'll happen to you. Speaking of passes." Aurora came over to pause before him. "Just what's wrong with me?"

"Wrong? What the devil are you talking about?"

Aurora raised curiously dissatisfied eyes. "I—I've never been so disappointed."

"Good Lord, Aurora, if I've done something—"

She dropped her eyes. "That's the whole trouble. You haven't!" Petulantly she crossed to the sideboard and uncapped a bottle of soda water. "I might be cross-eyed, half-witted and paralytic for all the attention you pay *me*. Oh, you flatter and feed an assistant you may find useful b-but—"

North went over to join her, completed two highballs before he demanded, "You think that because I haven't made any passes?"

"Oh, I don't know," she smiled suddenly. "I guess I don't understand you or myself either. I spend half my time fighting off hombres who want to tell me all about love by the Braille system. And—and now when—when—I want—" she suddenly turned her back. "Oh, the d-devil with you, Hugh North!"

He took her into his arms. A neat, trim figure, buoyant with life and fire, too, he found. She struggled. Provokingly he let her go, immediately stood back.

"Thank you for nothing, Watchdog," she muttered, picking

up her glass. "When the day comes that I have to coax somebody into—into . . . I—well, I'll marry a Rumanian first!"

"I'm being clumsy," he apologized. "Lord knows I love to fool. I enjoy every last thing life has to offer; but maybe the stature of this job has thrown me off stride. When I think of what's just around the corner for Rio, for you—for all of us if—well, I guess I can't do a Pagliacci."

He felt really contrite. True, for years he'd disliked and been contemptuous of Aurora's type and philosophy. Such a mistrust had been ingrained too long to be readily shaken off. Her bewilderment at not finding her whim of the moment granted without delay, was at once pathetic and disingenuous.

A damned shame they'd met under these circumstances. Or was it? Unsuspected qualities were beginning to break through the brittle shell of thoughtlessness, selfishness and cynicism. Would her steadiness crack as fatigue set in and the golden patina of adventure began to wear thin? He rather imagined so.

They sipped their drinks in silence, stared down at the Avenida until a buttons appeared bearing a chef's uniform. North paid the boy off, then went into the bedroom.

"You know, Infant, it might be a good idea if you were to keep that date with Altrocchi after all."

"What about Dr. Rupp?"

North emitted a brief laugh. "He won't show up. Not that lad."

They talked through the partially open door as he removed the green uniform, peeled off the false hair and scrubbed his face back to its natural complexion. For all his contempt of the practice, he needed a new disguise.

With grease paint from Aurora's kit he prolonged his mustaches, all but erased his eyebrows and otherwise altered the proportions of his face. Fifteen minutes later, a plump figure in starched white duck emerged from the bathroom.

Aurora sat with feet cocked up on the window sill, smoking and staring moodily out over the city, oblivious to the fact that her garish yellow and red skirt was riding high above her knees.

"Nuts," she snapped in a way that somehow expressed all the inevitable futility of her milieu. "Who's crazy now?"

On impulse he bent suddenly and kissed her on the forehead. Her hands crept up, closed over his neck, imprisoned him.

"Please, dear—just a minute more like this. I—I want to say something."

"I've been a lug," he said softly. "Sorry."

"No, you haven't," she said without looking up. "You did right, Hugh, a while ago. I was being smart Alec—out of step. You must feel a lot of contempt for my sense of values."

"Nonsense. I don't believe in passing judgment, except as it affects the future of our country. You see—"

"Oh bother," Aurora sighed as the telephone began to jangle. "Two bits says that's my pet ferret reporting on the B.B."

Aurora was right.

In decidedly sketchy English—one Paulo Almeira—the detective Aurora had so blandly assigned to duty, gave his account. Twice he had phoned the hotel only to be told that no Mr. West was registered.

North gave his companion a look of mock agony over the play on his name. She hung breathless at his shoulder, tried to listen into the receiver.

Returning to facts, the man with the mole stated that Senhorita Harte was now presumably at number 1081 Estrada do Redemptor, apartment 5E.

Why "presumably"?

Because the senhorita had been there for a long time now

and twice—three times now—he had had to interrupt his vigil long enough to telephone. It looked as if the senhorita might have stepped out. Did Major North require a detailed report of the lady's movements?

No, not now, North begged. Senhor Almeira would please return to his watching post with all speed. Oh, one thing. Had Senhorita Harte left any instructions?

Only that a Major North was expected at six o'clock.

Aurora winced. "You're a shining wonder, Watchdog."

North ignored the jibe, stated slowly, "And that seems to be that. So, Infant, suppose we go hunting together—separately?"

He shifted the .32 out of its holster and slipped it into the waistband of the chef's too-ample white trousers.

"What do you want me to do with Gino?" Aurora inquired absently. "In a nice way, that is."

"Pretend an interest in cross-word puzzles," he instructed. "Find out which are his favorites, and above all, find out if he loves Rupp as little as I suspect."

Green Eyes in the Dark

THE sun was swinging low over the housetops and the hills behind them were becoming edged with gold when Major Hugh North, vastly relieved to be out of that too-identifiable green uniform, commenced a cautious reconnaissance of Number 1081 Estrada do Redemptor.

He found little difficulty in locating the detective whom Aurora had so blithely assigned to duty. The watcher, a fox-faced individual with a great brown mole on the side of his face, seemed vastly relieved at North's arrival. What with all these comings and goings and the dislocation of normal life, it was hard to keep track of a person, he complained.

Succinctly, Almeira elaborated his report given over the phone. From the residence of Dom Luis da Evaristo, the Senhorita Harte had driven by taxi to the hotel Itajubá on the busy Rua Alvaro Alvim. No. He was very regretful but he had been unable to ascertain the number of the room.

She had then lunched by herself in a modest café on the Avenida Aparicio Borges after which she had visited the Embassy of the United States. This item dealt North a considerable jolt which he took care to conceal. From there she had visited an address he recognized as that of Captain Stuart Maitland. Apparently the Junior Military Attaché had not been there, for the detective stated that the Senhorita had come out almost at once and had mingled with the crowds so quickly he guessed that she was fearing pursuit.

Twice she had telephoned from various points, each time appearing more uneasy. At length, the senhorita had returned to her apartment, entering by the service door.

North praised Detective Almeira's work and the completeness of his report in such glowing terms that the latter's swarthy countenance became wreathed in smiles. Was there anything further he could do?

Yes, there was a simple but important request. Detective Almeira would proceed to the lobby of the apartment house and note anyone inquiring for Senhorita Harte. The detective was, at all costs, to prevent any unannounced appearances at Apartment 5E.

North drew a deep breath, fully aware that an important, if not critical, moment was at hand. On turning the corner into the Estrada do Redemptor, North instantly became aware of a pair of green-clothed celebrants loafing just a bit too casually across from the entrance to Number 1081. One of them turned his head as North rolled a little unsteadily out of the sunlight and into the shadow of the lobby. He dared not look back to see what the fellows' reaction might be.

Simulating a hilarity he was far from feeling, the Intelligence officer approached the *recepção,* this time a fat, beady-eyed woman, and gave his name. Beaming, volubly enthusiastic over the success of the carnival, she indicated an automatic lift.

"Fifth floor, senhor, and turn to your honor's left."

Danger was strongly, if indefinably, in the air, North felt.

It was blowing like someone's hot breath on the back of his neck. Why had Paula Harte dared come to a point so obviously under surveillance? Strange indeed!

The late Luis da Evaristo's secretary did very well for herself in the way of apartments. Hers was situated by itself at the end of a long, cool corridor paved with brightly waxed red tiles. From a hall window he deduced that she enjoyed a wide terrace on the first set-back. It overlooked a patio around which the apartment house had been constructed.

To his rap came a soft, swift movement beyond the door. He glanced over his shoulder and held the .32 ready under his chef's apron. Then he called softly, "Paula? What price a cocktail? I'm dry as Outer Mongolia."

"Ah-h. Hugh. I have been wondering, hoping you would not forget."

Unmistakable relief was in the speaker's voice; and the door, heavily constructed of teak and wrought iron, swung inwards. He lost no time in entering, stood with an amused smile watching Paula Harte relock the door.

If he had expected to find her nervous and distrait, he was entirely disappointed. In her breathtakingly sheer ashes-of-roses and blue colored harem costume, no one could have been more thoroughly casual or more charmingly hospitable as, slipping an arm through his, she led the way into a large and well-furnished sitting room. On the far side of it two tall French doors opened onto a terrace decorated with flaming oleanders growing in pale green jars.

A sudden chattering drew his attention as a white-faced monkey with an enormously long tail came galloping out of a door to the left. The arrival ran to Paula and caught her hand just like a child.

"This is Virginio Gayda," she explained laughing, "so

named because he talks a lot and says nothing worth remembering."

North chuckled but felt no part of that instinctive apprehension drop away.

Teetering on the back of a chair was perched a *curupião* bird, black with yellow wings and otherwise rather like a magpie, North thought. By way of greeting, the pet whistled a bar of "La Paloma."

"And how do you like my committee of welcome?" Paula demanded, steadily regarding him from wide, smoke-tinted eyes.

"Unique, to say the least. And they won't talk behind my back!" He smiled. When he put an arm about shoulders gleaming with powder, she swung suddenly close to him and clung.

"I have been so worried over you," said she in an undertone. "Oh, Hugh, please believe I care very much for your safety." When she turned, a breath of fragrance reached his nostrils. "Hold me close, Hugh, so I can know you are really here."

Far from unwilling, North complied and, to improve on the suggestion, kissed her thoroughly—but kept his eyes open.

"So now you are a cook?" Paula laughed, straightening a stray lock of platinum-pale hair.

"Yes. I am brewing a lot of fun for us."

"Are you really?"

Moving gracefully and delicately as a deer in a thicket, she led the way past a piano and coffee table loaded to capacity with costly knickknacks. There were little crystal elephants, dolls by Lenchi, ivory puzzles from China, carved ebony bears and even a set of magnificent ivory and ebony chessmen. A divan designed in the modern fashion dominated the far wall. The furniture was rather like her—expensive and good of its kind, but without ordered purpose.

Thanks to several slow-speed fans, it was cool and a breeze kept lazily billowing a pair of mauve curtains screening the French windows. Another pair of curtains remained the focus of North's attention; they muffled the entrance to the rest of the apartment. Amid the sharply reminiscent scent of Flor da Noite, other perfumes were recognizable. They originated from a wide variety of flowers. Paula must have been inordinately fond of them.

The *curupião* now on an antique Spanish chair with an enormously high back became annoyed at the attention Virginio Gayda was receiving. It fluttered over to a little smoking stand and cocking an insolent eye at his mistress, picked up a box of matches.

"No, no, Nicky!" Paula called, but the bird uttered a derisive whistle and shook his prize so violently that it scattered matches far and wide over the dull green rug.

The monkey screeched and lumbered over to snatch at the bird, but the *curupião* vented a derisive whistle and flew out onto the terrace. There it bobbed up and down and taunted the monkey.

"Of course, today my children would appear badly mannered," Paula sighed.

North said, "I should like to see the rest of your apartment. Do you mind?"

She gave him a veiled look, laughed mockingly. "So Major Curiosity wishes to learn how the other half lives?"

Full lips parted in a mocking smile that explained how thoroughly she understood his motive in expressing curiosity. She parted the hangings and beckoned.

"Come explore the inner mysteries of Apartment 5E."

Her skirt of ashes-of-roses organdie billowing, she led the way down a short passage to a bedroom in which mirrors of all sizes and descriptions multiplied the visitor by the dozen. A wide bed had been rested upon, and the conservative gray business suit Paula had been wearing that morning lay over the back of a chair, a sharp contrast to the expensive and very feminine lingerie and stockings on its seat.

A dressing table bore at least thirty widely varying bottles of perfume in addition to the usual combs, brushes and minor cosmetics. Tucked into the mirror was a rotogravure picture of himself in polo clothes. It must have been clipped from some Northern paper.

"Do you wish to wash your hands?" Paula suggested, indicating the half-open door to a well-supplied and fragrant-smelling bathroom. He merely shook his head and peered inside briefly.

"Now that you have inspected my domain," Paula said carelessly, "shall we have coffee?"

"Lord, no. Something cool and light."

"Tea?"

"We-ell."

"Beer?"

"Splendid!"

He followed his thinly-garbed hostess out into a little kitchen where they found a very fat Negress was putting the finishing touches on a costume. She was obviously preparing to depart. In pleasingly pure Portuguese, Paula instructed her servant to amuse herself well and added that she need not return until the next morning.

North, meanwhile, was relaxing his vigilance not a whit. He was at a loss to understand Paula's apparently genuine lack of concern.

From a refrigerator she produced a plate of hors d'oeuvres and sandwiches, also a platter of little cakes.

"When I planned for tea," she said in reply to his surprised look, "I included the trimmings. Do you mind?"

"No. I'm always hungry in the afternoon."

His eye wandered to the doors of several closets.

"So you wish also to see how I hide my skeletons?" Paula demanded a little coolly. "By all means, look."

To look would have been to annoy her—and that was the last thing he desired. "No, thanks. Everything will be at sixes and sevens—if your closets are anything like mine."

"They are perfectly orderly, thank you," she said, tilting her nose at him. "I've just straightened them out."

It seemed very pleasant in the cool living room. Its Venetian blinds had been drawn to admit enough light for North to see and to admire Paula's costume and the figure it fitted with such pleasing fidelity.

Paula Harte poured beer and passed it over to him, asked with a small affectionate smile, "Before we—er—get down to cases, why don't you take off that jacket?"

"What about callers?"

"No one will disturb us," she said equably. Her eyes veiled themselves. "Please believe me."

"What makes you so very certain?" he demanded, slipping off the chef's heavily starched coat. "Unless my deductions are absolutely haywire, I figure quite a few people should be extremely interested in finding you."

Paula sipped her beer, gave Virginio Gayda a cookie and seated herself on the arm of the settee. From that point of vantage she considered her companion, comfortable now in his shirt sleeves.

"You are quite right. I should be in danger. Several persons would like to do me harm if they cannot have their way. So—" she smiled a little— "I keep all their hopes up. 'If you bother me,' I say, 'I will tell my other friends and I have taken such steps so you will not even get anything.' This I have explained to those people you are worried about. Long before they know what my decision will be, I shall be out of reach."

While North finished his beer, raucous noises, engendered by the carnival, increased in direct proportion to the sinking of the sun. How curious to reflect that in all this long day he had seen not a single instance of ill-temper. It must be much as Nabuco had said, Cariocans were sometimes quick, but almost never bad-tempered.

Wandering over to a refectory table in search of a sandwich, he noted that, with the advent of carnival, the maid had neglected her dusting. A ray of sunlight, entering at an oblique angle, showed a layer of unflattering thickness. It also revealed something which interested North far more. He took a mental photograph of a pattern which he would later draw as

A great light broke over him but his lean features remained impassive.

Pleasant as this moment was, time was escaping, flowing relentlessly away. North lit a cigarette.

"You are an amazing girl, Paula," he remarked, "and I prefer amazing girls on a sofa."

"If only you had kept on the hussar uniform!" she complained. "It was so swagger, so very seductive. Since twelve I have had a passion for well-set-up cavalrymen. Nevertheless—"

She gave him a surprised smile and almost came running over while Virginio Gayda, in a fit of jealousy, retired to hunt fleas. As for the *curupião*, it swaggered about the floor with an evil look in its bright black eye.

It was a pity to shatter the iridescence of the moment, but there was no help for it.

"How did you know where to look for Miss Morrow?"

"By simple reasoning, my dear Major," Paula said, settling at his side. "I reasoned that that spoiled brat would go to an obvious place. One of these was the residence of her friend, that brainless Virginia Carpenter." She slipped her fingers inside his, curled them happily. "Once I located her retreat, the rest was ridiculously easy."

Said North in genuine admiration, "Brains like those could earn a fortune in espionage."

"That, my darling, I intend to do," came the almost demure reply. "Some more beer?"

"Not yet." North sighed. "That was a good act, too, you put on at João da Evaristo's."

Paula gave a small-girl wriggle and swung up small white satin sandals beside her. "When I found you in the library was a most frightening moment. Yes. I was in terror you would have me arrested. I felt certain you guessed I had—er—taken charge of certain valuables."

A dull red wave climbed to the ridge of North's cheek-bones. "How could I know what you'd been up to? Dom João had his brother's ring and I didn't yet know what was in it."

"That is true, darling," Paula murmured, raising her eyes. "No one could have guessed."

"Thank you, my dear. And now—"

"I imagine, *muy amigo mio,* you wish to know what was in Dom Luis' safe?"

"There are many things that interest me less," he admitted and began tickling the back of her neck.

"Um-m." She stretched and bent forward. "That is a delight. Tell me, Hugh, do you know how to scratch a back?"

"As a back-scratcher, I have no rivals," he assured her. "But to return to our muttons, as the French say. I am very worried about my mission. Will you tell me what you found in that safe?"

"What I put into it three days ago, praise God!" Paula straightened on the sofa and enumerated on fingers tipped with vermilion. "First, certain most confidential correspondence between Dom Luis, Dr. Rupp and the Estrella del Mar Company. Second, certain contracts arranged by Dom Luis for José Pujol. Third, copies of leases negotiated by Dom Luis for Baron Setsukada—"

"What kind of leases?"

"For certain coffee lands. I do not understand the need for secrecy in that instance."

North did, but only said, "Please go on."

"Third, there were lists of newspapers and persons interested in the Patriotista movement. Fourth, a list of shipments by the Americus Company." She looked him in the eye. "And last, plans for movements and actions to be carried out on a day simply designated as 'C 3.' These, by the way, only came in before the last time I opened the safe."

With her left hand she began scratching the monkey's head.

North drew so deep a breath it inflated his chest like a bellows. So? If she were speaking truth, Paula Harte had in her possession the proof, the ultimate proof to expose, to smash the Patriotistas.

"I understand," said he slowly.

"Understand what?"

"Why you are so confident. You have simply warned the Estrella del Mar group that if anything happened to you, Luis da Evaristo's documents would be turned over to the police. Is that it?"

"Yes, darling, the Estrella del Mar people—and one other of whom I stand in more danger," she said. Kissing him on the chin, she left a tiny red mark. "Am I not a clever one?"

"So much so that I am becoming afraid of you."

"Oh, no." Her levity vanished. "Whatever happens, Hugh, from me you have nothing to fear. On the contrary, I want for you nothing but success, but happiness."

Paula turned her head, studied the sun-lashed terrace.

"I wish to negotiate a—well, an arrangement with you. I am afraid to you it will sound outrageous?" She paused. "But—"

Hugh North tried to clarify the indefiniteness of her expression. "Suppose you don't handicap yourself in advance? I may not be so shocked as you anticipate. After all, one has seen a little of life."

"I fear only that I am going to insist upon my plan." She turned, took one of his hands in both of hers. "You see, Hugh, I want *you*. So far, what I have wanted from life I have taken."

"Isn't that a dangerous boast?"

"Of course; I know it very well." She was speaking rapidly now. "These, dearest, are the terms on which I will release the documents from the safe of Dom Luis."

He got up, poured himself a new glass of beer, faced her and said, "Paula, my dear, long ago you impressed me as one of those rare women who know exactly what they want. Now I am sure of it."

One foot slowly a-swing, Paula briefly enjoyed the power she held over this man.

"It seems low to play on a sense of patriotism, Hugh, but it is only in that way I stand any chance of persuading you."

"To what?"

"To grant me an opportunity of demonstrating what a really superlative Mrs. North I could make."

Hugh North's response was a quick, almost boyish grin. "I've never understood why men are supposed to do all the proposing. You underestimate your appeal, Paula."

"You are very sweet," Paula said, then added, her face brushed by desperate knowledge, "but your type doesn't marry until they—they have to. I know men. Maybe that is just what is wrong with me?"

"Please go on."

"Very well," she said in flat, business-like accents. "You know I can get no less than a quarter million from at least two sources. But I don't want that—even though somebody would be very very angry."

North entertained a shrewd suspicion as to who that somebody was, but said nothing.

"From you I will ask but ten thousand dollars and that only because I really need the money." Paula seemed to be selecting her words with care. "Your government can give it to me—or perhaps you can?"

North laughed. "What do you think an Intelligence officer is paid?"

"Well then, it will have to be from your government."

"That is most generous, Paula." He remained wary. "It shall be paid to you tonight."

She rose, came over and took his face between her hands. "Oh, Hugh, don't you realize that's only part of the price?"

"I do, my dear. What else?"

"You and I will go on a voyage—a trip lasting not less than three months. If at the end you do not care to marry me, that will be my loss."

It was all ridiculously simple and, after all he had expected! "Then you don't expect me to marry you straight off?"

She nodded her lustrous pale head as if to herself. "If I did that you would hate and despise me. It would be rather like shooting a bird sitting, wouldn't it?"

"You do understand men," he declared, with real admiration. "You do understand the importance of sportsmanship."

"Thank you."

"But what about Captain Maitland? You must know he is desperately in love with you."

"I suppose so. But I have never promised him—anything. As I said before, Stu-art is too self-righteous, too narrow, too ignorant of women. Therefore, *je m'en fiche!* After all, emotionally he is just a child in—"

North flung himself clear of Paula as the hall closet's door swung violently open. Stuart Maitland parted a pair of raincoats and emerged, perspiring heavily. Still in the white dinner coat he had worn to the German Yacht Club, he was haggard, his eyes red, and a day's beard cast a dark shadow over features that twitched. It was unmistakable that he had stood in that closet a very long time.

A dreadful, stricken look in his eyes, Maitland stumbled out into the middle of the living room and, swaying a little, faced Paula with a look of tragic bewilderment.

"You'd really rather be his—his mistress than my wife?" he

choked, his hands clenching and unclenching themselves at his sides.

"Yes." She dropped her eyes, said, "But I am most sorry, Stu-art, that you learned it in this fashion."

A silence descended in the shadowy, fragrant-smelling living room. Only Maitland's heavy breathing made any sound. Slowly, his bloodshot eyes traveled to North standing quiet, but poised for action, beyond the settee. It was surprising how nearly similar the two men were in their physical proportions, how different otherwise.

Maitland started to speak again but instead his jaw closed with a little *click!* He gathered himself to rigid attention, head up and shoulders flat and stood so a long instant, then executing a precise left face, he marched, not walked, to the door, opened it and disappeared. On the tiles outside his footsteps rang three, four times.

Paula had turned to look at North in silent apology when the darkened hallway resounded to the reverberating crash of a pistol shot.

"With My Compliments, Major"

"*DIOS! Que horror!*" Paula Harte's eyes had grown simply enormous. "Who could have imagined he would—"

"Stay here," North snapped as his ear caught a faint pattering noise. There were regular, yet disproportionate, impacts on the tiles outside. Taking care to shield himself with the door, he peered out into the corridor.

He could make out Maitland's white-clad figure sprawled, face down, on the red tiles. The fingers of one hand were curling and uncurling and already a shiny area was creeping away from the stricken attaché. Reassured that the passageway was indeed empty, North drew close, aware that subdued activity was taking place in Paula's apartment.

"Call an ambulance," he directed succinctly. "Tell it to hurry."

Pale as a berg, Paula appeared. "Thank God he is not dead."

That Maitland was critically hurt North could tell with half a glance. A wound through his chest was bleeding with terrifying rapidity when the Intelligence officer half lifted, half dragged Maitland out of the corridor where, surprisingly, no one had appeared. Doubtless, other residents were remarking that some reveler must have touched off an extra large firecracker. Nor was there a sign of weapon—not even an expended cartridge case.

"Sorry—sir." Stuart Maitland's lips moved in his ghastly yellow-white face. "You—right."

"Don't talk," North ordered, ripping open the dreadfully sodden shirt.

In the background, Paula could be heard telephoning, demanding a hospital.

Maitland's eyes rolled slowly upwards. "Couldn' believe— you said—'bout Paula. Had to know—"

Aware that Maitland felt he must justify his conduct, North asked, "Who shot you?"

Maitland tried to raise his head. "Don' know. Hear voice say, 'With my—compliments, Major.'"

North worked with expert haste, bound a compress, improvised out of his own handkerchief and the wounded man's belt, as tight as possible. For all that, copious rivulets still escaped down the wounded man's side.

"Made silly fool—of 'self. Must have been crazy." Maitland whispered though his eyelids sagged steadily lower. "Meant find out—she knew—"

"You did right," North soothed. "Take it easy, old man."

"Don't trust—Paula. Sell—you out, too."

The wounded officer's eyes closed.

"Maitland?" North asked sharply. "What language did your assailant talk?"

Stuart Maitland made a futile effort to rally, but lapsed into unconsciousness. Rather tight about the mouth, Hugh North straightened, sought the bathroom and washed quantities of dark venous blood from his hands. Paula paused in the hall.

"Poor Stu-art. How childish to have done such a thing!"

"He didn't," North said. "Somebody was in the hall."

"But he *must* have."

"He didn't try suicide. Somebody shot him."

"*Somebody shot him?*" All in a flash Paula's self-possession deserted her and she swayed as if slapped by an invisible hand.

Brushing by her, North gathered up his chef's coat and began to button its plastron while Paula, very white, crossed to the sideboard and took a long gulp of straight Scotch.

"I don't—I can't understand this."

"Can't you?" He was terse as a prescription. "No one wanted to kill Maitland. It was *me* the killer was after."

"You? Oh no! *No!*" she panted. "How could—"

"The gunman made a natural mistake. He saw only one of us go in. The corridor was dark. Maitland and I are of about the same build and are both in white."

"That cowardly dog!" Paula put down her drink when, not very far away, sounded the wail of a siren. She rallied. "You must go at once—but first, where can I reach you?"

"Name of West, Hotel Avenida," said he, tying on his apron and thinking sixty to the minute.

"Hugh," said she with extraordinary calm. She looked at him with an expression that denied analysis, an expression which puzzled and baffled him. In her eyes shone fear and tenderness, but no greed. "I have changed my mind. I shall want the quarter million after all."

"I will do my best to get it," he told her, then turned, drew his automatic and ran like the very devil down the service stairs.

After some search, the Intelligence officer located a cab driver sober enough to find the Hotel Avenida. Now that the sun had set, the real splendor of the carnival began to manifest itself in great clusters and festoons of colored bulbs, spotlights, banks on banks of Chinese lanterns and fireworks.

Shouting children in weird false faces yelled shrilly and swung sparklers in ecstatic circles. Idiotic, exotic, hideous, stupid and pretty faces kept swinging past the windows of the cab. This assignment was crazier than existing for days in the heart of a Democratic National Convention.

Um. It was now going on seven o'clock and now the tempo of events was accelerating like the puffing of a locomotive taking speed. He hoped very much Maitland would pull through, but recollections of the Attaché's pallor and feeble pulse left little room for confidence.

Um-m. The more he thought about that dust pattern and that irregular pattering noise heard in the hallway, the more sure he became that he knew who had lain in wait for him. Ironic, that Maitland should have been so indispensably useful after all.

Once back at the Hotel Avenida, North immediately put through a call to the Naval Intelligence Bureau. Lieutenant Nabuco was not in, an assistant informed him. No, he had no ideas as to where Lieutenant Nabuco might be found.

"Damn," North murmured. "Now isn't that convenient?"

The man on the other end of the phone had some information for the estimable Major North. Lieutenant Nabuco had left word that the fingerprints on the eyeglass corresponded exactly with the missing set on the cake of soap.

Upon receipt of this intelligence, North seated himself, uttered a long low whistle. It only went to prove what he had come to suspect. Swiftly, hitherto obscure lines of reasoning opened up and Paula Harte's amazing *volte face* became explicable.

Where the devil could Nabuco be? No doubt supervising the forging of that all-important letter intended to break Ernestine Berthier's heart—and to unlock her lips.

It seemed truly a despicable thing further to torture that unhappy soul and yet—and yet—in her head undoubtedly lay the means of thwarting a political hurricane gathering to disrupt the peace and security of a great, happy and inoffensive nation.

Before replacing the receiver North asked that one Captain John McCabe be located. Yes. He was to be kept under surveillance until further orders.

The sight of Aurora's nightgown hanging in the half-opened closet set him to wondering how she was faring with her guest at the Gávea Golf Club.

What an extraordinary mixture. Probably Aurora had a foolish, spendthrift, un-moral mother to thank for her lack of manners and warped point of view. Morrow, *père,* probably had had to work so hard to foot the bills he'd very likely seen but little of his child. Too many American families were like that—in the great cities particularly.

Well, she was shaping up unexpectedly. Her brazen playing of that hunch about assigning Almeira to watch Paula had smoothed his path not a little.

From the small rank on the bureau he selected a bottle of rye, poured a stiff drink. Next, he thrust his head under the shower, rubbed the back of his neck vigorously as was his custom when he needed to think quickly.

"God, but I'm tired," he muttered. "Side's hurting too."

Selecting a sheet of paper from the desk, he set about reviewing the matter of the Bolivar messages. The first message which had been stolen from Hugo Becker, shipping manager for the Companhia Americus and Axis agent, by Paula Harte.

That message had been solved by correctly reading a cross-word puzzle in *A Sentinella*. This had warned that the mission would arrive some time on Tuesday—day after tomorrow.

The two radio messages identified as Bolivar 2 and 3 had been picked up the day before. Um-m. Mlle. Berthier, there-fore, must have received key words to be included several days ago, if the corresponding puzzles were to appear on Tues-day. Allowing for distribution delays, the number sequences of the final instructions for the impending putsch were likely being distributed at this very moment. So if la Berthier were brought into camp the instructions might be very interest-ingly revised.

Where the dickens had Nabuco betaken himself? Too bad there had been no opportunity to keep the appointment with Herr Koerner from Recife. A conversation with that amiable Fifth Columnist would have been fun, and very likely instruc-tive, as well. Alas that a day consisted of so many inelastic minutes!

Presently the phone buzzed. A courier from the United States Embassy was below. He appeared, tendered a note and disappeared without comment.

The communication was terse:

> Dear Major,
> We very much regret we can promise not more than one hundred thousand. Have exhausted every possi-bility.
>
> > Yours in haste,
> > Edward Prescott.

North turned towards his drink and to it revealed his true sentiments. What a fine time to let a man down! He felt that sickening sense of revolt a person feels when some idiotic practical joker jerks a chair from under him. What in the great, good God's name possessed those spendthrifts in Washington?

In a twinkle they'd appropriate a couple of millions to throw a useless dam across Little Turtle Creek, or earmark five million to put deserving drum majorettes through ballet school; but when it came to saving the country from a hideously costly disaster, they niggled and cheese-pared. The weekly fuel bill for a single squadron of cruisers would amount to more than the sum Prescott had been able to secure.

As never before, a poignant discouragement, a mordant hopelessness ate like acid into his soul. Why should an overworked handful of trained United States Army Intelligence officers risk their lives, wreck their nervous systems if they were to get but grudging, wholly inadequate support from those very bureaucrats whose lives were at stake?

In the end he tossed off his drink and, as so often before, remembered those others who had not quit because the going was hard.

He was recalled to practicalities by the clicking of a key in the lock. Because he had thrown a supplementary bolt, it did not open.

The Praça Paris

"HI! This Hugh's place?" called Aurora's voice.

"Yep. What's the high-sign?"

"Okay, Watchdog. You can open up. Gino's dropped by for a quickie."

When, cautiously, he opened the door, he saw Aurora, still in her Bahiana costume, and in company with Count Altrocchi. The Italian, suitably enough, had adopted the costume of a Roman centurion but the bright green horsehair crest of his helmet was at ridiculous odds with his eyeglass.

That neither of the arrivals was in a hilarious mood North realized immediately. Soft-footed as a cat among glassware, Aurora Morrow secured the door and turning said, "Hugh, I've brought Gino because he wants to talk."

"Not till he's had a martini."

The Italian smiled faintly, offered his hand. His long, thin nose more than ever suggested a greyhound's and under the carnival rouge and grease paint his color was bad.

What was in the air?

"I have had conversation—a most serious one."

North smiled. "Then it's high time to lift the cup that cheers.

There's a bottle of champagne sweating its life away in a bucket. What say?"

Aurora shook her well-modeled patrician head. She had at last got rid of her fruit basket turban. "There isn't time for fooling, Hugh."

The Italian uttered a rasping little laugh, pulled off his helmet and mechanically smoothed the scant hair lying limp on his high, sloping forehead. "Is anything more important than good champagne, *Carissima?* Shall I?"

As he worked at the wire cage securing the cork, Count Altrocchi commenced to speak, hurriedly, as if he might change his mind or lose the thread of his discourse. North kept his eyes on the Italian's powerful hands but listened with all his might.

"During even so short an acquaintanceship as ours, Major, one perceives that you are a man of deep sensibility. Yes. Therefore, I am confident you will understand what lies back of what I am about to do."

The Italian commenced to pace up and down so rapidly that his green-and-yellow-lined centurion's cloak billowed out behind.

"For a long time every clear-sighted Italian has recognized that Italy already is a hopelessly defeated nation. Yes. No matter who wins. If it should be England—and she will win—or those unspeakable barbarians from Berlin."

Count Altrocchi swallowed hard and stood still, his chin outthrust a little. He was perspiring quite heavily and his fingers clenched and unclenched—rather like poor Maitland's. Aurora sat motionless.

"In brief, Major, it required only Aurora's urging to seal a decision which is most difficult to make—one that will be much misunderstood. Yes. It is all logical, truly patriotic, what

I contemplate. Yes. I have come here because I believe that my country will be more generously treated by a victorious England than by those Prussian liars and sadists."

He stood straighter, mechanically readjusted his eyeglass. "We are an ancient and proud people, Major." Altrocchi had never appeared to better advantage. "We cannot longer endure the insults, the contemptuous arrogance, the greed of our allies."

When Altrocchi accepted the glass North handed him, his fingers quivered.

"We must have been mad that spring of 1940. At heart all Italy hates, despises the Nazis, their incredible poisoning of the truth, their ruthless killings, their godlessness, their distorted thinking and, above all, their arrogance."

Hugh North, attempting to evaluate this declaration, found it difficult to decide whether Altrocchi was in earnest or not. Inept Axis agents had been weeded out long, long ago. Still, from the very inception of the war, he had pondered the success of an alliance between a tolerant, carefree and life-loving people and a sadistic, masochistic and humorless race.

"You are a far-sighted man," North murmured as Aurora held out her glass. "Some day I hope you will be blessed for that."

"Gino tells me that Hermann the German has been acting more Boche than ever, lately." A vivid picture in her gay, full-skirted costume, Aurora raised her glass. "Well, here's sand in the gears of Rupp, Pujol and Company!"

As they all drank solemnly, it occurred to the Intelligence officer that time was fleeting. Cautiously, he conveyed that fact to Altrocchi.

"I must be careful," Altrocchi announced, his tin breastplate making a brave show. "Rupp's men watch me. *Cospetto!* They shall have reason." He again removed his eyeglass and began nervously to polish it. "Already orders are out calling for concentrations at the *Stützpunkt*. You will have to act quickly."

A breeze honed on glaciers seemed to blow through Hugh North's being. There it was! Concentrations. Tomorrow, in the controlled press, would come a terrific blast of anti-democratic lies. Traitors at work. Lying rumors spread to widen like rings on a still pool. Communications paralyzed by saboteurs.

Altrocchi picked up his helmet. "You must come at once with me. Yes. Mlle. Berthier will be at work."

"A moment, please." North hated the thought of venturing into the bedlam raging outside. "Will you answer a few questions before we go out? I feel it's most important."

Count Altrocchi supplied a key to his nature.

"No, Major. If I am to help you, I must do it in my own fashion. Yes. Believe me. I know all there is about this business and I say we must reach Mlle. Berthier *at once!*"

North hesitated. It seemed decidedly dangerous to risk another visit to the Berthier woman's apartment. Especially since by now she must have received the counterfeit message.

"Let us make sure she is at home. Do you know her telephone number?"

"*Si.*"

"Then call Mlle. Berthier, please. Ask her to meet us at some safe place and," North's voice deepened, "tell her to be sure to fetch the lists of words she was to introduce into those puzzles."

"Lists of words!" Count Altrocchi caught his breath with a sharp click. "*Dio!* For a long time I have heard of your cleverness, Major, but already to have solved the secret of these Bolivar messages is—amazing."

"Thanks," North said shortly.

"My compliments, Major." Altrocchi's horsehair plume swayed to his bow. "For once I believe that our friend, Rupp, has underestimated an opponent."

When the other added, "Where shall we meet?" North felt a little surer of the situation.

"Instruct her," he directed, "to wait on the corner of—" He flung a questioning glance at Aurora.

"—Of the Praça Paris and the Rua Teixera de Freitas. And Gino, you might tell her we will be in a light gray sedan with number plate 2217-AZ."

The folds of his military mantle swaying, Altrocchi sought the telephone, gave the number. Presently he said, "Mlle. Berthier? This is Signor di Bono, B87F."

In machine-gun rapid French, he gave his instructions, then listened, hand held over the mouthpiece. Presently he spoke in an anxious undertone.

"She is most fearful about Rupp. Besides, she says she has suffered a great family sorrow." He shrugged under the bright brass clasps securing his cloak. "She seems incapable of doing any work."

"She need do none," North said in a sudden, most effective tone; but no one could have guessed what a colossal gamble he was about to risk. "Tell her the letter she got today was very likely a forgery." He saw Altrocchi's pale eyes widen momentarily over that. "*Make* her bring that material to the Praça Paris."

During the harsh conversation which followed, Aurora looked very thoughtful. To North she murmured, "How *can* he threaten the poor thing so?"

"Practice makes perfect, my dear."

"So they say, Watchdog, so they say. But this isn't quite so jolly, is it? Queer, I'd always imagined Intelligence work as being kind of exciting, romantic and fun."

"It isn't. It's a sordid, brutal game with no more chivalry to it than a lumberman's gouging match."

"Hugh, when was it you last slept for a whole night?"

He smiled. "Two, nearly three weeks ago."

"No wonder you're beginning to look as though you had been pulled through a knothole."

Hugh North felt as happy as a fish being taken off a hook so, under pretense of refilling a glass, he muttered, "What about all this?"

"I'd bet my shirt on it Gino's on the level," she declared earnestly.

He smiled, looked at her bare midriff. "Shirt?"

"Well, dear, hypothetically speaking."

Though deep within North's being stirred a persistent feeling of unrest, there seemed no choice but to attempt this coup.

If heretofore the carnival had been noisy and colorful, nothing short of incessant, raucous pandemonium now reigned on the Avenida Rio Branco. Huge floats mounted on trucks and illuminated by hundreds of electric lights were rolling slowly toward the Avenida Beira Mar. All four sidewalks were overflowing with a mad, kaleidoscopic mingling of costumes. Overhead, huge searchlights played back and forth. Countless dozens of hot-air balloons were climbing into the sky to hang there like weird green, red and blue astral bodies.

On the sidewalk Altrocchi paused, viewed the scene and laughed. "How happy they all are. No pretending—simply gay out of the heart." He sighed. "This is as Venice once was, and Florence and Milano and Cannes and Santa Margherita and Rapallo. Long, long ago, before we Italians allowed Il Duce to hypnotize us into delusions of grandeur."

The Italian spoke quietly, his long features set in serious lines.

"Yes, I believe seriousness and sorrow already have dulled too many peoples." He glanced at Aurora's lithe figure getting into the coupé. "Aurora is quite right. To rob the world of a sight like this would be a tragedy."

Hugh North dodged a jet of etherized perfume from some reveler's *lança,* piled in beside Aurora Morrow. He was ruminating on Altrocchi's last words. These, as nothing he had said before, lent a sense of reassurance. Altrocchi really had no business, either temperamentally or practically, in the same league with Dr. Rupp and Baron Setsukada.

Um. Ito Setsukada should be a subject for well-considered reflections. From past experience, North knew his old friend to be immensely proud of his nation and its achievements. On the other hand, Setsukada was much too well informed to entertain any illusions as to the true might of America. Far better than most of his countrymen, the Baron was familiar with the excellent morale, the vastly superior aircraft and the superlatively equipped ships of the United States Navy.

Strange, strange, that this Japanese would go so far, do things not countenanced in the Bushido, all to plunge his people into a war which he must know to be hopeless. Why?

Altrocchi sat gazing unhappily at the gyrations of celebrants dancing the *coração*.

"Yes. The Berthier woman will do as I say," said he as if to himself. "After all, it was I who discovered poor Ernestine starving so quietly to death."

North began to feel still better. Such hatred as rang in Altrocchi's voice could not have been counterfeited. What utter idiots the British had been not to have driven a wedge of some sort between the unnatural partners of Rome and Berlin.

In low gear, Aurora nosed her car through the packed humanity on the Avenida Presidente Wilson, through denser crowds surging around the Praça Deodoro. At the entrance to the Rua Teixera de Freitas, the coupé was finally halted by a solid barrier of revelers watching the expert clowning of some carnival club. North found it disturbing thus to be hemmed in on all sides, to be half blinded by handfuls of confetti, whirling sparklers and mists of *lança-perfume*. One couldn't hear a thing over the braying horns and booming drums. Colored spotlights transfixing the paper particles caused them to glow briefly, like handfuls of gems thrown into the air.

A flash of green shone in the window, another was in front of the coupé.

"Look out!" North warned Altrocchi. The Italian half opened the door of the car but shrank back as a square-shouldered figure in a green lancer uniform squirted a jet of acrid-smelling tear gas into the car. Another jet shot in through the window on Aurora's side.

"Help! Hugh!" Aurora choked. "It's—it's—"

North's eyes stung as, futilely, he grabbed his gun. No good. He was effectively blinded. A fresh smell drenched the car and when he tried to open a door, he couldn't. Outside the din was so terrific his frantic yells went unheeded.

Briefly he heard Aurora screaming, then, strangely, it faded and he began to cough great, racking coughs which left him dizzy and weak. Everything became confused, blurred; the crazy blaring of the horns, the banging of drums finally died into silence.

Fazenda Number Nine

THAT daylight was beating against his eyelids was Major North's first realization; that someone was bathing his face was his second.

"Pleasant, very pleasant," he sighed. It seemed a terrific effort to rouse from this delightful oblivion.

"Well, Watchdog, it's about time! Thought you were running on Ephesian Standard Time."

An unmistakable pressure of lips followed. They were very warm and tender.

"Dear Hugh." Very gently his head was shifted from a lap onto a harder substance. Then he felt lips on his again. "I've never been one to neglect opportunities," a voice observed tenderly. "Oh, but it's nice to have had you helpless for a while. You're so—so damn' capable the rest of the time."

He managed to open his eyes though their lids were red and swollen. Aurora Morrow was bending over him and, because the paint was gone from her face, it seemed finer, gentler in line.

"Hello, Infant. Fancy meeting you here." He struggled up on one elbow. "By the way, just where is 'here'?"

Aurora shook a head that would have looked prettier for the application of a brush and comb. "Take a guess, any guess up to a hundred."

"Oh—"

"Here, have some of this coffee. It did wonders for me."

"Thanks," he mumbled once he had swallowed a very large cup of black coffee. "Some gal. You came to first."

"Only because you were all in, dear," came the quiet response. "Your system was hollering for rest. Good thing you've had it. You—we are going to need all that famous resourcefulness of yours."

"Eh?"

"Look at that window and you'll see why."

Heavy bars interrupted a vista of fantastically tangled vines and treetops. Though his head spun and nausea assailed him, the Intelligence officer sat up and saw that he and his companion were occupying a small room, barely furnished, with walls of corrugated sheet-iron.

He had been lying on a crude cot fashioned of canvas, wood and wrought-iron pipe. There was a grass rug on the floor and a table and chair of such extremely light construction that they would stand no heavy stress. The floor was painted and showed that, at no distant time, a desk, bookcases and filing cabinets had been in use here. There were even pegs from which maps might have hung.

Dividing the structure in half was a solid, ugly wall of cinder block.

A steady dull *chunking* noise piqued North's curiosity, that and the staccato barking of several tractor exhausts. Though decidedly weak in the legs, he made his way to the window and, clinging to the bars, peered out. His interest was immediately sharpened. Some six feet from the window ran a high barbed wire fence with baffles at its summit; regular prison-camp type.

A crushing sense of defeat flooded his being.

"Poor Watchdog." Cool fingers slipped into his. "You've made a grand try in a hopeless game."

"I shouldn't have trusted Altrocchi."

"I'm not sure you were wrong," was Aurora's curious statement. "Better eat something—there's a tray in my room."

He shook his head, stared out over row on row of young coffee trees which obscured all view beyond the barbed wire. He could hear the rhythmic pacing of a pair of sentries over that inexplicable crackling, snapping sound in the near distance.

"Has anyone been here?" he asked, turning heavily away.

"No, only a soldier who brought breakfast."

"Soldier?"

Aurora ducked a head no longer so sleek and well arranged. Her eyes were a little red and she needed powder on her nose. "Yes. And he's a Jap. Believe it or not!"

"A Japanese!" North choked. So it was his old tennis partner he had to thank for wrecking a career he'd been nearly twenty years in building.

"The soldier boy also left a copy of *A Sentinella,* which is just ducky because my Portuguese is more full of holes than a Swiss cheese."

"Where is it?"

"In my room," the girl jerked her head towards a stout door to her left. "It's my guess, Hugh, that we've been locked up in what used to be some overseer's quarters but all the windows are barred and you can't get a knife through these sheet-iron walls." She laughed a trifle stridently. "It's all very cozy, dear; we've two nice little bedrooms and a johnny between."

The gay costume skirt a-sway, she disappeared briefly. When she reappeared it was with a tray between her hands and a determined set to her lips.

"Breakfast for my Lord Twindaddle. And you've got to eat it!"

North forced himself to swallow more coffee, then fruit and bread and butter.

"You're right," he sighed. "I do feel better."

His long sleep—he suspected he must have slipped from unnatural to natural slumber without awaking—had left him with renewed energy.

"And so, what next?"

He almost laughed at the vision of himself in a soiled chef's uniform crouched on a cot with America's Number One ex-glamour girl; she wearing a gaudy Brazilian peasant's costume.

A short, bandy-legged sentry in a gray-green uniform walked up to the window. Flat, yellow-brown features peered in. The apparition was unmistakably Japanese and wore a heavily loaded cartridge belt that also supported a brace of potato-masher-type hand grenades. To his bright yellow shoulder straps was affixed the soaring condor-and-lightning device of Pujol's Patriotistas, neatly executed in glistening brass.

The sound of chopping and the machine-gun-like reports of the tractor exhausts had grown so much louder that North sought the window. Aurora joined him.

"Well, I'll be—!"

At first he thought he was in the grip of delirium for, even as he looked, a whole rank of young coffee trees swayed, metal flashed and a swarm of workers busily cutting off trees very close to the earth came into view. The rank next nearest the improvised prison wavered, shivered and fell. Axes, hatchets and scythes glittered for acres and acres.

North was too fascinated to reply, for now that the nearest trees were falling, a wide and very interesting vista suddenly disclosed itself.

Aurora asked, "But why should they ruin all those young coffee trees? They must be worth a fortune."

At the moment North could find no explanation for these queer activities but noticed that a large number of these workers in printed cotton shirts were chunkily built Japanese of the peasant type. Others looked to be of the bourgeois and small businessman class.

About two hundred yards away a series of long low warehouses had now become visible. Also a concrete road, watertower and garage.

One gang of workmen was busy at the door of a warehouse and even as he looked, a whole section of wall was detached and carried away; then another and another. The warehouse quickly became metamorphosed into a very capacious hangar. Another gang, with the aid of scoops and tractors, was removing a thin layer of soil from what looked like a wide apron of concrete. Other laborers were affixing searchlights to the top of what once had been an innocent-appearing tractor shed. As for that great area on which the young coffee trees had been growing, it now looked flat as any airdrome in America.

"Look well, my dear," he invited bitterly as from the sky came a sound of droning motors. "Not everyone is privileged to eye-witness the birth of a *Stützpunkt*."

A monoplane of military design skimmed low over the field and, squarely in front of the ex-warehouse, dropped a message cylinder equipped with bright yellow streamers.

"Oh, Hugh, it's simply incredible!"

Try as he would, North could not speak—there was nothing to say. If he could only get away. But he wasn't going to. Not if Baron Ito Setsukada hadn't slipped a long way from his old efficiency.

Now that his eyes had become accustomed to the blazing tropical sunlight, North could distinguish within the new hangars the wickedly sharp outlines of a quartet of Messerschmitt 110 pursuit ships. Over them mechanics in khaki jumpers swarmed like monkeys.

Tractors appeared, commenced methodically to rake up the fallen coffee trees. Others began harrowing the earth behind them. A pair of heavy steam rollers came chugging into sight as a wind sock was run up to the summit of that water tower which was no water tower at all, it seemed, but a concrete pill box mounting a set of weather gauging instruments.

North said, "Well, you've got to hand it to them again—talk about organization!"

Aurora came over, slipped her arm through his. She looked dazed.

"It's dreadful, Hugh. I can't believe my eyes." She laughed bitterly. "Oh, I read a little now and then about Holland and Belgium, but I didn't care. There was always the Stork, 21 and Piping Rock. What *fools* we Americans are. Isn't there *anything* can be done to stop this?"

North said, "God only knows."

Though the clearing swept away for many acres to the right of the little prison, the hot green jungle rose like a wall immediately beyond a big pale green structure on its opposite side. A fly buzzed in and sailed about. The tractors roared and the steady t-chunk of ax and adz blades being driven home continued.

Feeling as helpless as an oyster on the half-shell, North deserted the window and gloomily caught up the copy of *A Sentinella,* flipped it open. It was for that same day, Monday.

He felt his breath halt in his throat. There was a Bolivar cross-word puzzle—a new one doubtless issuing orders for that stealthy assault taking shape outside.

"Escape! Man, you've simply *got to get away!*" infernal voices roared into North's mental ears. "This has got to be stopped."

Yes, he must get away, but how, *how,* HOW? There was no knife on the breakfast tray and the spoons and forks were fashioned of such very soft metal that they yielded under the least pressure. The floor, scrupulously clean, met the walls flush and was of green painted cement. The windows were barred and glassless, though mercifully equipped with screens.

In each room was a pipe bed and thin little mattresses covered by a single sheet of extremely thin muslin. The bathroom equipment included a crude shower, cast-iron washstand and toilet—all very solidly built in.

"From your expression, I gather they've left us nothing to play with?" Aurora remarked as she sat, elbows on knees, on one of the flimsy camp stools.

"Correct, my dear. And how! Not even Houdini could break out of here."

Absently Aurora scanned the paper North had abandoned.

"I figure this *carcere* is on the outer edge of the fazenda," North announced presently.

"Why?"

"Because they haven't even run the electric lights out here. The water, I suspect, is supplied by gravity, from a tank filled by the eaves."

"If they'd give us a pencil, we could play tic, tac, toe," the girl suggested.

When a bugle sounded at the far end of what undoubtedly was rapidly becoming a perfectly adequate small airport, the workers shouldered their implements, fell into column and marched off the ex-coffee field. Methodically the tractors continued to haul aside great mounds of crushed green branches. Everywhere, on tractors, trucks and autos, the green-star-on-yellow-globe insignia of the Estrella del Mar Company was to be seen.

Moodily the prisoners were still watching preparations at the four ex-warehouses when a very thin Japanese officer with heavy pince-nez and buck teeth led a detail of four men up to the *carcere's* door. In guttural accents he issued commands which caused the door—it was in Aurora's room—to be unlocked.

He clumped in, very spruce in bright brass buttons, well-polished leather gear and uniform of gray-green cotton. His oblique eyes seemed opaque as he gave North a military salute, and when he bowed to Aurora Morrow, a row of campaign ribbons on his tunic breast gleamed.

"Pleas-s, His Excellency, Divisional Commander Baron Setsukada, presents compliments," he announced as if speaking a piece learned by rote. "He requests Honorable Major accord him extreme honor of immediate interview, pleas-s."

"Left at the altar," Aurora sighed. Then she smiled winningly at the wooden-faced intruder. "Please, may I have a pencil?"

The Japanese officer hesitated, then a smile as mechanical as that of Charlie McCarthy flitted across his countenance and was gone.

"Much regretting, honored lady, that un-possible."

"You could tear out paper dolls," North suggested to cover his mounting apprehension. "Be back soon."

Apparently, Aurora was quite ignorant of the implications of this summons, never dreamed that this might very well constitute a final farewell. The Axis had a short way with those whom they found troublesome.

North forced himself to notice this officer's equipment. Though he carried an unmistakable Luger automatic, he nonetheless wore a Samurai sword as Japanese as himself.

The thin-faced officer held out a broad-brimmed straw hat. "Outside it iss hot," he explained. "And now, pleas-s?"

Still buttoning his dirtied chef's jacket, North gave Aurora a jaunty wave of the hand and she blew him a kiss as he stepped out into the blazing sunlight. Ominously, the sheet steel door clanged to and four hard-faced guards with bayonets fixed fell in around him.

When Aurora called through the bars, "My regards to Ito and remind him I'm fresh out of silk stockings," the officer looked inexpressibly shocked.

They marched the prisoner past the rear of the line of new hangars. Here, hundreds of laborers, mechanics and office workers were being issued uniforms and equipment from trucks backed up to a concrete drive. There was no excitement among the Nipponese, just the calm of well-drilled men performing a familiar duty. Parrots and monkeys frolicking along the edge of the jungle made more noise than they.

What appeared to be the new *Stützpunkt's* headquarters lay sheltered amid a dense grove of satinwoods. Not by accident was it painted green.

Hundreds of eyes examined the tall, wiry prisoner as he passed, and so many were charged with hatred that North felt increasingly sure he would not return from this march. The simple fact that the Japanese officer *followed* his four subordinates, all of whom were very evidently on the *qui vive,* served as a very grim omen.

The air-conditioned apartment into which North's escort marched him was on the second floor of the green-painted building. At first he stared in surprise because this room's furnishings appeared to have been transported *en masse* from some Nipponese home. Delicately tinted gray-blue walls were hung at correct intervals with a number of excellent *kakomonos*. Featured above a comfortable settee was a restfully somber sketch of night herons rendered in pastel by Setsubara.

An exquisite cloisonné vase supported a group of flaming blossoms skillfully arranged in front of a black lacquered letter box. Rugs, upholsteries and window hangings blended to create a restful atmosphere. The only inharmonious note in the *décor* was introduced by a row of prize cups, plaques, and trophies.

"Seat yourself, pleas-s." The officer waved North to an armchair, removed his kepi and laid the sword across his lap. Hand on holstered revolver, the guard officer sat bolt upright; his bright black eyes remained fixed, uncommunicative until a door swung open briefly revealing two sentries on duty in the hallway.

Baron Setsukada stalked in, very straight in a simple uniform of badly bleached khaki. Diamonds set into a Star of the Order of the Chrysanthemum twinkled bravely on Setsukada's left breast. He, too, wore the condor-and-lightning ornaments on a collar from which other insignia recently had been removed.

"Thank you, Captain Otuma. You may go."

The officer arose, bowed profoundly and backed from the room. Once the door lock had clicked Baron Setsukada hesitated, then offered his hand. The Intelligence officer accepted it coldly.

"I am so sorry."

"Sorry?" North smiled. "Haven't you chaps been working for this day a long, long time?"

Setsukada seated himself, fumbled in his breast pocket and brought out the same pigskin cigar case he had used at the German Yacht Club. "Please do not mock me, Hugh. One may plan *seppuku*—honorable suicide—for many years. This is the most unhappy day of my life."

North thought hard, permitted himself to appear surprised. "But why? You and your collaborators have successfully done your groundwork—the usual bribes have been paid, the usual newspapers have been bought, the usual lies about the democracies have been spread."

The big Japanese fixed his eyes upon a dwarfed pine decorating a wide desk. "Yes, certainly we shall win here in Brazil—but for whom? I do not think it is for Dai Nippon. That, my friend—if I may continue to call you one—is the doubt which makes this the unhappiest day of my life."

In his armchair the Intelligence officer relaxed. It seemed utterly bizarre that two men who had twice won the doubles championship of Virginia should be conversing thus, and in these roles. In his mind's eye he could but too readily remember Setsukada, always well liked, always the good sport, posing for the photographers with himself; Setsukada sailing in a regatta on the Potomac, almost English in his enthusiasm.

North asked, "But if you foresee what must happen in the long run, why do you do this?"

The Baron's smooth, sensitively formed features contracted. "Yes, Hugh, *I* know very well; but there are others in whose judgment the Son of Heaven has placed much confidence. They cannot, or will not, or dare not retreat and so lose face."

The Intelligence officer leaned forward, his face drawn in fine anxious lines. "But Ito, why must you go through with this?"

The figure in bleached khaki plucked a yellow jasmine blossom from the demure vase at his side; when he poised it he looked as if he belonged in another era. There was nothing of the harsh militarist about Ito Setsukada now. He shrugged, unhooded flat dark eyes.

"My dear friend, if I were to talk for a year I could never explain why I go on with this bad business—unless I remind that, on occasions, you too have obeyed orders which you knew to be both evil and futile."

"But I have never murdered in cold blood, Ito."

The Japanese started and the jasmine blossom floated to the dark blue rug, beautiful even in its fall.

"I do not understand."

"May I have a cigar?"

"Certainly." Setsukada passed over his case, and politely raised the clamp of joined rings.

North selected a perfecto and held it to the light. On its side were two small circular impressions.

"I shall not examine the end of this, Ito. But Luis da Evaristo should have."

The big man in bleached khaki sat like something wooden.

"How did you learn of my—my unforgivable crime?"

Hugh North hesitated. For a Samurai to stoop to cold-blooded murder, and poisoning at that, was ignoble beyond words. Clearly Setsukada was suffering, tortured.

"Please to go on, Hugh. I have no shame left."

"There was tobacco in Dom Luis' mouth. Philippine tobacco. The cigar that killed Dom Luis was, of course, not to be found, but the stub of a cigar rolled of Philippine tobacco and bearing two such impressions as these was found.

"I recalled this case—it is really too beautiful to be safe for such work—and its patent clamp." He paused, aware that Setsukada had slumped in his chair, glossy boots extended and close-cropped head heavy on chest. "There were no other cigars made of Philippine tobacco. An oversight, Ito. Tonight I planned for your arrest, but—like so many Anglo-Saxons, I waited too long."

It became so still in the room one could have heard a spider spin, and a faint odor of lilies became apparent.

Baron Setsukada spoke heavily, as if each word were measured with a medicine dropper. "Can you believe it, Hugh? I, a prince of the illustrious Clan Teshio, very honorable during seven hundred years, am become a murderer. And why?" He raised weary eyes. "So that Dai Nippon shall make an enemy of the United States, of that nation which helped us so generously after the great earthquake? If we win—" he sighed—"the Germans—" he almost hissed the word—"will ruin us. Not yet are we as proficient at treachery, at cynicism as they."

North felt prompted to point out that certain Japanese were learning fast, but he did not. The poignancy of the other's tragedy was too evident.

Outside, arose the whining roar of one of the pursuit ships being warmed up.

"No," Setsukada said, heaving himself to his feet, "not even your shrewdness shall stop us. Everything is arranged. To-morrow will come all help; the money, the technicians, the advisers that we need. I shall not tell you where or when, my friend, because I know you. You would risk your life to get away and so spoil our plans, and I—I do not wish you to die."

The glittering dark eyes regarded North with a warmth which was at once touching and tragic.

"Yet you killed Dom Luis."

Setsukada blinked. "You, Hugh, are my friend, honorable and brave, a real Samurai. Last night I almost killed that butcher Rupp. He wished you shot, killed as you lay unconscious. Shot as he ordered executed that futile and unhappy Italian. Was it not typical this German could not distinguish between a brave enemy and a traitor? That you both obstructed his plans was his only consideration."

"Then Altrocchi is dead? Poor devil."

"He deserved the fate of a jackal," came the reply, loaded with contempt, "the fate that will be the fate of his nation. No, Hugh, I have risked much to bring you here."

"Thank you. But if I escape?"

A rather surprised furrow appeared on Baron Setsukada's pale bronze-hued brow. "You will not escape. I have seen to that, old friend. At the first attempt—or sign of one—you will be shot."

Briskly he clapped his hands and a neat young girl in an obi entered bearing a small tray set with the inevitable pale green saki bottle and two tiny cups of exquisite lacquer-ware bearing the tiger's head crest of the Teshio clan. Ceremoniously she bowed, set the tray down and departed.

All smiles again, the host poured out the colorless liquor, raised his cup.

"Our last drink together, Hugh. As soon as the field is cleared, I must go south; and in two hours I shall be at Pujol's headquarters." He sipped his drink with dignity. "I fear I shall never see you again, old tennis partner, so is there anything you would like to know?"

"What are you going to do with Miss Morrow and myself?"

"For the present I regret that you must be kept close prisoners," came the quiet response. "What happens later depends on the success of the Patriotistas—and us. Please make any reasonable request."

North thought hard, remembered something and said, "Naturally, Miss Morrow and I shan't be able to sleep well. Could we have a deck of cards, a score pad and pencil and, of course, a lamp to play by?"

Baron Setsukada looked relieved at so simple a request.

"Of course. I will send you a fine lamp." He smiled as he said, "You will not use the glass from its chimney for suicide?"

"We Americans don't go in for *seppuku,* you know. Well, again thanks for saving me from Rupp."

Baron Setsukada put down his saki cup, glanced briefly at the jungle blazing just outside the window, then started to offer his hand.

North said, "Don't be a fool, Ito," and took it. "At least we played good doubles together."

The Japanese looked long and hard at his prisoner; then without a word, turned and on silent feet left the pleasantly shaded room.

The New Card Game

WHEN Hugh North regained the *carcere,* Aurora Morrow very sensibly was taking a nap. How slight she looked in her scanty bandeau, petticoat and bare feet. Because of the blistering heat of midday, she had removed all but the utmost essentials and so he got more than a passing impression of what her bath mirror would recognize.

The pencil, pad and cards arrived, so North occupied a torturingly hot two hours in trying to do the cross-word in *A Sentinella,* yet found he could not. His knowledge of Portuguese was far too imperfect.

Accordingly, he spent more time in sketching the sleeping girl; damp curly hair, long, relaxed limbs and all. It was not a bad sketch, but he ridiculed his effort by drawing above her the conventional buzz-saw eating through a log of wood.

Aurora was quite indignant about that when at last she sat up rubbing heavy eyes. "You lie like a gas meter! I never snore. Anyway, if I do, you'll be the first man who has ever heard me," she laughed and began to put on her sandals.

"Sorry you woke," said he, wiping perspiration from his

forehead. "You looked positively surrealist. Reminded me of Dali's show at the World's Fair in New York."

Aurora reddened. "I've more clothes on than that—and a better figure, I hope." She wrinkled her nose at him. "Well, what did our friend Ito have to say?"

North told her, began to pace up and down the room. More and more that nebulous idea trapped in Setsukada's quarters captivated his imagination—and apprehension. Would it work? If so, would it work too well? One simply couldn't gauge this matter. That was the catch. Too great a success would be just as bad as too great a failure.

"Yes, Pujol's boys and the Fifth Columnists are really rolling now. The airport's all been cleared."

"How do you know?"

"Two planes have come in from the south. Wonder where in God's name we are?"

"Maybe I can give you some idea," Aurora volunteered. "We ought to be south and west of Rio."

"Why?"

"It's hot but, from the temperature, I'd bet my prettiest pretties we're on a plateau. That's the only really high land for miles."

"Right," North agreed. "Coffee does call for a moderate temperature."

"What have you been doing?" she demanded from the washroom where she occupied herself washing the last marks of sleep from her features.

"Been trying to remember an odd card game," he confided, sickened to hear still another plane taxi down the new field and take off. Then another came over, circled and lit. "A prisoner in San Quentin Prison invented it."

"What is this? A new brand of solitaire?"

"You might call it that."

"Who did you say invented it?" Aurora demanded over a weak gurgling of the water.

"A convict by the name of Kogut."

"How do you play it?" she demanded as once more the whining roar of an airplane motor being warmed shattered the stillness of late afternoon.

"Tell you later, Infant. It's too hot now." North winked. After all, the guards could hear every word spoken aloud. "The game is better played at night, so we'll play whatever you like in between."

"Cribbage?" she suggested, and inclined her head towards the window. There stood a Japanese peering, grinning, through the bars. "I generally can take J.P. for a month's allowance."

"We've no score board," North pointed out casually. "Ever try piquet? Best two-handed game there is."

She had not, so he occupied the time with instructions. After they had played a good while, Aurora stared because her companion suddenly dropped a couple of cards into a cup of stale coffee.

"What in the world?" she demanded quietly.

"Quiet," he whispered. Louder he complained, "Oh, damn! That's spoiled our game. You can recognize this queen a mile off. Guard!"

Apparently orders had been given to humor the prisoners in this respect. Before long a noncommissioned officer appeared, passed a fresh deck under the screen. Certainly no chances of escape were being taken.

The new deck was of cheap paper, worse in quality than the first deck. Instantly North flared, banged the table and roared in a manner well calculated to command the respectful attention of the sergeant outside. Aurora gaped, utterly amazed at this sudden display of temper.

"What is the meaning of this? I am used to playing with cards of decent quality. How dare you bring me these cheap, flimsy paper apologies? I shall complain to the Divisional Commander."

The Japanese flinched, bowed and returned considerably later with a deck which must undoubtedly have belonged to Baron Setsukada himself. The crest of the Teshio clan was done in dull red on a pale blue background.

"Satisfactory, Honorable Sir?" demanded the sergeant.

Carefully North riffled the cards through, bent them a little, while Aurora looked on, quite mystified. "Yes, they will do."

Aurora raised a slender, quizzical eyebrow. "That was a pretty song and dance for an American officer and gentleman," she observed softly. "What, pray, is the wherefore and the why?"

"*Qui vivra, verra,*" North replied shaking his head. "Perhaps, like Hamlet, there is method in my madness?"

Aurora started to say something but changed her mind, only lifted her bandeau free and blew inside. "If Jack or Charlie could see me now! Hotter than the W.K. hinges, isn't it?"

"And then some. Suppose you take a gander out on the fair face of Nature?"

The girl looked her surprise. "Why? I've seen all there is to—"

He signaled frantically for cooperation, knelt beside his bunk as Aurora wandered over and looked out on the dreary barrier of barbed wire. It was electrified, the sergeant had mentioned ever so casually.

Obediently the girl kept her one eye on the sentry, the other on her companion now busily wrenching free a length of wood from the bed frame support. Successful at last, he spread a sheet over the resultant gap.

"I say, Infant, do you really need those?" He indicated Aurora's stockings discarded beside the bed.

"They are pretty near shot, but whatever do you want with them?"

"I might wash them, and again I might not." The Intelligence officer smiled. Just as a new guard with a fat, cruel-looking face peered in, he stepped into the washroom, jauntily waved his hand and began to divest himself of his clothes.

Presently, he began to sing in a voice more notable for volume than quality, all about "The Wreck of the Old '97." Next he rendered "Bell Bottomed Trousers," censoring frantically as he went along. Meanwhile the water splashed merrily in the shower.

North meantime had braided both stockings with his shoe laces, then had thrown a lumberman's hitch very tight about that section of pipe connecting the spraying apparatus with the riser pipe. With the short piece of wood applying leverage as a windlass, he tugged, all the while caroling at the top of his lungs about "The Old Maid and the Tomcat." Funny, he'd never sung that song before save during the lighter moments of a duck-hunting trip.

A sentry came running around the house to peer in the window, but North was there ready to greet him.

"No hot water, no good!" he shouted and playfully flipped a wet hand at the outraged Oriental. Insulted, the sentry scowled and drew back so quickly he just missed touching the cruel, blue-white points on the barbed wire.

Because, fortunately, no red lead had been used to seal the joints, the desired section became fairly easily loosened until merely a twist would be required to free some six inches of cast-iron one-inch pipe. His next step was to loosen both faucet fittings in the same manner.

"Hey, Watchdog! Isn't that what they call a God-given voice?" demanded Aurora.

"What do you mean?"

"God gave it away because He couldn't sell it!"

He thrust a dripping head through the door, grinned cheerfully.

"For that dirty crack I'll warm your pantalets first chance I get."

"Try and do it!" she challenged while her eyes asked a dozen anxious questions. When he nodded, murmured, "O.K." she relaxed and smiled.

By the time an orderly brought a far from Spartan supper tray, and with it a kerosene lamp with a round wick and shade, North felt almost optimistic—if he didn't stop to think.

"What's got into you?" Aurora demanded, stirring a cup of maté. "You'd think there wasn't a bar, a guard or barbed wire fence in miles. I suppose you know they've added another ring of sentries outside the wire?"

"Yes. Isn't it great to be so popular?"

She bit her lip. "If that's popularity, I'll risk B.O. They must be scared stiff of you."

"Let's have another go at piquet," came the imperturbable reply.

Presently she said, "Hey, that's my trick! Have you gone nuts?"

Said he in an undertone, "Keep on playing—go through the motions but listen carefully." He dealt a hand at random. "This has got to be played carefully. The Japs act suspicious."

"What are you up to?"

She had never looked more naturally lovely than now. Gone

was the ordinary effect of lipstick and brow pencil. Her large clear eyes were serene in their quiet self-confidence.

"I'm game, Hugh. Game for anything that will do Hermann the German and all his merry men in the eye."

Game, that was it. But she'd no idea of the terrific, appalling risk he was going to ask her to run. Yes, Aurora Morrow had declared she'd be game, but would she be if she realized that it was fifty-fifty they'd both lie dead inside of an hour?

Briefly his fingers closed over hers and his steady gray-blue eyes peered out from deep under straight black brows.

"My dear, for the sake of what we know is right I—well, I'm going to try a gamble. It may well cost both our lives."

While speaking he picked up cards and passed them over to her by twos and threes.

"This offers your only chance of getting back to Rio?"

"Yes. But I warn you it's a thin one at best." His lips formed a tight little smile that paralleled his mustache. "If you're frightened, you can demand to be put in separate quarters."

"Wouldn't that rouse suspicions? We've been pretty clubby, you know."

He hesitated, shrugged just a trifle. "Well, it might."

"Then I stay," she announced, mechanically shuffling the cards. "The password tonight's going to be 'Mizpah.' My grandmother had it engraved on a funny old locket. Means something like 'We will stick together through all kinds of weather,' doesn't it?"

"Not exactly," he smiled. "Means almost the opposite. 'May the Lord watch over you when we are parted, one from the other.'"

Completely unabashed, Aurora grinned. "It was a good try, anyhow, wasn't it?"

"A for effort," he smiled. "Come on, let's get at our game."

Fireflies by the millions lit the night which, unfortunately, was clear as a bell with the Milky Way drawing a chiffon mask across the purple-black heavens. Great bats chittered and swooped and off in the tangled forest, nocturnal monkeys whooped, and an *ai,* or sloth, complained.

More and more Oriental Patriotistas reported, were equipped and sent marching away in long gray-green columns. The jungle swallowed them up without effort.

Until eleven that night the prisoners played piquet. A moon had risen and was dusting the new airport, hangars and the surrounding forest with silver when, around twelve o'clock, North yawned.

"Getting tired of piquet, Infant. What say let's try Willy Kogut's solitaire?"

An electric impulse passed between them and Aurora went a little pale in the light of the lamp. Her lips looked a bit stiff as she mechanically brushed a lock of hair from her eyes. Twice she caught her breath before she could speak.

"I c-can't wait," she said in a clear, almost even tone. "You have m-me all hot and b-bothered about it."

The crunch, crunch of the sentries' boots beat a deadly reminder that this game would be for higher stakes than matchsticks.

Said he then in a soft whisper, "I'll fix the layout. When I tell you, go to the window. Keep an eye on the sentries."

Her eyes grew quite round. "Sure thing. Any last words, Watchdog?"

"Yes. I've been wrong about you, Aurora," he murmured earnestly. "Very wrong. I want you to know that, before we go any further."

Her face came close and there was no fear in her look. "Thanks. Example goes a long way, Hugh."

Let the guards think what they would. He took her into his arms, kissed her gently. She responded sedately, then hungrily. He could feel her trembling a little as he released her.

"Thumbs up?"

"Thumbs up, Watchdog."

"Just make some remark about the weather if one of those yellow boys comes around the corner."

Immediately she had sought the window and stood apparently absorbed in the busy patterns of light created in the hangars, Hugh North ducked into the lavatory, disconnected the length of pipe and removed both faucets from the washstand.

After screwing a faucet tight to one end of his length of pipe, the Intelligence officer then commenced to tear Baron Setsukada's glossy new cards into little shreds. After wetting them, he crammed them into the cast-iron pipe, packing the shreds as tight as possible.

Every so often he poured a little water into the fiber. It was well that Baron Setsukada indulged himself with such excellent cards. Perspiration stood out like blisters on North's forehead before the pipe was packed to his satisfaction. This operation completed, he capped the open end with the second faucet fitting. He now held in his hands a curious dumbbell-like contrivance.

Aurora called, "The moon's really divine, Hugh. Makes the tops of those palms all shimmery. Reminds me of a dress of green sequins I had once in Biarritz. How's about that game?" Her voice was like that of a patient waiting to learn whether her disease was curable.

"In just a minute."

Unhurriedly, North moved their kerosene lamp into the one corner of his room where it would be difficult for a guard to see. Supporting his contrivance between an edge of the bed and a chair, he then shifted the lamp until the vent of its chimney lay directly below the center of the pipe.

When a furious blast of heat was beating steadily on the iron, he felt his stomach writhe. Well, it was neck or nothing now. Striding to his bed, he pulled off the mattress and dragged it into Aurora's room.

"The night still fine?" he panted. From now on a curious guard would wreck everything. He'd just have to trust to luck.

He saw Aurora standing steadily at her post, her head and shoulders framed at the window.

"Come on, Infant."

"Don't call me Infant. I like 'darling' better."

Once she came out of his room he closed the connecting door, pointed to the two mattresses stacked in the farthest corner. "Lie down in the corner next the cinder-block wall," he whispered.

"Mamma said not to."

"Please—there may not be much time."

He lay beside her, protecting her as much as possible, then drew first one mattress and then the other on top of them.

"Curl up. Turn your face to the wall."

"This is a nice game," Aurora murmured when she had obeyed. "It's got sardines in a box beat a mile."

"But it's a trifle stuffy," he objected. "Now put your fingers in your ears and open your mouth wide."

"Sounds silly!" She tried to sound casual.

"It's not. Do as I say and—and—God bless you."

Minute after minute dragged into eternity. Sweat began running in streams from both of them. He could feel the violence of Aurora's heartbeats against his chest. Damn! Something was wrong. Cards weren't right? Pipe was too thick? The story of Willy Kogut was just a wild yarn?

Miserably he stared into the dark, listened to the vicious hum of insects dashing themselves at the window screens. One of the guards belched, a cur began to howl down by the pseudo water tank.

"Watchdog?"

"Yes?"

"What's wrong?"

"Don't know—sh-h-h."

The tread of the sentry just outside sounded heavy as the footsteps of doom. A new relief of guards was tramping up. Surely one of them must recognize the reek of hot metal permeating the whole *carcere*.

"I'm stifling, Hugh," Aurora said, breathless. "Really I am."

"Quiet, for God's sake!"

A sudden babble of Oriental voices broke out. Feet pounded around the corner of the house. Sharp yells echoed against the wall of the forest. The fat was in the fire now, and no mistake about it! Oh, damn, the whole—

It seemed as if a meteor had struck the earth. A terrific yellow-green blast blew the connecting door bodily across the room, the floor heaved, and it seemed as if North's head had been caught beneath a trip hammer. His senses reeled as chunks of cinder block and rubble cascaded onto the mattresses. Billows of dust and smoke filled the air.

Choking, bleeding from his nose, North could only lie motionless a long instant. Then the spur of necessity goaded him to action. Dizzily, he struggled to his knees and began to tug at Aurora Morrow's limp wrist.

Night Road

BEMUSEDLY praising the memory of Willy Kogut, condemned murderer and suicide in San Quentin, North staggered away from the shattered *carcere* through a great gap in the wire. Not conscious thought, but blind instinct, prompted the Intelligence officer to snatch up a rifle; then, tugging his dazed companion, he plunged into the jungle.

Amid the swirling fumes he glimpsed a pair of bodies. Two others were squirming, groaning dully. Something slashed at his ankle—barbed wire. He ignored it.

As for Aurora Morrow, she, too, was bleeding, from the mouth, and reeling like a yacht in a gale, clinging blindly to his hand.

At the end of ten minutes' blind, headlong flight, North blundered into a tangle of lianas strong enough to check his branch-buffeted, thorn-lashed flight. Sobbing, panting for breath, the fugitives let their trembling knees give way and collapsed onto the damp ground. Behind rang shouts, the trampling of men in the jungle, the wild clanging of a bell.

The moon, now well up, penetrated the jungle, lit the perspiration-bathed pair as they sprawled, wildly disheveled, on the earth. Aurora seemed in bad case. Her bandeau had been ripped and dangled useless. She was breathing in violent gasps that lifted erect, small-nippled breasts in convulsive jerks.

North produced a handkerchief, drenched it with the copious dew on a nearby branch and wiped away the spatter of blood on her chin.

God above! His head still rang as if he were imprisoned in a boiler and a hundred riveters were at work on it. Before his eyes the whole dim scene rocked and swayed, but a little less violently. Mechanically, he wiped his own face and felt better. Then he re-wet the handkerchief and, lifting Aurora's head on his knee, bathed her face. Clumsily his fingers brushed aside hair drenched with dew and matted with bits of leaves, bark and twigs.

She was breathing easier now, but still lay with eyes closed. Fanning away viciously singing swarms of mosquitoes, he tried to think.

Well, at least now, he knew what cellulose, wetted and sealed in, would do when heated. Only that solid cinder block wall had stood between them and instant death.

"Hello, Watchdog. Some game." Aurora's eyes were open and she smiled faintly. "Guess you bid and made a grand slam —or did I trump your ace?"

Presently she sat up, noticed her deshabille. "Say, do I look like Ann Corio after the third encore, or don't I?" she mumbled and, producing a pin, set about replacing the bandeau.

"Well—it worked after all," North commented stupidly. "You all right?"

"Sure, but my head feels as if I'd been drinking champagne with brandy chasers. How are you doing?"

"Okay, even if I seem a bit messy."

To be truthful, his hurt side had been torn open, his shirt

was ripped to tatters and that barbed wire loop had snatched away a leg of one trouser. Using a liana, he hauled himself to his feet, then helped her up. A sorry pair they looked. But they were free.

"Come on—still too close."

He had a rifle containing five shots. With it, a determined man might accomplish a great deal.

After following a half-choked trail through the insect-filled dark for nearly a mile, North thought he heard the sound of a motor passing not far ahead and called another halt. Yes. There was a road and it had been in recent use.

He found a rotten, but solid-appearing, dead tree which would, with a good push, fall across the road. Expectantly, he squatted beside it with Aurora resting quietly alongside.

At last the lights of a motor car appeared and wavered near, nearer, along an incredibly bad country road. When the vehicle was barely a hundred feet away North sent the tree crashing down and, stepping suddenly out of the underbrush, covered a pair of startled uniformed Japanese on their way to Fazenda Number Nine.

In German which, oddly enough, both Fifth Columnists spoke with ease, he ordered them to get out. They were to remove their tunics and visored caps. Aurora relieved the Japanese of their side arms and tossed a pair of pistols into a battered little runabout which stood panting faithfully in the road.

Next the prisoners were directed to face the woods and walk to the edge of the road.

The pair glowered, hesitated, but under the threat of North's rifle obeyed and stood patiently with hands held shoulder high. Aurora stifled a little scream when her companion, his jaw set in an ugly line, suddenly brought his rifle barrel smacking down once, twice.

In perfect silence the two prisoners collapsed into a weed-choked ditch, became lost to sight save for a faint gleam of their white cotton undershirts. Whether he had killed them Hugh North neither knew nor cared.

Keeping one ear cocked, the Intelligence officer turned the car around while Aurora struggled into the smaller of the two uniform coats. Presently some distinctly unsoldierly curves were filling a gray-green tunic decorated with flat nickel buttons.

"I can't seem to think," she complained. "You will have to tell me what to do."

"Push your hair up under the cap," he directed. "Keep up the good work, Infant. You've been fine so far."

"Thanks. Will we be too late?"

"God only knows," he grunted. "Depends on a lot of things. We're far from out of the woods."

The remaining Fifth Columnist's coat was so small North's wrists protruded from its sleeves like those of a boy outgrowing his clothes, but he managed to get it on. The cap was a better fit and did much to hide his countenance.

A hasty inspection revealed the runabout to be of cheap manufacture, but on the other hand its gasoline tank was full and a sack of hand grenades on the back seat promised to be of real service if need arose. Beside him Aurora's fragile features looked very like those of a young cadet in some military academy.

Where was he headed? God only knew. He had no choice because, so far, this moonlit track neither forked nor crossed any other highway.

So Baron Setsukada was contemplating a two-hour plane journey southward? Mm. Once the situation of Fazenda Number Nine became identified one might draw useful conclusions as to what might have been the Japanese destination.

As fast as he dared, North forced the car along a wretched backwoods road. Inside of the first half hour they encountered two other cars, and once a Japanese in a round steel helmet attempted to bar the road. However, North's Patriotista collar ornaments, reinforced by a furious blast of German profanity, caused the Oriental to fall back and hastily to present arms.

The moon was high and was etching inky shadows behind the scattered buildings of Campanha, the first little town to appear on the route. Here North went to the *prefeitura* and roused the mayor, a very stupid fellow who merely giggled when warned that an insurrection was rising with appalling speed. Finally North got the idea across and left the *magistrado* pulling trousers over a long-tailed nightshirt.

On plodding back to the commandeered car, he found his side was hurting infernally and, from a sogginess of his tunic, he deduced the wound must have begun bleeding. When Aurora saw him limping into the headlights' beam, her eyes flew wide open and she jumped out in a hurry.

"Good heavens, Hugh, you're hurt! How'd it happen? I swear I never heard anyone shoot."

"They didn't. It's that old cut. Messy, but nothing much. Can you drive?"

"You bet," she declared. "I feel heaps better. Guess I pulled sort of a blank a while back."

Under her expert guidance, the touring car fairly roared eastward along a considerably better road.

The rest did him good, gave him opportunity to think. Two points, North saw, should immediately be checked, followed up. Mlle. Berthier and McCabe.

"Damn! Pujol's boys are right on the job." He pointed to a

succession of telegraph poles. From them severed lines drooped in all directions. Always the wires were cut between settlements.

Still the fact was not without compensations. It stood to reason that any alarm for the stolen car would be hard to spread. His misgivings grew as village after village seemed absolutely unalarmed.

By three o'clock of the morning a glow on the horizon, like that of some vast foundry, indicated the direction of Rio and, three-quarters of an hour later, Aurora was turning into the Estrada Rio São Paula. Here brigades of street cleaners were stolidly hosing down the streets, pitchforking tons of streamers and confetti into trucks. A few belated revelers were singing long songs on two notes, and cats slunk about in search of tidbits from well-filled garbage pails.

Everything seemed so normal, so utterly peaceful, it seemed incredible that, unless a miracle happened, these same streets tomorrow would be spattered with blood and littered with corpses—not confetti.

In none of the moonlit squares, praças or avenidas were to be found soldiers or tanks. No armored cars were patroling the streets. Why? Certainly many traitors had been at work.

At the Bureau of Naval Intelligence, however, many lights were blazing and when North swayed up the steps, Almeira, the fox-faced detective, came running out.

"O senhor Major. What has happened?" His eyes widened when he saw the bloody patch on North's side. "We have been in a desperation."

"*Gloria a Deus!* I had thought you dead." Nabuco, wild-eyed and distracted, appeared, flung both arms about the apparition and led him into a private office. "I am so glad you are safe. So many terrible things are happening."

"Correct. Now get this!"

In rapid-fire succinct sentences the Intelligence officer described the mobilization at Fazenda Nine, a scene no doubt being repeated at dozens, if not hundreds, of points throughout the Republic.

Once Nabuco's assistants and superiors had dashed off to make telephone and telegraph wires hum, they began at once to curse an extraordinary disruption of service. It was more serious than even the celebration could have caused.

North drew Nabuco aside.

"Can you get me patched up for a while?" He began to take off his tunic. The blood was still flowing.

"But of course. Sergeant! Send for Dr. Ribeira."

"What news of Mlle. Berthier?"

"We have her."

"Where?"

"In safe keeping at the Carmo Hospital," Nabuco said, his dark eyes snapping. "Her nerves are most bad. She appeared around seven o'clock of this evening, in terror of her life. She escaped during the excitement of your capture. Dr. Rupp, of course, had caused her line to be tapped. He heard her conversation with the Italian."

"How much does she know of Rupp's plans?" North demanded quickly.

"Practically nothing." The Brazilian looked his disappointment. "She has given me a list of words she was told to use in a cross-word puzzle which is to appear in the papers tomorrow. Mlle. Berthier swears it was composed three days ago. It has been distributed as far distant as Recife and Rio Grande do Sul."

"Good," North grunted and tried not to wince when a police surgeon set to work. He scanned the cross-word puzzle.

"You have the third Bolivar message?"

"Yes, my friend, but it is not for this cross-word," Nabuco explained angrily. "So far our listening posts have heard no new broadcast or other distribution of number sequences. It is my opinion the sequences will be radioed in the morning."

North did some hard thinking, then said slowly, "That may be all to the good. So long as we possess the cross-word itself, we should be able to throw a real monkey wrench into the Patriotista gears. Where are the words Berthier was to employ?"

Nabuco passed over a list written in unmistakably French script:

brigade	mission
staff	Tuesday
noon	disregard
field	pending
hold	Iguape
instructions	former
divisional	base
assemble	orders
at	officers
delayed	immediate

North's head felt rather light when he seated himself at a desk with pencil and paper.

"There are, of course, many extremely significant words present," he commented. "Take 'staff,' 'divisional,' 'assemble' and so forth."

Nabuco nodded, "But what can one learn unless one possesses the number sequence or—"

A general officer in a half-buttoned uniform burst in. Unshaven and red-eyed, he seemed bewildered, angry and very anxious.

"What is wrong? All telephone cables leading from the Ministry of War have been severed! Three of my staff have disappeared."

"The Patriotistas are on the move, Senhor General," North told him. "If your provincial garrisons can be warned by radio, there may yet be time to halt them."

The general officer stared an instant at the grim, gaunt figure with bloodstains splashing ragged trousers that had once been white.

"*Senhor Deus!* You are sure?"

"Absolutely."

Without further comment, the officer wheeled. He was running before he left the office.

Reverting first to Rupp's list, North then studied additional quite innocent words appearing on Mlle. Berthier's puzzle. From these the Intelligence officer made a rapid selection:

Victoria	halt
future	six
Pará	suspect
treason	Sunday

To Nabuco he said, "How quickly can you put a message on the air?"

"Within twenty minutes," came the prompt reply. "I have requested, and received, authority to transmit any message you may wish."

"This idea may not accomplish all we'd like," North admitted, "but it *should* serve to confuse the opposition a bit."

His pencil flew over the yellow pad as he designated the following words by their position in the puzzle:

Bolivar. Field officers brigade staff disregard former instructions. Assemble Victoria six Sunday. Mission delayed. Suspect treason. Field command hold forces at bases.

North flung down his pencil and as quickly Nabuco bent over the message which now read:

BOLIVAR 22-3-18-31-6-15-21-14-36-5-13-30-8-17-7-20-40 19-34-9-23

"And now," Nabuco demanded as an orderly sped upstairs to the radio sending apparatus, "what next?"

Thanks to a long pull of brandy followed by a cup of coffee strong enough to float an ax head, North began to feel better.

"Lieutenant, suppose you have somebody, with sense, prepare more confusing messages? Send them out every two hours until further notice and from as many points as you can. We'll jam this communication system. Suppose also you instruct your listening posts to keep their ears skinned for anything they can pick up?"

When he stood up, the bandage stood out starkly white against his bronze and muscular torso. A sudden sense of guilt galvanized him to action.

"Lord, but I'm a stupid fool! Lieutenant, will you detail someone to see Miss Morrow to her home?"

Nabuco promised. "And in the meantime?"

Hugh North permitted himself a faint grin. "I think we had better start looking for an interesting gent called Masibi Jack McCabe."

Virginio Gayda Chatters

"A MESSAGE for Mr. West?" yawned the night operator at the Hotel Avenida. "Please to wait one moment."

The two Intelligence officers smoked, stared into space until the operator returned. No. There was no message. A thousand pardons but a thorough search had been made. Definitely, there was no message for a Mr. West.

A blank wall once more. Where would Paula most likely be? Had she run in terror of her life? No telling, no way of learning.

As from a previous incarnation came a recollection of assigning a watcher to McCabe's rooms at the Hotel Neptuna. Since the hostelry was not far distant, North lashed his aching body back into harness, suggested that the watcher be questioned.

The man on duty was all subdued excitement. *Sim.* An hour ago Senhor McCabe had come home, more than a little *bêbado,* and very, very angry about something. He had cursed his taxi driver over nothing at all. Yes. Senhor McCabe was certainly in his apartment. He, Detective Ulloa, had bribed the porter to report any movement.

In the empty moonlit street North deliberated an instant, then reached a decision.

"We'll go up. I—"

All of the group, experienced in such matters, flinched into the shadows of a covered driveway when the first rays of light flashed from an elevator's opening doors.

Wearing a green, nondescript uniform, Masibi Jack appeared, his scarred face set in an expression which argued intentions of no pleasant nature. The uneven sound of his limping progress was loud and reminded North of that moment before he found Stuart Maitland prone in the corridor.

The flyer limped out onto the moon-silvered sidewalk after first casting a careful look up and down the sidewalk. Setting his cap at a jaunty angle, McCabe walked to the corner, turned right and presently the roar of a car's motor being too quickly warmed, reverberated down the street.

It gave North's party opportunity to regain their own conveyance.

To follow the other's mad progress down the deserted streets of Rio was not difficult. The flyer's lights were visible from a safe distance, if a pursuer kept his lights out.

As the aviator's progress took a general direction, North's amazement grew. Unmistakably, Masibi Jack was heading for the Estrada do Redemptor! Could Paula have been such a fool as to revisit her apartment? Not likely! You wouldn't find so wary a campaigner thrusting her head into so ready a noose.

What could McCabe be up to?

A smell of dawn was now in the air. Dogs and cocks began bugling the fact. Down the street appeared a peasant driving a line of donkeys mountainously loaded with vegetables. The delicate patter of their little hoofs on the macadam sounded like gigantic raindrops.

A cat maioued mournfully. Suddenly, Nabuco's dark eyes grew enormous. Out of the shadows at the entrance to the second apartment house below 1081 had stepped a man.

"Senhor Major!" It was Almeira, the fox-faced detective. "A message—"

It appeared that the night operator at the Avenida had made a mistake—there *had* been a message for Senhor West.

North's heart soared as the fox-faced man passed over an envelope.

"And why did you look for me here?"

"It occurred that the senhor might come back. One hears that Senhorita Harte is most fascinating."

"If I could give away medals," North declared, "I'd award you a dozen, my friend."

By the light of Nabuco's pocket flash, North slipped his thumb under the flap of the envelope and read:

2:30 A.M.

Sneaked home to pack. For God's sake come quickly. Leaving at daybreak.

Devotedly, P.

Familiar with the surroundings, North halted his group two blocks short of Number 1081, kept Nabuco and one detective with him. The other two were to drive by and to dismount two blocks beyond. They were to close in, covering the apartment house front and rear.

For some moments he stood peering up at the fifth floor. Were there lights in Paula's apartment?

Once McCabe came limping back from the car he had parked up the street, North felt his fatigue drop away.

Straight into the lobby swung Masibi Jack McCabe. A shifty-eyed woman on duty at the desk started up expectantly. He paused, muttered something and passed a bill into her eager hand. North watched the flyer glance sharply about, limp over to the automatic elevator. As he turned, the light beat briefly on his hard red features, glistened on the scarred area.

Easing in his pocket a clumsy automatic captured from the Japanese Fifth Columnist, North nodded to Nabuco, rapped, "Keep that woman quiet. Then come up," and went pounding up the fire stairs at a rate which did his injured side not a bit of good. A serious expenditure of energy, this, but it would consume valuable time to recall the elevator; besides, its use would very likely alarm Masibi Jack.

He gained the fifth floor landing just in time to catch the *click!* of a key. In the shelter of that identical arch from which McCabe had fired his mistaken shot at Maitland, he watched the green-uniformed figure ease open the door. Was it significant that the flyer left the door open a trifle? A split second would be saved in case of a hurried retreat.

How quiet it was. Someone's snoring in an apartment down the corridor was distinctly audible.

Kicking off his shoes, North advanced as soundlessly as a shadow. There was a light, a very dim light in the living room. The rug was pulled back as it had been when Maitland had lain bleeding on the floor. The flyer of fortune halted.

A tingling began in Hugh North's fingertips when, peering in the front door, he glimpsed Masibi Jack tiptoeing forward into the living room. Then he moved on out of sight. There followed the sound of furniture being moved very, very quietly.

Immediately, North advanced in his turn, entered the little vestibule. The familiar odor of Flor da Noite roused a dozen vivid recollections. He'd never forget that scent if he lived to be a thousand!

Paula, he deduced, must already have fled. From where he

stood, the Intelligence officer could see her clothes and belongings scattered in wild disorder.

A slow rasping sound held him immobile. Then after a little, a man's voice muttered, "The bloody fool!"

At the entrance to the living room North shrank back, for all of a sudden began the shrill chattering of a frightened monkey. McCabe darted behind a curtain, clutching a handful of documents. Rigid, he waited, his back turned to North. On the back of a tall chair Virginio Gayda was jumping up and down, baring his teeth and squalling in outrage.

In from the terrace came Paula, still in costume but looking pallid, very far from gay. She was loosening the fastenings of her turban.

"Oh, be quiet! I—" her sentence ended in a gasp. "Jack! what—please—"

McCabe moved not at all from his position. "So, on top of everything else, you'd try to run out?"

"Oh, no, Jack." Paula was speaking soothingly, in a calm, low-pitched tone. "I had no such intention. I swear I hadn't. The money has been promised."

Hugh North calculated that a series of informative accusations and counter-accusations would follow. Braced for instant action, he prepared to listen. He miscalculated, for, without any further ado, McCabe shot from the hip with a small revolver North couldn't see.

For an instant, he imagined the aviator had missed. Paula stiffened convulsively but remained where she was, an expression of incredible surprise spreading over her lovely features. Uncertainly, one hand went out to the chair back as from it the white-faced monkey leaped, all the while squalling in terror.

"How d'you fancy that?" snarled McCabe. "Try to diddle

me out of a quarter million, would you? Well, I've had enough of your bloody lies!"

Paula's eyelids wavered, shut suddenly, then opened again. Very slowly she doubled forward, clutched the chair for support and commenced to cough so hard she lost her balance and sank to her knees, coughing still.

Like an acid, North's voice bit into the situation. "Drop that gun and don't move!"

McCabe started to obey, but when he heard the shrilling of whistles below, heard Nabuco racing up the corridor, he spun suddenly about and fired. His bullet whistled harmlessly, but the Intelligence officer sent a heavy .38 caliber bullet crashing into the flyer's shoulder, knocking him clean off his feet.

In no time at all, Nabuco burst in and took charge of Mc-Cabe while residents of the three other apartments on the floor appeared armed with everything from automatics to golf clubs. Apparently, shots fired in the small hours of the morning produced a very different effect from ones fired in the late afternoon.

Like a diapason chord on an organ, excitement swelled. Two detectives appeared and prepared to hustle the now sobered and sullenly defiant flyer of fortune down to a nearby drugstore.

"You fancy you've won this round, my dear Major," he gasped. "All the same, you'll get yours later today, and then, by God, I won't envy you."

"There is nothing can be done," declared the bald, fattish doctor who had appeared in gay lavendar-and-pink striped pajamas. "There are many arteries cut. She bleeds internally."

"Call a priest, someone," cried the man with the golf club.

"No," Nabuco corrected. "The lady is not of that faith."

North returned to the group standing in awe-struck silence

about that same settee upon which Paula had propounded her extraordinary offer. It was clear now that Paula, in making her original offer, had intended calmly to sell out McCabe's share in this more or less joint property, not for money for once, but for those things she had always craved.

Naturally, a hard-bitten type such as Masibi Jack did not intend to surrender his share of a fortune to humor his partner's belated sense of patriotism. North's lean features were further sharpened by gravity and a grinding fatigue, as more fully he comprehended the nature of her sudden reversion to a demand for the quarter million.

"Hugh, *alma de mi corazón—*" Paula spoke faintly in Spanish. Her smoke-colored eyes were wide open but those appealing bluish shadows above them were going violet. "Come close to me."

Still in that blue and ashes-of-roses harem costume she had worn that afternoon, she presented a theatrical impression as she lay smiling, but deathly pale on the light green of her settee. It was curious how little blood was in evidence. The doctor's first-aid compress was hardly discolored at all. The bullet, evidently of a .22 or .28 caliber, had caused only a small wound and had not emerged.

When her fingers twitched towards him, North turned heavily, faced the group standing in respectful awed silence. One or two of the women were praying silently; another's eyes were running over. Her tears slipped smoothly over the olive-brown of her cheeks and made small dark spots on the blue silk of her dressing gown.

North murmured, "Would you leave us, please? There are things to be said in private."

Following a trail of bright splashes sketched by McCabe's

shattered shoulder, the onlookers crossed themselves as they retired.

Nabuco's face was wooden when he stooped to collect the documents McCabe had lost. Then he emptied into his portfolio the contents of a small safe which had been let into the wall behind a reproduction of a painting by Gauguin. He bestowed on the stricken girl a look full of compassion, nodded to North and sped from the shadow-ruled room. Outside on the balcony Virginio Gayda began whimpering softly, bewilderedly.

"*Muy querida—*" he began.

"No. Please in English, my dearest."

North dropped on one knee beside the sofa, took Paula's hand. There could be no doubt that not much time remained. Her lips were going lavender.

"And so," she murmured, smiling a little, "you were right once more. One cannot always win at such a game."

"No. I expect my turn will come sometime, too. McCabe's too. Tell me, *querida,* how did he know you had taken—er—opened Dom Luis' safe?"

She sighed. "Because it was all agreed. He was my partner, to do the—the rough stuff—like Becker in São Paulo. He even drove me to Dom João's home. He saw you arrive there."

North held her hand closer, tried vainly to dispell the increasing chill of it. "When did he suspect you were going to give, so to speak, the evidence to me?"

"I refused to accept a huge offer from Rupp, and Rupp must have told him—implicated you, my heart's heart. Then all day today—" she paused, drew several deep breaths, "—I avoided him. Of course he guessed I intended to leave—Oh Hugh, if— if only you had got here first."

"Would to God I had!"

To remain practical at such a moment seemed barbaric, yet there was no help for it. "Paula, dear, where have you hidden the real evidence?"

Her fingers stirred between his. "What makes you so sure your friend Nabuco has not taken it away just now?"

"You are much too intelligent, *querida,* to have kept such evidence here."

He bent closer, felt a hardening in his throat. To think that there could be nothing more in life for this lovely, vital young woman was sickening.

"The evidence from Dom Luis' office I have left for safe-keeping in the vault of the Hotel Itajubá," she murmured.

The lashes fluttered down, rested an instant, dark on the smooth pallor of her cheek.

"You will find there, my beloved, everything you will require to reveal those ones in high places who are traitors. The treacherous workings of the Estrella del Mar and of the Companhia Americus, the locations—" She struggled suddenly for breath and a fine sheen of perspiration began to glisten at her temples—"of the *Stützpunkte,* the port and the hour for the arrival of the Axis ship, the *Andalucia,* which brings the saboteurs, the technicians, the gold and Herr Hitler's own *Gauleiter* for Brazil."

North knew he should tear himself away, rush immediately to the Itajubá; yet to desert Paula like this would have been inhuman.

A long shuddering sigh like that of an autumn wind through a spruce shook the girl's body.

"—And so," she smiled, "there shall be no homeland for me after all. I really wished to make the United States, your country—" a long pause— "a gift of the evidence." Her fingers tightened briefly as he kissed her. "Will you believe me when

I say—that it was because of that Masibi Jack has killed me? Kiss me once again, my darling, and then—and then speak to me of America, for I *am* half American, you know."

He kissed her tenderly, then, his lips held close to her ear, he said gently, "No, Paula, you are wholly an American."

Presently he began to talk, to tell her of their country's future until, at length, Paula gave a weary little sigh and crossed the frontier into that realm in which there is no hatred, no greed, no envy.

THE END